CONFESSIONS OF A SIREN SINGER

ARTISTIC DEMONS SERIES #3

IRENE RADFORD

Book View Café

Published by Book View Café Publishing Cooperative.

Publication Team: Jennifer Stevenson
Editors: Alma Alexander, Phyllis Irene Radford
Proofreader: Alma Alexander, Patricia Rice, and Maya Bohnhoff
Formatter: Patricia Burroughs
Cover Designer: Maya Kaathryn Bohnhoff

Book View Café Publishing Cooperative
PO Box 1624
Cedar Crest, NM 87008-1624

http://bookviewcafe.com

ISBN 978-1-61138-933-3

PROLOGUE

I held my breath, one, two, three, and gently pressed the false eyelash to my lid, felt the adhesive cling to the sensitive skin, and...

A sneeze gathered. My face twitched. The lash slid to the inside, decorating my nose with spider legs.

"Storm coming," my back-up singers said in unison.

My insides trembled from the warning. I couldn't hope to battle or control a big storm from the basement dressing room of a small Las Vegas nightclub.

Brittney and Joycelyn knew that those words were as much a curse as a warning. We shared this dressing room as we shared everything, from hairbrushes to clothes to sensitivity to weather changes.

The girls were really my nieces but raised with me as if we were triplets.

The one thing we hadn't shared was our reaction to the recent plague vaccine. They'd breezed through the procedure last month while I still had a red welt on my upper left arm.

The vaccine didn't like my siren blood any more than the plague did, but I couldn't perform in public without proof of vaccine. As we stepped onto the stage a black light would flash across us and the light sensitive dye in the injections would flare briefly as proof to the audience.

"Another storm, Celia?" Brittney wailed. "So soon?"

"That's three times already this winter." Joycelyn sighed deeply, heaving her ample bosom high above the constrictions of her red spangled bodice. The men in our audience fully appreciated the moments when she needed a deeper breath. Sometimes they were rewarded. Mostly not. In Las Vegas, few cared. But they loved the anticipation.

"It's winter. Even Las Vegas suffers from rain and wind upon occasion," I replied, ripping the false lashes free of my nose and reapplying a few drops of glue. I needed to show my sisters calm in the face of a storm, like I always did, not the quivering mass of gelatin that my belly had become.

This storm was something more than the usual clash of air masses over the desert in late February.

"It's called a monsoon," Joycelyn grumbled. She shivered too, like she had caught some of my own anxiety.

"I thought we'd moved to the desert so we'd be as far from the sea as possible." Brittney looked longingly to her blue lace woolen shawl on the rack with her street clothes.

Lately wind and rain, born of our great-grandmother, the StormMother, the goddess Tiamat of old, (we called her Mummy because the generations got confused and tangled) threw temper tantrums, that flooded the streets too often.

Call it climate change if you must. We three, born of a siren, knew better.

During a storm, water calls to water even more than usual.

Lake Mead, hundreds of thousands of gallons of water trapped behind a flimsy dam, lay to east of the city. I could feel its longing to join the storm.

The itch at the tip of my nose crept upward. I held my breath to avert another sneeze. Gradually the itch dissipated. Another deep breath and I was free of the storm portent.

A distant grumble rolled across the horizon. If lightning

accompanied it, I couldn't see or feel it in this windowless basement dressing room.

"Do we need to alert management to gear up for a power outage?" Brittney asked. "That one three weeks ago was a doozy." She stood before her own lighted mirror and added a tiny dusting of glitter powder to her cleavage.

I checked my own chest above the sparkling white gown and the artful airbrushing that gave a visual suggestion that my own boobs were bigger than they were.

"Never hurts to be prepared," I murmured.

"Two minutes, girls," Gus the stage manager called. "Places."

I took a swig of water and gargled lightly. My backup singers did the same. We each warbled our favorite warm-up vocalizations. Thirty seconds later we marched out of the dressing room, down the dimly lit cement corridor, up a set of stairs with a metal tube railing that near froze my fingers. The inefficient air conditioning was aimed incorrectly, again, to chill the railing but not the stairwell.

As I turned at the landing to climb the last half story, I felt like I walked into a wall of water. Not the soft, warm welcome of a tropical sea. No, this was the cold, unrelenting push against humidity from a different location, a different coastline, and different climate.

My nose twitched again, so aggressively I was glad I wasn't looking into a mirror. My sisters would have crossed themselves and quit this gig, if they saw my nose pull a Samantha witch wiggle. We were all a generation, or more, removed from sea magic. Still I had the greater talent for it than the girls.

That coming storm was a big one and I was pretty sure it was going to hit directly overhead.

Time to pull out all the stops. We stood in a line, arms around each other's waists, me in the middle, a unified trio, promising amazing harmonies.

"Plan B," I whispered.

My girls looked at me with raised eyebrows. Then they nodded. "Just give us the pitch and the opening phrase and we'll follow," Brittney said.

I gave Mitch, our pianist, a two-handed Vulcan salute. He lifted his lip in a sneer. If I hadn't worked closely with him for six weeks, I might have interpreted his expression as one of disgust. Instead, I knew he merely concentrated on a new placement of hands and calling up the muscle memory of a different set of chords and tones.

The curtain lifted before me. The black light panned across the stage highlighting our vaccination wounds. Then spotlights blazed, blinding me to the audience. Just as well. I didn't lust after enchanting men to blindness of their own thoughts and actions.

The wind outside this nightclub whipped to a new frenzy. The storm sought me. I sent my mind wandering through the web of winds, seeking its source. The note vibrating at its core, stabbed my heart and weakened my limbs with loving languor. By force of will alone I matched the tone in a single high C#.

A piano note softly joined me, then it followed through with a third and a fifth below that. My girls joined the chord, each taking a lower note to support me. With their underpinning intact, I burst forth with an ancient sea chanty I hadn't dared to sing for ages. It had a million verses I could adapt to the circumstances.

Water calls to water.

In Las Vegas there wasn't a lot of water to support the storm. It had to draw power from a different source. A source I would never acknowledge again. I had no compunction against stealing a mere storm from it.

What do you do with a drunken sailor?
Tie him to the mast and let him sing to the mother...

I heard a chuckle in the back of the room, a deep masculine exhalation of mirth. "Never that much water in Vegas!" he proclaimed.

Lightning exploded outside. The building shook.

Hysterical cries as my audience cowered.

The lights flickered. A unified cry of dismay.

4

I pushed more force into my song, shifting easily from the perils of the sea to a song about roses blooming in the spring. The lights died. Candles in jars on each table flickered cheerily.

The calming scent of spring roses filled the room and my senses.

Even I could not channel electricity through broken wires to feed hungry lightbulbs and voracious amplifiers. But I could keep the audience from fleeing in panic, stampeding each other, and letting the storm win.

This battle was between me and the StormMother herself.

Leave these people alone!

Mortals should die. Return to me, the wind keened overhead.

I shifted the song to a recollection of hot summer days, swimming, surfing, loving in the sand.

The wind slackened in confusion. Mummy pulled it one way; I coaxed it another.

Mummy shook herself free of my spell. The windows rattled. A car alarm pierced the beauty of the tune I wove around my anxious audience. Emergency vehicle sirens ramped up in response.

I heard Brittney falter in her harmony, unnerved by the closeness of the StormMother.

Joycelyn, bless her, strengthened her own notes to fill in the gaps.

Water calls to water. It also follows the path of least resistance and there was a bloody mountain between us and the lake. How could I direct the water-laden clouds to find the only water-laden land away from the city?

My blood wanted to burst free of my skin and create channels for rainwater to drain back into the Colorado River. I couldn't open a vein on stage, inside a cement building. I needed to be out there to fully battle this storm.

If I emerged from the building the wind would circle me, forming a tornado to lift me back into the bosom of the StormMother.

I wasn't yet ready to make that sacrifice.

Since the time before Ulysses, all my mother's kind had been born of a water nymph and a god, or a king, or a god-like hero.

Because of Mom and my mortal father, I had access to waters the

StormMother never dreamed of. Fresh water answered me as much as the sea responded to her.

This hole-in-the-wall nightclub hadn't renovated everything the last time a new owner came in. The water cooler between the ladies and the gents was still a glass bubble. Heavy glass to be sure. But full.

I look the last note about summer fun up and up and up again until it resonated with the glass, almost above human hearing. I urged the clouds to evaporate.

My throat grew dry, burning harshly. The top of my head threatened to lift free of my body.

I had to set that bubble of water free to attract the storm center to me and my control.

And still I held that piercing note.

Customer's drinks slopped all over the tables as glass containers shattered.

And still the cooler resisted.

The storm wavered in confusion.

Mummy, drat her, pushed harder, forcing wind and rain to obey her.

Another octave up and finally the cooler succumbed to the irresistible power of my voice. It crumbled with a low rumble akin to the thunder circling the city.

StormMother shrieked.

Thunder roared closer.

Lightning struck another power pole.

Water from the cooler fled the scene, seeking out all the creeks and streams and artificial aqueducts. Down, down, down the path of least resistance it escaped, seeking to merge with all the other water and hide from my voice.

The rain followed, pulling the clouds with it.

But the wind still shrieked at the StormMother's command, ripping the roof clear of this building, leaving me open to the sky.

I tingled from my hair to my bones from the electricity in the air. I knew what was coming and held up both hands, palms upward, pushing back with my will, my magic, and my voice.

Sleep my child and I will tend thee
  All through the night.
  Guardian angels God will lend thee
  All through the night

Brittney and Joycelyn crooned soft and soothing notes in gentle harmony. The first lullaby we'd heard from mom, from our own guardian angel, the invisible friend of our childhood. Perhaps the first song we ever sang together, or apart.

But StormMother had wind, water, and fire. All she needed was land to combat my lullaby.

The fire of lightning mindlessly sought the fourth element, its mate and its opposite.

Three bolts hurtled downward.

I returned one of them to the sky.

The other two found my backup singers, my friends, my sisters. I watched them writhing with their death agonies as great splinters of metal and wood and glass pierced their bodies and then their skulls.

CHAPTER 1

"And why do you, Miss Celandine Fisher, wish to audition for the *Here I Come, World* competition?" an anonymous male voice asked from the fifth row of the studio theater. The black light flashed across my vaccination tattoo for the third time since I'd entered the building through the front door.

These people were taking no chances for spreading the plague again. I'd heard that the producer and head judge of the competition had lost his wife to the disease just weeks before the vaccine became viable and available.

I resisted the urge to shield my eyes from the lights in order to see the speaker and the other two judges. Impolite. They had set the stage in order to remain invisible and anonymous. I must perform as if they were any other audience. And I must perform alone.

Alone.

"I've been stagnating," I said from the speech Mom had made me memorize. My gut clenched. Since the monsoon had killed my sisters, I hadn't been able to face singing alone in another club. I'd moved home to Cleveland, grieving, and clinging to my parents as an island of normal, as far removed from my paranormal great-grandmother as possible.

No singing, no paycheck for rent and the suburban house in Ohio had become claustrophobic. I hastened back to Las Vegas for the audition and a chance to move on.

"I hope that the challenge of a competition will push me to become a better performer in a broader venue."

I sensed the three figures hunched over their clipboards.

My toes constrained by my white sandals began twitching, begging me to sing something. No storm tickled my nose. I planted my feet squarely, hoping my casual look of denim capris and gingham camp shirt over a white camisole projected the image of innocence I wanted them to see. I was just another kid with ambition and few outlets.

"You list your talent as singing. Have you ever danced before?" This voice belonged to a mature female. The way she controlled her breaths suggested that she'd had extensive vocal training, maybe opera.

"Just a few steps on stage to go with my songs, nothing formal or official." Thankfully, my dad and I had actually read the contract when I signed up for the show. The producers wanted dancers to learn to sing, and singers to learn to dance, paired initially with pros and then with each other, for a shot at a Broadway musical. Paragraph six, sub-paragraph G stipulated no previous skills in the opposite talent. So, I knew the answers they were looking for even though Mom had insisted Joycelyn, Brittney, and I take ballet when we were five. I'd lasted three lessons because the recorded music wobbled on the antique cassette player and it drove me to my first migraine.

"You list your age as twenty-one?" A third voice asked. I couldn't tell if it was a very high tenor male or a very low alto female, but younger than the other two.

"Yes." The truth, as far as I knew. Mom had given me a copy of a birth certificate when I left home in Cleveland to find fame and fortune in the desert city of lights. I presumed it was valid and accurate. With my family I couldn't be certain.

"But you look very young, too young, for the rules of the competition."

I'd read the rules in the magazine ad looking for contestants.

"Must be between eighteen and twenty-nine." Old enough to sign a contract, young enough to inspire other young people. More likely young enough to attract horny old men to pay big advertising bucks to sponsor the show.

"Good genes and a better moisturizer." I shrugged and smiled. Mom had looked forty on her sixtieth birthday. Dad was even older and still looked no more than fifty.

"Celandine is an unusual name," the first voice said. I suspected he was the executive producer, and recent widower, Bryant Thomas.

"Mom's a florist. Celandine is a kind of buttercup." I cut in a little too quickly. "Mostly my friends call me Celia."

"What are you going to sing for us today, Celia?" the opera trained woman asked.

Something bright and snappy suited for musical theater audiences, or should I wow them with an aria? Either way, I had to step away from the mic and let the power of my voice fill the studio rather than the electronics. I had ninety seconds, without accompaniment, to impress three people to advance me to the next round of challenges.

I'd done my research and chose a bluesy barn burner, "That Old Devil Moon," from *Finnian's Rainbow*. I pulled low notes up from my toes to croon the opening invitation, tilting my posture forward, giving the illusion of meeting the gaze of every man in the audience.

Then I straightened, lifting up onto my toes, hands fluttering at my sides as if willing myself into flight up to that full moon hanging high above the desert, bathing us all in cool, silvery light and mysterious shadow. I wooed, I enticed, I challenged my audience to take that flight with me.

But I used no magic. I had to do this on my own.

I held that last high note longer than a square count allowed. At the apex of tone, I drifted back down to ground level, releasing the marionette strings that held them enthralled.

They collapsed back into their chairs with mouths agape and eyes glazed, my last note lingering in the corners, waiting to pull them back into my web of music once more.

11

Ten long, agonizing seconds of dead silence before they recovered and bounced to their feet in applause.

I made a full sweeping curtsey as if wearing a magnificent ball gown instead of homely casual clothes.

The stage lights dimmed and the spotlight on me went out so that I could make out the faces of the three judges. As they finally regained their seats, each of them pulled a piece of paper from their clipboards, an airline ticket to Los Angeles. "Celandine, you're going to dance boot camp for *Here I Come, World.* I really hope you make it through that ordeal and go on to the actual televised show," the first man said, his deep voice caressing each word.

Dylan McQuilleran kicked his heels against the legs of the plastic and steel armless chair in Abigail FitzWarren's waiting room. His butt sweated from the impermeable seat. Never, ever, had anyone designed a more uncomfortable place to sit. He'd be willing to bet good shillings that Mrs. FitzWarren used this seating to force flunkies to abandon their quest to see her in person.

But he had an appointment with her. He'd waited two weeks to see Madame Director and flown six thousand miles.

He had a problem and knew it. *She,* unfortunately, was the only person alive who could fix it, or authorize someone else to fix it. Madame knew that, and she didn't want to deal with him.

He stood, shaking his casual khakis back into some semblance of freshness. Casual clothing might be the dress code for Hollywood, California, but it wasn't his idea of appearing professional. Of course, Northern Ireland rarely got as hot as southern California and a tailored suit was more comfortable there.

Step by measured step, he walked across the wide room, turned at the window that overlooked short, squat buildings, and acres of blacktop radiating heat. He could feel the triple-paned glass trying to melt despite the internal air conditioning cranked up to polar.

Above, the perpetual pollution haze marred his view of the distant hills.

A headache began stabbing him behind the eyes. *Not again!*

Slowly he began visualizing and reciting the Mayan alphabet, concentrating on little variations in the script that changed the pronunciation.

Isolated tribal groups in the mountains of Mexico each had a different accent in their remembrance of their linguistic heritage.

Decades ago, when finishing his first dissertation, he'd worked his way through three remote villages studying the nuances of pitch and tone, and was just starting on a fourth when a vampire had attacked. A real vampire, not some Goth teen playing pranks. The beast killed three of the strongest and brightest of the young adults who retained some knowledge from their grandparents of the pre-Conquistador language and even older folklore. Then the vampire held Dylan and one hundred others hostage for his next feeding frenzy.

The very idea of ever encountering such a creature had never entered Dylan's mind. A werewolf, maybe. Those legends abounded throughout Europe and the British Isles, including his beloved Ireland. But never a vampire.

Fortunately, a Hunter from the International Guild of Demon and Vampire Hunters had arrived. He'd chased the blood-thirsty creature across half of Mexico and the Yucatan. Dylan had worked with him to save the village, and thus the speakers of the ancient language. On the flight home, the Hunter had recruited Dylan into the Guild. His gift for languages allowed him to work all over the world. But he preferred speaking Gaelic with his ancestral people in Ireland.

Overlooking Hollywood while awaiting Abigail FitzWarren, he ran out of Mayan vocabulary.

Coptic followed in his litany to banish his headache, grateful that some people in the world still spoke the language and he could actually whisper the syllables.

The twisted cords in the back of his neck relaxed but he still had hot pokers stabbing his eyes. Only one thing remained, Sumerian. He gave his imagination free rein to invent sounds to go with the symbols.

Relief at last, just like the first weeks of recovery from augmentation surgery at the Guild clinic in Geneva.

Not everyone survived and remained sane.

He turned slowly and aimed his steps past the receptionist toward the double doors that led inward to Her Majesty. It seemed that seeing Mrs. FitzWarren in person was harder than getting an audience with Queen Elizabeth. All he needed for a few words with his sovereign was to make a lot of money and/or perform an heroic deed. He didn't know the algorithm to get past Abigail FitzWarren's security.

The nameless receptionist touched the wireless bud in her ear and said, "Yes, Ma'am." The same phrasing and pronunciation she'd use if she did indeed work for the queen.

"Mr. McQuilleran, Mrs. FitzWarren apologizes for the inconvenience, but she will be unable to see you today." She looked up with her sparkling blue eyes and batted long, long eyelashes at him as if flirting, or begging forgiveness.

Must be a natural response for every blonde, natural and bottled, in Hollywood, for they were all really actresses, just waiting for their "Big Break."

"I have an appointment!" Dylan kept his voice under control when he wanted to shout down that solid oak, double door barricade that Abigail FitzWarren hid behind.

"We realize that, sir, but something has come up. Here is a voucher for meals in the studio canteen, and one night at the business suites hotel where we house out-of-town associates." She handed him a piece of parchment weight paper with the Studio Twenty-three masthead across the top.

He took it, not quite admitting defeat. At least she was putting him up for the night and not dismissing him completely.

"Abby!" a deep, masculine voice roared from the single door main entrance, quite a bit less impressive than the double barrier to the inner sanctum.

Within three seconds, the simple plywood panel burst inward and slammed against the wall. The rubber stops bounced the door back toward the face of the intruder. It came to a shuddering halt by a big hand and stiff arm.

"Damnit, where is she?" the man snarled.

Not just any man. The legendary Bryant Thomas, executive producer of musical competition shows, and, more importantly, retired Hunter for the International Guild of Demon and Vampire Hunters.

Not many Hunters survived long enough to voluntarily retire, especially after three augmentations.

Dylan had studied this man's stalking, fighting, and slaying techniques at the academy and used them in the field more often than he liked to count.

The receptionist blanched and frantically searched for something under her desktop.

Dylan heard a faint click and whirr before Bryant Thomas jerked the double door latch, almost dislodging it from its screws, and threw the panels inward with the same force he'd used on the outer, flimsier door.

Opportunist that the Guild had trained him to be, Dylan followed Mr. Thomas into the Holy of Holies: Abigail FitzWarren's office.

"Mr. McQu... you can't..." the receptionist protested, half rising from her comfortable executive chair.

Dylan flashed her the kind of flirtatious smile he reserved for waitresses who had been particularly gracious and efficient to his demanding tastes.

"Abby, I've told you too many times, you aren't my boss anymore. How dare you inflict this investigation on me? I'm in the middle of launching a new series. I don't have time to babysit a paranormal who probably hasn't a malicious bone in her body," Thomas shouted loud enough to be heard throughout the complex of his Studio Twenty-six.

Or was it Twenty-three? Dylan couldn't remember. More evidence that something strange was going on in his brain. Remembering details was a requirement for his job.

Mrs. FitzWarren shifted her glance to take in Dylan's presence, then back to Bryant Thomas. "Sweetie, we are not alone," she cooed with a bit of a British clip in the undertone, capturing Bryant's gaze with her own. She had her dark-blonde hair swept back into an elegant chignon and wore a professional blouse in dove grey with a double strand of grey pearls and matching earrings. Her charcoal blazer hung from a hanger, on a coat rack behind her. Dylan had only seen her a few times, but he guessed that her style tended toward a slightly flared charcoal skirt that flirted with her knees when she walked. She was not a slacks kind of person.

Like so many Guild members it was impossible to judge her age. She looked forty-five, but she'd been director over twenty years with at least another twenty in the field before that.

Every pencil, note, and file folder rested neatly aligned with the edges and corners of her massive desktop. Even her three computer monitors and keyboard lined up at precise forty-five-degree angles along with her landline that carried a launchpad of buttons worthy of NASA. If she used a mobile phone or tablet, they weren't visible.

Bryant Thomas whirled around to face Dylan. He performed a quick visual assessment, raking Dylan from hair to toes and back again. Then he gave one sniff and returned his attention to Mrs. FitzWarren. "He smells like a Hunter. Get him to do your dirty work." One quick pivot and he exited as rapidly as he had come, every line of his body graceful and controlled.

"Where will you be, Bryant, dear?"

"In my office, where I'm supposed to be, not babysitting your Siren Singer." And he was gone.

"Oh dear," Mrs. FitzWarren sighed. Then her gaze riveted on the heavy stationery Dylan still held. He hadn't had time to fold it and stuff it into his shirt pocket. "If you are anyone but Dylan McQuilleran from the Belfast office, I must ask you to leave."

"I'm McQuilleran and I was in the Belfast office yesterday until you answered my request for an interview."

"Good. Here's your new assignment." She typed rapidly, checked her words on the screen, then hit a double key command. In the outer office, a printer mumbled to itself.

Not very secure, he thought. *Anyone could be out there to read the printout. Anyone. Including a demon or vampire.*

"Marci at the front desk will hand you the details. A car will be waiting for you at the front gate of the studio to take you to your new lodging. Report to me at the mobile number in your instructions. I believe we can place you as publicity manager of Bryant's new show. But your real job will be to discover which contestant in the show is actually a siren and make certain she is safe from predators and the show is safe from her. You will start by monitoring the next set of contestant interviews. There will be outside press people there. Keep them orderly and contained."

Then she typed a few more commands and focused on her monitor.

"What the fu...."

"Language, Mr. McQuilleran. We do not tolerate foul language within my hearing."

Bryant Thomas got away with cursing *and* calling her Abby. What kind of relationship did he have with Madame?

And she still hadn't solved Dylan's problem.

CHAPTER 2

"Comb your hair behind your ear, sweetie pie," a woman wearing a press badge drawled as she tucked a stray curl of my short hair out of the way. The hairdresser had just spent twenty minutes trying to get that single strand to sweep forward into a half circle curl. I had chosen a no-nonsense pixie cut that never flopped out of place after swimming. The attempts by the professionals to soften the otherwise sharp lines of my straight blonde hair made me look... well, more friendly and approachable.

"Um...." I tried to protest. My skin tingled on the edge of a burn where her fingers had touched me.

What?

The press woman's gaze captured mine. I needed her to guide me forward. I couldn't break free of her compelling golden eyes with the oblong pupils...

"Trust me, sweetie pie. You want that beautiful face fully visible to the cameras, not hiding behind an inept coiffure. The casting couch may be illegal now, but every effing man in Hollywood expects you to go to bed with him. Straight no-nonsense lines and get a gun and a carry permit. You won't regret it."

I believed her. Her eyes told me that she spoke the truth, only she knew what was best for me...

"Oh and lose the fresh sea breeze perfume. Too much of an aphrodisiac."

"And who are you?" A tall man with dark auburn hair and an educated, but faint Irish accent, emerged from behind the fixed television camera and spotlights. He marched up to me, where I was seated at the precise center of the lighted area with a backdrop of a rehearsal hall behind me. He swept my hair forward again back to where it belonged, with a touch as light and as soothing as a water fern.

He broke my line-of-sight with the woman. I blinked rapidly, suddenly knowing she was wrong about my hair and the men I had to deal with, and about getting a gun. Dad had taught me how to defend myself against overly aggressive football players in High School. Most Hollywood producers were flabbier and had better control over their hormones.

Dylan McQuilleran, the head of publicity for the studio, turned to face the intruding woman. He'd introduced himself as each of the contestants entered the rehearsal hall for a recorded interview.

The almost burn from the woman's touch vanished as he withdrew his fingers from my face. Had they lingered a bit longer than appropriate?

His eyes kept moving, never fixating on any one thing or person—especially the intruder with the hypnotic gaze.

"I have full authorization to be here," she said in an insistent tone as she flipped the laminated badge dangling on a long cord between her full breasts. Her gesture challenged him to fix all of his attention on her assets rather than the dominating word "PRESS". Her yellow knit top that matched her bottle-blonde bob molded her figure a little too snugly for my taste. Her chocolate brown capris did nothing to hide an extra twenty pounds on her hips. But her yellow straw sandals with three-inch wedge heels gave her an illusion of height and therefore command.

Alpha Bitch came into my mind as the perfect description.

"You have permission to observe and take notes, no photographs, no interference, and NO questions." Dylan stepped toward her, menacingly invading her space.

A waft of musk rose out of nowhere, with no obvious source. Immediately I thought of the family dog. Prince had been a black mutt with a lot of, but not all, Labrador in his ancestry. After swimming with the family, he always needed to share Lake Erie with us. And he smelled just like that musk.

Meanwhile the camera operator straightened away from the eye piece and slumped against the nearest wall. "We're going to be here awhile," he muttered.

"Dylan, can we get on with this? We're already running an hour late," the show's hostess whined. Her west coast accent sounded flat and uninteresting compared to Dylan's Irish lilt.

She slapped a tablet against her thigh. The contestants called her Little Miss Bouncy as a pun on her exotic name that no one ever said in my hearing. She hadn't introduced herself. Her body language said that she was important enough that I should know her already. The open screen on the mini-computer told her who I was.

"Who are you and which tabloid do you represent?" Dylan demanded of the press woman again. He took another step forward, forcing her to step back.

The hairdresser scooted between them and me, brandishing a curling iron in one hand and a can of hairspray in the other. Her short apron bristled with combs, brushes, scissors and other arcane tools of her trade.

I accepted her ministrations while listening closely to the music in Dylan's voice. Even when sharpened by anger and indignation he reminded me of a bard extolling the history of the land in poetry.

"Call me Stevie, sweetie pie," said the alpha bitch trying to engage Dylan's gaze with her own.

"I need your full name and your employer so that I may have you both banned from this studio."

He almost cursed under his breath, something about an interfering bitch. *Bitch.* That word again.

Personally, I wouldn't insult my female dog at home—the latest replacement for Prince—by calling this woman a bitch.

"Stevie will have to do." She lifted her chin and faced him down.

I'd call her audacious as well as interfering.

Dylan snapped a picture of her on his phone and quickly emailed it somewhere with a few words of text. He cocked his head, one eye on the woman and the other on the screen.

"You don't want to do that, Mister," Stevie's voice turned steely. "People listen to me in this town. This is your first show, and by the way you are mangling these interviews, it will be your last job in this town. I'll still be around when the world has forgotten you."

Dylan's nose wrinkled in distaste. "If you leave now, you will avoid the indignity of being carried out in handcuffs and dumped in the street." His lip curled showing his eye teeth. "The full moon approaches and you stink of it."

She lifted her own lip showing a full set of very sharp teeth.

There was something going on here I couldn't comprehend. Unfortunately, my nose was not as keen as my ear. The nuances in their words still evaded me.

He pulled a glowing pendant from beneath his golf shirt and brandished it at her.

She snarled and ran out of the room shielding her eyes as if she'd looked directly into the sun. Her wedged heels clomped on the floor too loudly. "You won't live long enough to regret this," she growled.

"Go ahead with the interviews. We won't be bothered again," Dylan said, consulting his tablet. Then he turned abruptly and disappeared into the darkness outside the spotlight.

"Finally," Little Miss Bouncy said on a long exhale. She pasted on a bright smile and sat in the canvas and wood folding chair beside mine. With a snap of her fingers the cameraman returned to his post and a red light blinked to indicate recording had begun. "Celandine Fisher, Celia, what made you accept the challenge of the long and arduous audition process?"

I almost believed her smile as I took a deep breath and sought appropriate words while wondering what had just happened between Dylan and the reporter "Stevie".

~

Dylan counted impatiently while grinding his teeth, as Elevator B slowly ground upward toward Mrs. Abigail FitzWarren's office. For once all of the nanobots in his brain were firing in sync. He had his full range of powers available. When the lift stopped on the fifth floor at the top of the flat-roofed building, he blinked twice to engage his infrared vision. The heat signature of the last person to use this conveyance shone on the keypad above the normal floor number panel.

Ah, the code to open the door had changed since this morning. He punched the new code based upon the fading red glows, faintest first, most dominant last.

Silently the door slid to the left. Dylan sidled through before they finished opening and slammed into the outer office of the Guild's director, just as Bryant Thomas had earlier.

The scowl on his face must have convinced the receptionist he meant business. The electronic lock buzzed before he could knock on the double doors to the inner sanctum. He hit them with a flat palm and straight arm with all of the super strength the Guild had given him.

"We have a security leak," he said before he'd cleared the entry. He didn't have time for cowering petitions for help with a problem. Mrs. FitzWarren had given him a job and a cover story. He intended to do both properly, like any highly trained Hunter for the Guild.

His cover story named him press-secretary to Bryant Thomas, specially chosen by the big man himself to feed positive information and filtered gossip to the media. He had control of email accounts, a web site, and twitter feed. He sent his releases in English, Spanish, Vietnamese, and Japanese.

Boring languages. But useful in getting along in a multi-cultural world. He'd rather play with ancient Hindi, or Sub-Saharan tongue clicks.

Abigail FitzWarren half rose as she put her computer on lockdown with a single key stroke. The blue light from the monitor shut off abruptly. So did the tablet.

"Explain," she barked. She already had her hand at the back of her waist where a holster snugged up against the small of her back. She hadn't left her field training behind when assuming administrative roles in the Guild.

Dylan had been visiting the Guild clinic in Geneva for his migraines when Abigail FitzWarren was discharged from her latest augmentation. Her speed and agility should be phenomenal.

"A werewolf with a press pass just tried to rearrange one of the contestant interviews. I took her photo and emailed it to the guards at all the gates. On my own authority I have banned her from conventional entrance. That does not mean she can't climb a fence or dig under a wall."

He went to the western wall of windows and engaged his long-distance vision. The guard shack snapped into view as clear as if he was within five meters instead of three hundred. One uniformed man removed the handcuffs from Stevie, not silver unfortunately. Another guard opened the pedestrian gate in the wall with one hand on his still-holstered weapon. His eyes roved constantly, taking in Stevie as well as the foot traffic outside.

A shadowy figure lurked just beyond the gate and to the side. An extra blink and Dylan's focus zoomed in another degree of magnitude —the highest he could manage and he couldn't hold it long. The profile of a swarthy man, middling height and aquiline features emerged from the static of his vision.

As he lost his ability to keep the high degree of magnification, the image of a thousand ancient coins flashed through his memory, Roman and Greek mostly, some earlier, some later. The man could have the face of any one of a hundred legendary monarchs from the oldest of civilizations.

Then Dylan was back to the limits of normal vision and the beginnings of a headache.

The man faded from his view as he watched the first guard say something rude to Stevie and shove her unceremoniously through the gate. The second guard spoke words that Dylan could not hear. And didn't care to lip read.

He kept searching for the achingly familiar face from antiquity. But the man had disappeared.

His adrenaline rush faded, and his knees grew rubbery. His lungs deflated.

"Why didn't you shoot her?" Abigail touched an ear bud and sank back into her throne of an office chair.

"No silver bullets in my gun and the place was much too public." Dylan stumbled into the armchair that faced the desk. He had to lean his head back, resting his neck on the back of the chair and pressed his index fingers into his temples. He no longer cared about niceties and polite supplications. "Now about those screwy nanobots you put in my head that give me blinding migraines."

"Any other symptoms?" Abigail asked. She brought her computer back to life and typed a twelve-stroke command.

He let his mind drift while she did what she needed to.

He'd reached way beyond the point where examination of an obscure language could ease his pain. Damn he wished he could hear some Sumerian. He thought that the sentence and phrasing cadence followed a musical context...

He drifted some more, maybe slept.

"How long?" she asked after an unknowable amount of time.

He jerked awake, the migraine mostly gone. His vision cleared when he opened his eyes.

"A few months. It came on suddenly after a job. I bespelled an English Billy ghoul back into his grave."

"Which cemetery?"

"Small church about two miles from the border. Back in the time of the Troubles the English would bury a Catholic in a Prot cemetery if they were informants—Billys."

"But the guy did not rest easy because he betrayed his own. So, he hangs around his little plot, eating the flesh of fresh corpses and of teens who go there thinking it's a private place to snog." Her original London west end accent came through more clearly when she used slang from her childhood.

"Did he bite you?" she continued.

"I... I don't know." Dylan sat up straighter and winced as the headache threatened to return.

"What triggers it?"

He had to think a bit about that. "Surges of adrenaline, at first. Now they are random."

"Hmmmm..." She tapped a fingernail against her teeth. "When you aren't fighting this, try to remember the exact wording of the spell you used to quell the ghoul and write it down. I'll get the medicos in Geneva working on it. You've done your job today. Go home and get some rest. I'll get back to you when I know more."

He snapped his fingers at a pad of paper and a pen on the side of her desk. Words evaded him as he pictured the ancient Gaelic he'd used in his mind. She handed him the writing implements.

Quickly, neatly he let the spell flow through him into his fingers as he wrote. The musicality of the words floated in front of his eyes. On a long sigh he finished writing with a wild flourish like an opera singer trilling scales upward to finish an aria.

He handed the paper back to Mrs. FitzWarren, his headache banished.

She turned back to her computer and started working again.

He and his problem were dismissed.

CHAPTER 3

I slid into the steaming, bubbling water of the hexagonal shaped hot tub. I shifted until I found the right spot and let a jet pound my lower back. My legs drifted upward in the water and I didn't have enough strength left to force them back down.

Adding dancing to my repertoire wasn't easy. I even dreamed of endless repetitions of shuffle ball change. There were days I was certain I'd never master the simplest *plié, pointe.*

The three other people spread out around the pool also let their tortured legs drift free, each sighing in the relief that only hot water can give. This hotel had added the luxury of sea salt to the hot tub for extra healing properties. All four of us were singers who'd endured dance bootcamp.

Combine the rehearsals with our professional partners, staging of a group number to open the show, interviews, and costume fittings, my head was as tired as my body. I dreaded the sessions with the irascible costume designer most. Millie cursed us when our musculature changed due to the unnatural exercise and therefore so did our sizes and the fit of the sequined costumes.

Frankly, I'd rather sing the most challenging opera ever composed and turn over the dance numbers to those born to that talent.

Three weeks ago, one hundred singers and one hundred dancers had descended upon the studio complex in Hollywood. Each day some were eliminated, packed their bags, and went home. We were down to ten in each category. Only two of us, one dancer and one singer, would survive the coming weeks of competition.

Next Sunday, three days from now, we'd begin recording live performances. At the end of the season, the last two standing would win cash prizes and solo roles in a Broadway Musical. The musical had yet to be announced, but rumor had it that a revival of *Hauntings*, written and composed by our music director, Margot Tremayne, was the front runner.

I thought I knew every piece of music written for the theater, but I'd never heard of this particular play, nor any of its music.

"Anyone seen Terry and Trish this evening?" Lisa, one of my roommates, asked.

"Heard they went surfing," Brad replied, his voice slightly slurred with total relaxation.

"That's what, four times this week?" I asked.

"Yeah, they live at the beach when they aren't in rehearsal," Brad replied. "I *wish* I had that much energy and stamina. "Have you heard them belt out songs with Ethel Merman gusto?"

"Lots of vim and vigor but slightly flat, *a la* Frank Sinatra," Lisa replied.

My eyes listed at half-mast as my mind played catch with the few white clouds above. Memories of letting my body drift upon tropical seas surrounding an isolated island edged toward dreams. The scent of salt permeated the air, as it should.

Salt! Tropics!

I'd never been to Hawaii, let alone Fiji or any of the other top tourist spots. My family avoided proximity to saltwater oceans for good reasons.

Not *my* memories.

My nose twitched.

My mind and eyes snapped to full awareness of how the air, grey/brown from pollution and not rain clouds, had cooled ten degrees in the blink of an eye. The puffy white clouds had begun to tower. I sat up straighter, no longer concerned with my aching body.

A shadow flitted past the inside of a low stone wall that surrounded the pool patio. Then it disappeared through a wrought iron gate. I hadn't seen that particular shadow since early childhood when my sisters and I played with our invisible friend, a grandfatherly "Fred."

I banished the memory as I concentrated on the shape of the clouds, looking for trouble.

"Did I just see a flicker of lightning?" Jenny asked.

"I smell ozone," Brad added. "You only get that when lightning strikes."

"The rumble in the distance has a different tone from traffic," Lisa said. She stood up and reached for her towel even as she glided to the ladder and climbed out.

Dangerous! Metal railings and water, both conductors of electricity if the storm came any closer. "Looks like it's time to go inside and stay there." I warned them. The itch inside my nose began to burn.

"Margaritas in my room." Brad licked his lips and reached for his own towel. He disdained the ladder and used the various ledges of the pool to climb out, but then his legs were longer than petite Lisa's, or mine. "The tequila is cheap, but I have a really cool blender, and few tricks up my sleeve." His voice took on the lilt of the Caribbean.

That's one of the things special to singers, our ears are so attuned to tiny nuances of sound that we can mimic almost any accent upon first hearing.

"Did I tell you I work as a bartender between singing gigs?" Brad continued as he mimicked a two-step suggestive of tropical rhythms.

I waited until I had the hot tub to myself and the others were out of earshot before I too climbed up to the pool deck. When I turned due west and lifted my face to the first drops of rain, I whispered an incantation in a language older than time.

Then I added my own stern warning. "I've had enough of you,

Mummy. I'm two generations removed from my elemental roots. Go find someone else to play with."

But I need you, granddaughter. I need your voice and your power to finally rid the Earth of the infestation of humans. I'm tired of doing this alone. Even my beloved mate has deserted me.

"Get over it, Mummy! We humans are much more numerous than your descendants will ever be. We are a dynamic force that has great genius, and vital energy. We've grown beyond our ancient Earth-bound beginnings and now reach for the stars."

You have no right to count yourself among humans. They kill each other with gleeful abandon and pollute our Earth and Oceans.

"And you and your kind don't do the same? Don't tell me you are innocent. You sent my mother and her two teenage daughters into a mating frenzy during a huge storm. All three of them got pregnant that night. Mom raised me and my two nieces together as if we were sisters. Triplets with the same birthday. And you killed both of them. You stole them from me. My heart aches with emptiness every minute of every day now. I sing to honor them, not you."

Silence.

"Did you ever think that I might need my *sisters* to complete my talent?"

The thunderheads moved northwestward taking their rain and wind elsewhere.

My nose ceased to twitch.

I turned my back on the storm and the StormMother and walked back to the hotel, grateful that I had a poolside room and didn't have to climb any stairs. My legs felt like soft, hot rubber.

A whisper of a breeze echoed around the back of my head.

Your nieces had no power. No-account half-breeds! You do not need them. You need only me to complete your talent.

Then silence, as if a door had closed between me and Mummy, just as had happened in childhood when Fred protected me and my sisters from my grandmother.

~

Bryant Thomas, the producer and judge of the competition stood in front of the gathered contestants and staff. Dylan held a stylus over his tablet to take notes. Mr. Thomas had banished the cameras. The press release Dylan had to write would be all the more powerful for its simplicity.

"Ladies and gentlemen," Bryant said in a strong, theater-trained voice. Then he had to pause and cough into his clenched hand.

Uh oh! Dylan scrambled to open a new window on his tablet and pulled up local news feed.

"I'm terribly sorry I have to inform you of... of the death of two of our fellow competitors." The knuckles of Bryant's clenched fist showed white.

A gasp of horror rippled around the room—one of the rehearsal studios—just as Dylan spotted the glaring headline on the news feed. A freak sneaker wave; two surfers, both strong swimmers, caught in the undertow.

"Trish Finellero, a singer, and her older brother Terry, a dancer, drowned last night while surfing," Mr. Thomas continued.

Dylan scanned the room as his thoughts raced through various phrases slanted toward an emotional press release. Most of the eighteen remaining contestants, and their professional partners looked dismayed. Celia Fisher lost all color to her lovely face, her eyes looked glazed as she swayed on her feet. Paul, her short and wiry Asian partner, caught her around the waist until she found her balance again.

Dylan shouldered his way through the crowd and took a position on Celia's other side, just in case he needed to help her out of the stuffy room.

He wondered just how close she'd been to the siblings that their death affected her so deeply. He thought that Trish and Terry had stuck pretty close to each other, and no one else. Celia seemed friendly enough, always in the middle of a crowd with no one person in particular closer than her partner Paul.

Mr. Thomas said a few more words about a memorial before the Finellero parents came to take their children home for burial.

Celia turned her back to the group and let tears flow down her cheeks. Paul reached to support her once again. She shook him off and marched out of the room, head bowed, shoulders shaking with heavy sobs.

Dylan eased through the mingling people and followed her back to the empty studio where she and Paul were scheduled to rehearse. He considered going to her, offering her a shoulder to cry on or a neutral figure to pour out her emotional distress.

Just as he reached for the doorknob, the nanos in his brain started screaming at him that there was a connection he should pay attention to. But they were so strident he had to back off, down the hallway past three more studios, and press his fingers hard against his temples.

Before the pressure could contain the warning signals, Paul had rushed into Celia's studio. "Mei Mei, talk to me. Tell me what you need!" He slammed the door after him, cutting off the girl's response.

Dylan retreated, finally coherent enough to write the press release the siblings deserved.

Wallowing in self-pity would feed the StormMother's wrath and rob me of the strength to resist her. So, I accepted Paul's compelling hug, clinging to him only long enough to gain control of my fear and turn it to cleansing anger.

I had to stay strong to fight Mummy with my intellect and guile. Paul couldn't help with that. But he could help me learn our first competition number.

The music came up. I counted the notes and matched my breaths to the rhythm, taking in as much air as I needed to complete a full phrase of lyrics. The influx of oxygen sent strength and energy through my lungs and out to every muscle and tendon. My increased blood flow made my toes and legs and arms beg to move with the compelling music.

If I gained nothing else from this competition, the professional training in both song and dance gave me new confidence and mastery. It was all about breathing.

Mummy, of course, would discount the training. According to her, I needed only my instincts to fulfill her needs.

To make it in the mundane world, I needed training. Music had grown far beyond Mummy's simple siren call, made up on the spot, to match the secret desires of her victim.

Paul ran a scale on the practice piano. He had a lovely tenor voice but little training or power behind his songs. He'd featured in three different musical shows on the road as a dancer and chorus singer, but never made it to solo roles or to Broadway. I was doing my best to coach him in song while he taught me to dance. Twice a week we met with professional coaches for both skills.

"That's not like you, Celia. You went off pitch on an easy high C." He frowned at the keyboard and ran the scale again.

"It's out of tune," I said.

"Shouldn't be. The board on the door says it was just tuned yesterday."

I didn't remind him that I had perfect pitch and was matching the piano. That's a skill you learn when working the night club circuit in Las Vegas: you make the most out of your accompaniment or you sing a cappella. One or the other. No compromise.

"Report it to management. We'll work on your vocals later. Right now, I'm still floundering with the dance routines." I grabbed his hand and pulled him upright. "You can fake singing. I can't fake dancing."

He ran me through fifteen minutes of intense ballet warm up exercises. They came easier today than any of the three weeks before. Maybe the change in air pressure from Mummy going away in a sulk helped me move through the air.

But when it came time to put on tap shoes and twirl a baton to the tune of "76 Trombones," I tripped three times just getting to the middle of the studio.

Paul shook his head at me. His straight, black hair flapped into his eyes. "I wish I knew a better way to help you develop your sense of space. From the waist up you are beautiful, and graceful as all get out. Hips down you move like a fish out of water. All flop."

I hung my head in disappointment. For three weeks I'd been learning the steps by will power alone and bullying my way through the competition primarily on my voice.

Fish out of water! His words hit me in the gut. Well, duh. Technically I was a fish out of water. A sea nymph for a grandmother, a siren for a mother, and saltwater in my veins. I might not have a mermaid's tail, but I swam like one.

I didn't want to know if swimming in sea water would let me grow a tail, or if such a tail would be permanent. I liked my legs.

"If I'm a fish out of water, why can't we rehearse in the hotel pool?"

He stilled, then his eyes brightened as he looked me full in the face. "Worth trying. You learn how the moves feel when supported by water and hopefully muscle memory will kick in when we hit the stage." He grabbed my hand and ran with me down the stairs and into his car in the back parking lot.

Ten minutes later, wearing a bathing suit—skimpy as it was it still felt like too much fabric between me and the life-giving force of the water—I dove into the hotel pool, smooth and sleek, accepting the water as a natural habitat.

Mid-morning on a weekday meant we had the place to ourselves. All the other competitors were busy in their studios. Except Dylan, the guy from publicity who was always on the periphery, sat at a poolside table with a big sun umbrella shading his Irish fair skin. He had his laptop open, his tablet at hand, and phone to his ear. I wasn't sure if he even knew someone else was in the area.

Paul stepped cautiously into the shallow end, adjusting to the change in temperature inch by inch. Not a natural swimmer.

I came up for air right beside him, the water lapping at my hips. We walked through the steps, slowly at first, then a second time closer to the tempo of the recorded music that awaited us in a boom box on the cement surround.

The weight of the world lifted from my muscles. My blood

warmed and flowed more smoothly, aligning salinity as well as temperature.

Shuffle ball change, strike right, cross, strike right again. Repeat on the left.

"And remember to point your toe."

Paul assured me these steps were basic, raw beginner stuff. For the first time I believed him. I rolled into the next sequence without having to think about it.

An hour later I felt like a dancer! I'd gone through the entire ninety second routine five times without stumbling or hesitating. I glowed with joy.

And working in sync with Paul made my heart flutter. My chest swelled with new emotions. I could fall in love with this guy.

But Paul drooped with fatigue.

"You don't swim much," I confirmed on a long, regretful sigh.

"Not by a long shot." He shuffled over to the ladder and hauled himself out of the water. He sat on the side of the pool, feet dangling in the water while the sun dried his back and his hair. "Pools were a luxury in my neighborhood. Membership in a gym with a pool cost even more."

"You rest a bit while I swim." He'd said the opposite to me many times, offering to let me sit and sink into my own doldrums while he worked out steps to new music.

I took off in an easy crawl, undulating from my hips and knees in imitation of the fish I called my brothers. I lost track of time.

"Hey, mermaid, it's time for lunch. Then vocals," Paul called to me.

Coming out of my unfocused melding with the water, I noticed the angle of the sun had shifted and shortened the shadows.

Just to prove to myself that I remembered the dance, I stood squarely on the pool deck, took a deep breath and walked through the dance.

A big smile filled Paul' face. "I'll make a dancer out of you yet."

CHAPTER 4

"This's weird," Dylan said, slapping the screen of the production sound board. The line indicating tonal volume remained flat.

He looked to Jeff Baumeister, the sound engineer sitting beside him in the booth above the television theater at the heart of Studio Twenty-Three. Dylan had finally seen the number on the side of a building and memorized it.

Memorizing things kept the nanobots in his brain from trying to break free and make him see things that weren't there. Like the red and teal dragon flitting among the lights in the shadowed audience seats at the top of the theater.

"She turned off her mic," said Margot Tremayne, musical director for *Here I Come, World,* and a bunch of other Bryant Thomas Productions. She'd just walked into the production booth with a stack of sheet music covered in red scribbled notes all over every page.

"Then why do I hear every note she sings coming through my headphones?" Jeff gestured toward the ear cupping device that blocked out every nuance of sound except what the microphone wiring fed him. He pointed through the glass barrier of the booth to the projection on a huge screen of a lean girl with legs that went on forever, dressed as if ready for a day of gardening. She'd used the simplicity of her clothes as a guise for the temptress she truly was. The cameras had shifted from the singer to the judges at her audition who had sat in stunned silence for a full minute when she finished. This recording was for some of the filler material in tomorrow night's performance.

Dylan had lurked around the studio all week, watching and listening for anything paranormal. Even benign entities could be pushed into violence to keep their talents hidden. The girl had pipes to spare. Who cared if her feet were often a nanosecond behind those of her partner? He doubted anyone without Guild enhancement could see the difference.

Margot stilled her hands and paused with the pile of papers inches above the desk. She stared; eyes squinted in concentration. "I don't know," she whispered. "But it is weird. I think Bryant Thomas needs to know about this." She dropped the papers, sending sheet music sliding in a dozen different directions, and scooted out of the booth as if her flared denim skirt was on fire.

Secondary instructions from Home Office in London—now only second in authority since Abigail Fitzwarren had moved the bulk of her operations to Hollywood—had told Dylan that he could trust Margot with sensitive information. She was knowledgeable about the Guild but not affiliated. If she said that recording was weird, then he needed to pay attention.

His primary target was to observe and report activities of a Siren.

Not many of them around. The Guild had only ancient sources to guide him. This girl, originally from Cleveland, looked to be the one he needed to follow. He'd suspected her the first time he heard her sing.

Mrs. FitzWarren was always vague about the identities of the people the Guild watched, just in case an innocent was fronting for the true paranormal.

He turned his attention to watching Jeff as he tried to get the screen to show the natural spikes and dips of a human voice.

"Let me try something..." Jeff mused, half to himself, half to Dylan. "Sometimes if there's a gremlin in the programing, files will go to

Trash rather than into a designated destination." He twisted his chair to a side desk and a computer monitor. Six clicks later he raised his arms over his head and fist bumped the air. "Yeeeas! There it is, a temporary back-up file with the right time stamp." He pulled it up and replaced his headphones.

Dylan grabbed a second pair and placed them over his ears, making sure they were plugged into the right jack so he could hear what Jeff heard while watching clear images on multiple monitors, each from a different camera.

He listened closely to the brief discussion among the judges before the audition. No anomalies, just a slight nervous breathiness from the girl. That irregularity was filtered out in editing, if anyone but Dylan noticed it.

The lights changed. The girl, Celia, stepped back from the stand-up mic and crooned softly, eyes fixed on the second balcony where one might expect the old devil moon to hang enticingly in the sky. Images of hot summer nights, a full moon tinted blue around the edges, the sweet smell of freshly mown hay, and the feel of a loving girl in his arms…

Celia's voice built into an ecstatic crescendo, then slid softly back into remembered bliss.

Dylan jerked awake, suddenly aware of the absence of sound. He resisted the urge to check for dampness in his groin.

Celia Fisher was the most sultry of Torch Singers he'd ever heard.

He understood the long, astonished silence from the judges, before bursting into applause so loud Jeff had to tone down the higher range of sound and boost the bass to compensate.

Dylan fallen under the girl's spell in this *recording* just as the judges had at the live audition.

Something weird indeed. He needed weird to report to Abigail FitzWarren so he could get the boss's attention long enough to find out if there was a fix for his brain, or if he faced a lobotomy and early retirement.

～

A whole trailer to myself! Not bad for a dressing room. I wasn't used to the luxury that Hollywood considered normal. What was more beautiful was that I didn't have to deal with my own hair and makeup. I *did* have to take care of the costumes the studio provided or answer to Millie, the wardrobe mistress. No bent sequins, or loose elastic straps, or creased chiffon allowed.

I breathed in the unique air of a tiny trailer parked outside the back door of Studio Twenty-three. The perfume of old meals and body sweat from previous occupants lingered, the universal essence of theater dressing rooms. But someone other than me had cleaned the place with bleach and put fresh linens on the single bed in the back compartment and added thick, fluffy towels in the bathroom with a tiny, metal shower stall. The closet might hold three costume changes and one set of street clothes. A fat person couldn't squeeze into this place, and a tall person would bump his head, but I fit nicely.

Up front, I had a padded bench that doubled as a sofa, or possibly a second bed, two dinky swivel armchairs, a kitchen table with bench seating shoved up against an outside wall, with a kitchen counter complete with microwave, coffee maker, and mini fridge.

And light! Lots and lots of light streamed in through the windows —one in the bedroom and one in the parlor. I also had recessed ceiling lights and lamps scattered about.

I turned a full circle in delight. This was my space and mine alone. So much better than a dim basement I had to share with at least two other people. I loved Brittney and Joycelyn, truly and deeply. But I remembered our silly arguments over space and occasionally over trampling each other's costumes. That brought a half smile to my face, tempered by grief. We always sang in better harmony after a fight.

Delicately I removed my sequin encrusted majorette costume and hung it up in the closet. The breakaway pink coveralls went onto another hanger. Millie, the costume designer would have my head if a single disc of shiny plastic got bent. Then I threw a robe over my nakedness and stretched out on the bed.

I'd survived dress rehearsal and had two and a half hours all to myself before I needed to prepare for the first live show of the competition.

Tap, tap, tap. A delicate fist knocked on the screen door.

I sighed. "Who is it?" I wasn't about to heave myself off the bed for just anyone. But there was so much activity surrounding a television show that I didn't understand yet, I never knew when I might be needed for a lighting, or sound check, for a costume alteration, or even a group photo shoot for publicity.

The flimsy door creaked open and soft footsteps climbed the two steps at the entry.

Didn't that press secretary have any sense of privacy?

"Sweetie, are you in here?" came a syrupy voice.

"Mummy!"

"Of course, dear. You don't think I'd miss such a monumental event as my favorite granddaughter's first television performance."

When the StormMother came down from the clouds long enough to take on human form, she usually chose to be a society matron wrapped in an ermine stole (she'd never wear the pelt of a sea animal) and pearls (she gladly liberated shellfish from an irritant that grew into pearls) and a unique gown commissioned from the best Paris designers for the event. Today she wore sea foam green, of course. The same color tinted her white hair, coiffed in multiple braids coiled around her head like an arrangement of seaweed and coral.

And she'd clad her feet in iridescent pumps, also in sea foam green, with four-inch spike heels worthy of a sea serpent's spines—weapons in themselves.

"You don't usually approve of my human activities. They aren't worthy of your notice." I collapsed back onto the mattress, for the first time fully aware of how thin and lumpy it was.

"But then, you drowned two expert swimmers who were strong contenders in the competition." There. I said it. I knew she was responsible as soon as I'd heard the news. I hadn't known Trish and Terry well, but I liked them. They were innocents and didn't deserve to die.

They weren't truly worthy of Mummy's vengeance.

Mummy shrugged off my accusation and began wandering the tiny trailer, about three steps in any one direction. "Well, I have decided that your father, while not a god or a king, is regarded as a hero among his peers. That means you are a true Siren of my breeding and I should nurture your career."

"Thanks, but no thanks. The studio has provided me with names of approved agents and business managers, if I survive tonight's competition."

"Oh, you will, darling. Did you know that late last night your producer, Mr. Thomas, approved a change in the voting rules?" She continued barely pausing to draw breath. "The judges scores count for half; they are present and thus vulnerable to your magic. The live audience have one quarter of the votes and are also present and vulnerable. Lastly the television viewers only have a quarter. They are not subject to your powers but with only one quarter of the votes, they barely count. Other shows give half the score to call in votes. Now they can still feel like they are participating, but without enough sway to truly skew the scores based on... whatever it is that counts in television land. That means you are a shoo-in." She flipped open her fingers into a parody of jazz hands.

Her attitude reminded me of the arguments she presented to Mom and Dad the day Brittney, Joycelyn, and I started kindergarten. She'd argued against us going to a public school. According to her, she would arrange for private tutors who would nurture our singing talents and our need to swim in saltwater under her command.

Dad went all Hunter mode and physically picked her up and threw her into our pool, where he'd just refreshed the chlorine.

Mummy shot upward into the clouds, a roiling column of mist—or smoke—screaming at how the chemicals burned her.

My nieces had laughed at the time.

Fred had manifested for a moment and joined their laughter, then faded from reality as he followed Mummy upward.

Upon that memory came the realization of why my girls had died in Las Vegas.

So why was Fred hanging around again? I hadn't seen him since...

since second grade when most children gave up their invisible playmates. Joycelyn, Brittney, and I had all agreed that it was time to let Fred go.

The StormMother was not someone you laughed at, ever.

"Mummy, I don't want to win by magic. I want to prove myself a contender based on my talents, the whole package of personality, looks, dancing, and singing. I have to live in this world, unlike you, who only chooses to when it's convenient."

"You know it's harder to withhold the magic in your voice than to let it flow free like a surging tide." She narrowed her eyes as she peered at me.

I glared at her, willing her to be gone.

"Well, do your best, sweetie. I know your parents will be in the audience cheering you on. Perhaps I can persuade them to release you to me as they should have when you experienced your first moon blood." With that, she patted my foot and exited with the grace and regal carriage of a queen. Well she was royalty in the mythological sense.

But I was ever so tired of living a myth. I wanted normal.

More than that, I wanted revenge. I wanted her stuck in a cage. Forever.

"Here are the updated bios and headshots of the final ten competitors in each category," Bryant Thomas handed Dylan a flash drive. "I pulled in two back-up contestants to replace Trish and Terry so our numbers are complete. I want the new info up on the website two minutes before cameras roll and not a second before. The viewers can look at them during the performance but not before."

"Easier if you just shot me the computer file complete with interview sound bites," Dylan grumbled. The afternoon light coming in through the windows behind Bryant made him wince. A headache hovered around the edges of his mind.

He started counting backward from one hundred in ancient

Greek. The extra focus of doing that while keeping Bryant in the front of his consciousness sent the headache elsewhere.

"Too easy to hack and alter files in transit from my computer to yours. I've seen rabid fans 'enhance' this kind of material before it arrives at its destination. I didn't realize the alterations until a friend called me laughing at how the prettiest woman in a competition was made to look like an old hag." The producer dropped his face into his hands and shook his head.

"I can encrypt..."

"You do it my way or you lose your cover story. I'd prefer to hand you paper files but rescanning before you put them up on the site will also cause some distortions. Cybercrime is too prevalent to let anything slip."

"Yes, sir." Dylan dropped the flash drive into a protective envelope designed by the Guild and folded it into the inside breast pocket of his jacket. If anyone scanned him to get at that drive, they'd download only static, leaving the information intact on the device. Hunters used this kind of thing all the time in the field. He never thought Guild paranoia tech would end up in Hollywood.

"Is there anything you can do to quash the rumors of the show opening on a curse because two contestants were stupid enough to go surfing in a thunderstorm?" Bryant asked.

"I'll see what I can do. I already tracked the source of the rumors to a cyber-troll in Arkansas. He's attempted to sabotage a number of competition shows. I sicced the FCC and the FBI onto him for cyber-crimes."

"That will have to do for now. But once a rumor goes viral it becomes more real than the truth. Keeping trouble at bay for the length of the competition is the key to proving trolls wrong." He buried his face in his hands again, his fingertips massaging his temples. "Sorry if I'm snappish. The baby was up all night and therefore I was too. Nanny's night off."

Dylan nodded in understanding. He had taken attic rooms during grad school with a family with five children. He remembered how little sleep he got during final exams when the youngest was colicky and the mother too tired to deal with the baby. Responsibility for the crying infant fell to the eldest daughter, a child of twelve. Dylan took his turns bouncing and walking the baby until he finally slept in his arms.

Bryant's daughter was almost eighteen months months old and his wife had died last winter of the plague. Tthe producer's entire home life centered around caring for toddler Bryanna.

Best he change the subject.

"I think I have identified the Siren, sir. But so far, she's done nothing to endanger anyone, or even cheat with her performance. If anything, it sounds to me like she's holding back on her vocals and is not a natural dancer, except in the pool." Dylan mentally reviewed the audition recording. He'd felt some of her allure through the headphones but not nearly as much as legend said he should.

"Quite frankly, as long as she doesn't use magic to win the competition, I don't care. Report to Abby. I'm not a part of the Guild anymore," Bryant said, retuning his full attention to his computer monitor. Then he retrieved his phone from the desk and sent a quick text.

"You can go now, Dylan." Bryant didn't even lift his gaze from his phone until he received a return text.

"Sir, did Mrs. FitzWarren tell you I chased a werewolf with a press pass off the lot yesterday?"

Bryant stilled, hand poised over his phone. "Who?"

"She said her name was 'Stevie,' but didn't give up the name of her employer."

"I'm not familiar with her. Probably just another paranormal trying to get by with a day job to pay living expenses. I've met plenty of those. If she hunts at the full moon, she is a problem. But if she makes do with raw meat from the butcher shop and stays indoors, chained to her bed, we've nothing to worry about. Keep an eye out for her."

Clearly dismissed, Dylan backed out of the office on the fourth floor of the same building where Mrs. FitzWarren occupied the entire fifth floor. Should he report to her about Celia Fisher? That would mean going all the way down to the ground level, walking around the building and taking an express elevator all the way up to the top floor. Secure access.

He'd already done that once today.

He wondered if there was a back stair, for emergency exits as required by law to get a construction permit. He'd heard that Abigail's fifth floor aerie was a recent addition, so permits would have been necessary.

He didn't have time right now. Maybe he'd find blueprints for the building online at midnight when the nanobots were chewing on his mind and he needed a compelling distraction.

As he exited through the main doors, a middle-aged man in a dark charcoal suit brushed past him, almost knocking him down. "Excuse me, I'm sorry I was distracted," he apologized. Wisps of grey hair gracing his dark blonde temples put the man at the upper edge of his fifties. His trim body and the lack of wrinkles around his eyes, suggested a younger age. His sea green eyes engaged Dylan's compellingly.

Dylan's hackles rose. Usually those kinds of age anomalies and near hypnotic gaze shouted Guild augmentation. This guy could be anywhere from a real fifty with prematurely grey hair, or over a hundred if he was a Hunter.

Members of the Guild didn't know many other members. They shifted orbits frequently, and changed their names more often. Secrecy and paranoia clouded every aspect of their lives. Mrs. FitzWarren kept them apart.

"I don't suppose you know where Elevator B is? I keep getting turned around." The possible Hunter had a cultured accent only slightly flattened by years, (decades?) in the mid-west.

"Let me lead you there," Dylan said. The stack of press and web releases he needed to review took a back seat to finding out who this man was and why he needed to find Abigail FitzWarren's at the top of that exclusive Elevator B.

CHAPTER 5

"I don't know that I'll ever get used to this heat," Mr. Green Eyes said as he ran a finger between the collar of his white dress shirt and his clean-shaven neck. "Back home the trees are starting to turn, and I'll have to put the winter cover on the pool when I get home."

"Sounds delightful. M' home in Belfast is cooling down toward winter too." Dylan laid on his native accent full and thick as a ploy to encourage the man to talk.

"I haven't been in Belfast for close to thirty years," the stranger sighed. "Lovely city. Cleveland's home now."

Dylan punched the button to summon elevator B.

Cleveland rang alarm bells, along with the green eyes. Could this man be related to Celia Fisher? His suspected Siren?

Curiosity kept him close beside Mr. Green Eyes. He needed to know his connection to Abigail FitzWarren.

The first live performance of *Here I Come, World* was due to start in less than an hour.

Dylan was going up to the director's private aerie.

The elevator doors slid open. "After you, sir." Dylan gestured his companion inside the small cubicle.

A tall blond man wearing a ubiquitous blue security uniform stood firm and solid and made no move to exit. He looked like a recruiting poster for the Third Reich with his strong jaw, square shoulders, and keen blue eyes. His holstered weapon was a Guild Issue piece with a custom grip. Dylan had one very similar made to fit his hand and be uncomfortable for anyone else to handle. Upon the death of a Hunter his gun would be consigned to crematorium fires along with his, or her, body.

The guard held out a hand to prevent Dylan from entering. He hadn't been there earlier, the last time Dylan had used the lift.

"Sorry, sir. Mrs. FitzWarren is not expecting you." He rested one hand on his weapon.

Dylan said something rude in Cantonese under his breath. But he backed away. Abby had an agenda that he was not privy to.

Yet.

He left to take up his post outside the public entrance to the studio theater, understanding for the first time why Bryant Thomas so gleefully referred to their boss as "Abby", a name she clearly hated.

Where is he? Of all those who need to be here tonight, he is the most important. Oh, my Anshar, how can you desert me tonight of all nights? Celia is your grandchild as well as mine. Her triumph reflects on you as much as me.

Where are you, beloved?

<Where you can't find me even if you look, beloved.>

Just like a man to desert me when he is needed or wanted most. He may be the ancestor of the gods, and my life mate, but I'll make certain he pays for this desertion, along with all of the human pets he calls allies.

They need to be eliminated. Soon.

Dylan tapped the "send" button on his email, closed down the laptop, and stowed it into his shoulder carryall. The first show in the singer/dancer competition would start in just a few minutes.

He was still miffed that an armed guard inside Elevator B had barred his entrance while allowing Mr. Green Eyes to travel upward to the lofty offices of Mrs. Abigail FitzWarren.

If there had ever been a *Mr.* FitzWarren, he wasn't talked about or even mentioned.

From the shadows by the street entrance to the theater of Studio Twenty-three, he had a clear view of the arriving audience. Celebrities abounded. Most of them currently starred in programs aired by the same network as *Here I Come, World*. They'd get two seconds of airtime as the cameras panned the audience, unless the network had paid for the show's host to point them out.

Dylan ducked behind a support pillar as Abby joined the arrivals. In her maroon-colored cocktail dress of draping layers of silk and chiffon, dark blonde hair in a French twist secured by a diamond and pearl comb and her inevitable double strand of pearls, she blended in with the Hollywood glitterati. She neither stood out in the crowd, nor faded into the woodwork. She could do either.

Sure enough, right on Abby's heels, Mr. Green Eyes emerged from a stretch limousine. If you knew what to look for, the darkened bullet proof glass windows and extra armor on the frame stood out like a sore thumb compared to the other vehicles disgorging elegantly dressed people onto the red carpet. Mr. Green Eyes held out a hand to assist three women from the depths of the limo, one middle-aged, probably a wife, and two younger women. They were all dressed in semi-formal and flashed passes to the televised competition like they were winning raffle tickets.

Association with Abby secured his belief that the man was a Hunter. He had to have serious credentials to be close on a social level. And they shared the same shade of hair—hers had less grey. More than associates, relatives, Dylan guessed.

He took a seat two rows behind and to the left of Abby and the Hunter's family. The place gave him a clear line of sight of both the stage and the Guild elite. He'd secreted a remote camera in the greenroom that gave him full view on his phone of the contestants.

A moment of panic sent his heart into overdrive for a nano-second. He had no escape should a vampire or demon attack. Then his training took over and he plotted a path along the back of the seats in front or behind him. He could easily balance on so narrow a platform, slightly wider than a tightrope. He'd been trained to prepare for anything—more so than the Boy Guides.

But the faulty artificial connections in his brain kept gibbering at him to get out now, before the world came to an end.

He listened to the conversations around him and began translating them into an Amazon River tribal language that had three native speakers left in the world.

The nanobots in his brain calmed down.

I sat back on the padded banquette that encircled three sides of the green room. All twenty competitors and their professional partners mingled and jabbered like anxious lab rats. I'd seen schools of fish do the same when a shark swam onto the horizon of their awareness. (My family was addicted to "Shark Week" and watched every program. That's as close to saltwater sharks as I'd ever gotten.)

Another night I could have joined my comrades-in-arms. Instead I fought to breathe through the pressure in my chest and churning of my stomach in a full out panic attack.

"Breathe, Mei Mei," Paul whispered, letting hints of an Asian tongue as his first language bleed through the endearment. "Breathe in deeply, hold it, let it fill your lungs, then breathe out slowly. You made it through auditions, bootcamp, and rehearsals. That's the hardest part. You can do the rest."

"This is my first time alone. I always had my sisters beside me before." I tried to breathe and failed. My feet wanted me to run away from here, far, far away to the deepest hole in the ocean, or up to the space station. Mummy couldn't find me up there.

And then a janitor wandered through with a push broom. As Little Miss Bouncy pushed him back into the corridor, he lifted his head and winked at me.

"Fred." My childhood invisible friend, the grandfather I'd always wanted. My protector when Mummy tried to overwhelm my senses.

And then he was gone.

"You've endured opening nights before. The theater here really isn't that big. You have nothing to fear," Paul continued his calming litany as he waved away an intrusive hand-held camera operator who followed us everywhere and recorded everything.

I didn't tell him that his litany wasn't the source of my improved breathing and attempts toward calm.

"Night clubs are a lot smaller than that small theater." My breath caught again as I gestured to the television monitor, one of a dozen, each with a different camera feed, currently showing the audience entering and finding their seats. I refused to look at the monitor showing me splay-legged and fighting for air.

Talk about a fish out of water!

I expected to see Mummy sitting up front and center in the audience, the focus of attention in her furs and sea gems. But she had taken a seat in the second row of the balcony. The camera panned in that direction only occasionally.

Third row center on the main floor held my parents and two sisters—my real sisters—much older than me and not my nieces who I thought of as my sisters. They were dressed to the nines for them; clean of iridescent scales and jewels—though Anemone's necklace looked suspiciously like sea glass and Zinnia's chunky enamel work looked like a chain of seaweed draped in coral—compared to Mummy.

"My family is out there. I didn't expect them. I can't let them see me fall flat on my face." I made to get up, ready to fling off my costume and quit this entire, mad, bid for freedom.

"Celia, don't." Paul held my hand so tightly I couldn't move if I wanted to.

A trick of the air currents opened the door a crack and revealed

Fred waiting to push me back inside.

I could sing Paul into obedience, or lust, or extreme violence against my enemies. But I hadn't the strength to break free of his hand.

Fred wouldn't let me.

And I'd vowed to myself and to Dad that I wouldn't use any of my magic in the competition. That meant I had to stay and listen to my partner.

"You have made it through weeks of grueling training and rehearsal. You've beaten out hundreds of other competitors to get this far. You can do this." He varied the phrasing but said the same thing over and over. Supposed to be calming in its familiarity.

"Think about why you were willing to endure these trials."

That brought me to a screeching halt.

I had a vague notion of freedom at the end of the contest. Freedom from what?

Or whom?

I loved my family. Our house on the edge of suburban Cleveland was great as far as childhood family homes go. We even had a pool in the back. I'd had good schools and teachers and cherished memories. My sisters and I were close enough to farmland to have lots of land to roam, trees to climb, ponds to swim in. There was one tree in particular where the top was tall enough we could see all the way to Lake Erie on a clear day. I couldn't remember the kind of tree it was, but I remembered the view and the sharing with my sisters. It was our special place.

We were close. Our secret heritage bound us all together. My much older sisters, Anemone and Zinnia had rebelled and left home after giving birth to Brittney and Joycelyn, then came back home with their husbands when they settled down.

But there was Mummy.

How did one gain freedom from the StormMother, chaos personified?

I didn't know yet. I only knew that I had to do something, and the contest seemed like a good start.

And Fred was around to lend me support.

Paul must have sensed the moment my body relaxed and accepted that yes, I could do this.

"Okay, I'll get you some water to sip. Then you and I can run through the lyrics to stay focused."

"Focus. I can focus." My feet began a walk-through of the dance steps all on their own.

The audience lights dimmed. Dylan straightened in his theater seat, anticipating something... anything. In the paranormal world of a Hunter, things happened when you least expected them, a.k.a when you wanted to sit back and enjoy something. A bright chord of music brought a hush to all conversations. Spotlights played across the curtains. Then the musical introduction burst into a vivacious overture that mimicked the style of musical theater without zeroing in on any one familiar tune.

Generic and almost identifiable, like the face of the swarthy man who had watched Stevie being exiled from the studio... He could have been any one of a thousand historical persons.

Lights up. The entire cast appeared stage center as if by magic, and burst into a simple song and dance routine to *Another Opening, Another Show.* They shuffled and mimed their way through sixty seconds, then froze until the lights went out and they faded backstage with more clatter than was strictly professional.

Dylan felt more than heard a collective intake of anticipatory breath. The announcer's compelling voice welcomed everyone to the first episode of *Here I Come, World.* Applause filled the theater. "And here are your hosts!"

A whoosh of moving fabric as the curtains split in the middle and draped to the sides revealing an up-and-coming comedic actor and a lovely spokesmodel wearing a glittering gown from the hottest new designer in town.

Dylan wasn't certain if the woman or the dress was supposed to dazzle the viewers into rapt awe.

Behind them the three judges linked arms and followed the hosts down a few steps across the peninsular shaped apron and over to the dais. The announcer identified them, two stars of Broadway musicals and Bryant Thomas, the lithe executive producer wearing a custom designer tuxedo. He had won almost every ballroom dance title, judged more than a few of them, and reportedly done some time in the chorus of some musicals in his youth.

Dylan knew that stint on Broadway had been before the Korean War in the late 1940s, but few others cared when he'd done the work, as long as the work added to his credentials.

The music paused for half a beat and then increased the tempo and the brass elements. Twenty contestants and their partners pranced down curving staircases on either side of the elevated stage, all wearing bright smiles and brighter costumes. A few looked exultant at having survived the group number.

In front of Dylan, Mr. Green Eyes and his family clapped and pointed and bounced eagerly in their seats as Celia's name was announced. Abby remained serene but smiling and happy. Madame Director was reputed to never be happy.

The nanobots in Dylan's brain clicked together, reminding him that every-one of his press releases for the show had highlighted Celia Fisher's hypnotic green eyes and porcelain pale skin, suggesting Irish roots similar to his own. Her blonde pixie cut might hold hints of strawberry if it didn't shade toward green from pool chlorine and bright sun. Yep, he'd nailed the connection between her and the man he figured was a Hunter—he had to have been retired a good long time in order to sire three daughters. Augmentation made Hunters, male and female, sterile. But Augmentations wore off or went awry, as he well knew.

So, if a Siren came from the coupling of a sea nymph and a god, king, or hero, that made the brunette with Mediterranean coloring (Greek?) beside Mr. Fisher the sea nymph, or a siren. But Celia's bio said she hailed from Cleveland. He wondered if a port city on Lake Erie was the same as access to the sea. A nymph, or a siren, even second generation, would have to swim in saltwater occasionally to maintain her essence.

What was the connection to Abby? Only the same shade of dark blonde hair between her and Mr. Green Eyes gave hints of shared blood.

Abby had assigned Dylan the task of babysitting a Siren. He didn't know why or if he was protecting the world from her, or her from something dastardly. He needed more information than the Guild could provide him. Interviews with the family? Abigail FitzWarren knew more than she had told him about his job assignment. She knew a lot more based upon the way she and Mrs. Sea Nymph tilted their heads together and whispered with huge smiles on their faces.

The host and hostess announced the rules of the competition, making jokes and puns along the way to keep the audience interested. They also demonstrated the use of the remote voting device velcroed to the bottom of each seat. The judges' scores counted for half the total points for each contestant. They explained the weight of the votes and how all scores were posted on a giant reader board above and behind the stage. Everyone involved could read the numbers as they were reported.

Meanwhile the contestants, with their spotlights off, retreated backstage to prepare.

Dylan checked his phone for his hidden camera feed from the Green Room. Bits of a fluffy yellow costume obscured the camera lens. Damn, he didn't remember who had worn that color. All his concentration had been upon Celia and her partner Paul.

A lot of Guild assignments consisted of monitoring the activities of suspected paranormals for signs of dangerous activities. He'd been on this job a week and hadn't noticed anything paranormal, except that fumble foot Celia had learned to dance in the pool. Who would expect a Siren, a sea creature to be graceful on land? Of course she learned her dance in the pool.

He sat back and decided to enjoy the performances, checking his phone occasionally and making sure that Abigail and her guests didn't wander off.

CHAPTER 6

Eight couples performed, alternating singers paired with professional dancers, and dancers paired with professional singers. They all performed their specific talent well, including the two late-comers who'd only had days to rehearse instead of a full week. Not all of the contestants meshed with their partners or managed their new training. Dylan gave them all pretty much middle of the road scores on the remote provided. Not that he was an expert on anything musical, but he'd sung in a choir as a child and seen his fair share of nightclub acts all over the world to know what touched his heart or mind.

Then Celia came up in the rotation. In the middle of the pack, she had the least memorable position in the line-up. He wondered briefly if that was deliberate on the part of management, or just the luck of the draw?

He straightened a little in his seat, as did Celia's family, and prepared to listen carefully. But he blinked rapidly four times to engage an infrared setting in his vision. If Celia's aura glowed with extra energy to tap into her innate magic, he'd see the heat signature.

Across the way, Bryant Thomas did the same. He was looking for a cheater.

The orchestra began the soft refrain from the love song of *The Music Man.*

Celia and Paul slipped through the curtains onto a darkened stage, nearly invisible to any without augmentation. He wore a faint halo of deep green energy: excited but not anxious. She flared a full body aura of bright red that had a defined edge about six inches away from her core—nervous energy tightly contained. None of the bright white of magic or paranormal talent.

They moved through a brief pantomime as the orchestra morphed into the boisterous finale music from the play. She shucked her sparkly pink overalls to reveal a red majorette costume with a miniscule skirt, big buttons and more gold sequins than fabric. After two beats of awe at the transformation, she grabbed a baton from an invisible wire, seemingly out of thin air, and they were off.

Dylan watched for the barely detectable hesitation in her steps. Celia and Paul weren't fully synchronized. The slight delay in her steps remained. But their voices flowed together like two streams slowly and effortlessly moving toward a bigger river. Paul carried his part of the tune with a lot more power and less flatness in tone than he had in the dress rehearsal.

Celia didn't just sing, she belted the music and dazzled the audience with her smiles and personality. No human vocal cords should be able to command the music as she did. The orchestra didn't matter. It was just her and her voice.

Who cared that she missed a step near the end? Bryant Thomas noticed and marked his score sheet. Dylan wanted to applaud him for his focus.

But still Celia's energy levels remained in the red without even hinting at leeching into the white paranormal levels.

"She's holding back," her mother whispered.

If that was holding back, Dylan didn't want to think what that voice could do unleashed.

No wonder ancient sailors crashed their boats and gave themselves up to the sea just trying to get to a voice like that.

~

"You've memorized the steps, and it's important you stay aware of where your partner is, but really Celia you need to dance to the music not as an echo of what Paul is doing," Bryant Thomas intoned, the last of the judges to make comments. "Still your voice is such a wonder, no one is going to care if you fall flat on your face as long as you command the lyrics like that. Good performance."

I remained standing in front of the judges' dais stunned by the comments. Bryant Thomas was right. He knew precisely what I'd done wrong. No one else noticed.

Paul tugged at my hand to break my stunned paralysis. All I could do was follow him. Still following him. I really needed to learn to move of my own volition outside the pool.

Once in the Green Room, my partner grabbed me in a hug and swung me around until my feet flew off the floor. "Good show, luv," he said in a mock Cockney accent.

The occupants of the Green Room added their own enthusiasm over the judges' scores for my performance. Two sixes (about as high as one could expect on opening night, mostly we'd seen fours and fives) and an eight. We had no way of knowing which judge had given which number. But from the comments I guessed that the eight had come from the lady with the operatic voice. She knew how hard it was to hit and hold some of those high notes and keep the tone from sliding into sharp or flat once reached.

None of us ever expected a good score from Bryant Thomas. He pushed for a higher level of expertise than any other judge on any of his shows.

Paul and I stood with our arms draped around each other while we waited for our tally from the studio audience. Loud whistles pierced my ears as the average of seven point six flashed.

"We're on the top, Mei Mei," Paul said, hugging me closer.

This was becoming a normal posture for both of us, holding each other up, or melding into one personality. I couldn't tell, didn't object to either.

"For now," I replied, eyeing the remaining competitors.

"I am happy, for now. The viewing audience counts for only one quarter of the score. Unless they are all blind and deaf, they won't move us any lower." He mouthed his counting and estimation of the performance level of those left to compete. Then he continued, "There are a whole bunch of people below us in the stats. As long as neither one of us blows it next week we'll be safe for a while." He shoved me toward the banquette while he moved toward the mini fridge stacked with bottled water.

I drank greedily and turned my attention to the monitor that continuously panned the audience. I saw my family clapping joyously. A little knot of anxiety in the middle of my chest dissolved. I hadn't disappointed them. In my last text to them, I'd dedicated this performance to Brittney and Joycelyn. Now I'd proved that I could continue on my own without their back up.

Then I noticed the publicity guy, Dylan something, sitting behind my dad. I'd seen him around the studio often over the past week. He always seemed to be watching me. *Me*, the flat-chested, limp-haired, no-fashion-sense nonentity from Cleveland, not the prettier and more glamorous girls who openly flirted with him.

Before I could decide if I needed to avoid or court him, the camera moved across the upper levels of the audience seating. Mummy's chair was empty. When had she left? Seconds ago, I guessed, since none of the standing room only viewers had yet moved to take her place.

What was she plotting now?

You may be only one-half siren my beloved granddaughter, but you have lost none of the ability I gave you, as your sisters did. Your mother wasted her essence by swimming only in freshwater lakes and rarely singing since the day she pledged herself to her hero. But you, you my lovely, can join me to combat the changes in climate that humans have forced upon us. I need the wind in your voice to dispel pollutants. I need your passion to root out the sources of contamination.

We don't need a man to partner us. Anshar has proven himself unreliable once again. Together, you and I will target all of the fossil fuel burning factories. Together we can target crops tainted by genetic engineering and artificial pesticides.

When we are done, the population will return to sustainable levels and they will all eat natural foods full of nutrition instead of useless filler.

I'm thinking a global heat wave followed by a global blizzard should set the tides to turning.

CHAPTER 7

The Green Room became more boisterous at the end of each performance. We had trouble staying quiet so that our noise didn't filter into the audience, except when the camera was on us.

Little Miss Bouncy, the show hostess (really that was her name, Samantha Bouncé I'd learned. She only bounced when men were around), shoved a microphone under my nose. "How does it feel to have top scores so far in the competition?"

I reared back as far as the high back of the Green Room banquette would allow, putting as much space as possible between me and the audio equipment. I could *feel* feedback building, something Miss Bouncy had to learn to control or suffer the ear-piercing squeal.

She didn't seem to understand why my amplified breathing rasped in the metallic mesh surrounding her instrument of torture.

Oh, well, she had to learn sometime. "I'm excited, of course, we put a lot of work into the number." *Squeal!* I winced and bit my lip.

Everyone in the room hunched shoulders and squinted eyes. They stared at Miss Bouncy with loathing.

She stared at the microphone as if it were an alien artifact designed to ruin her career. Thankfully, she pulled it back an inch from my mouth.

"But there are still nine couples who need to compete tonight," I continued. "Their scores could push me down to the bottom half very quickly. So, I'm still nervous. Just glad I'm done for the evening."

There, a perfectly suitable, neutral, and boring statement. I designed the sentence for her to seek more interesting fodder.

As one, we all turned silent attention to the monitors as the next couple stepped onto the stage. They were scheduled to perform to "If I Loved You", a poignant waltz from *Carousel*. I felt my heart sink as the tall blond man sang his baritone part with deep and mellow tones, a trained singer who glided through the notes with practiced ease. His dance steps were in perfect sync with his dark-haired and sloe-eyed partner. Her soprano reached the highest level of the balconies with whispered softness that was as distinct as if she sat right next to the listener. If I didn't know better, I'd say they were ringers, true professionals in both talents rather than untrained in one. The difference in their coloring offered a powerful symbol of the conflicts between the characters: he, the wandering carnival barker with few morals, she, the staid librarian. They gave us a truly poignant rendition.

I loved the piece and their presentation. I hated that right off the bat they were true contenders to win this competition.

Paul reached over and squeezed my hand. "Let's see how well they handle the rapid tap and syncopation of their number next week," he whispered. "It's *hard* to sing *and* dance with precision and retain any speed. We did that tonight." He'd been gulping lemon water since we came off stage. I wondered how much strain he'd put on his vocal cords trying to keep up with me.

Probably he'd pushed his voice as hard as I had strained my thighs and feet to match his dance moves. He needed one of my mom's special tonics, mostly honey and bourbon with a few extra family secret ingredients. I might find a tonic useful too. I definitely needed another session in the hot tub when this was all over.

But Mummy was still around. My nose twitched a little. How volatile was her temper tonight, and would she explode every time I entered water, even fresh and highly chlorinated water?

~

At the end of the show, Dylan followed Abby and the Fishers backstage to the special holding area for family and friends of the contestants.

"Sixth place on the first night isn't a bad place to be," Mr. Fisher said as he draped an arm around the shoulders of his wife.

A quick Google search on his phone informed Dylan that there was a Mike and Jeannie Fisher in the telephone directory for Cleveland, Ohio. Nothing else came up on a quick internet search. Even the aerial maps site showed a knot of tall trees dominating their address. No way to see the house or even see if they had a pool. But they were only a quarter mile from the shores of Lake Erie.

Abby must have close ties to the family to have access to this exclusive meet and greet. Bryant Thomas was very protective of his contestants. He wouldn't clear her entrance on Guild credentials alone—or even her pretend administrative assistant to the executive producer I.D.

Dylan shifted his posture from anonymous observer to head publicist. With an authoritative hand he gestured for one of the ever-present cameras and Samantha Bouncé to follow him with her microphone.

He fetched up beside Mike Fisher with Samantha directly in front of the family.

"Not here, not now," Abby said, stepping between the camera and the family.

Mr. Fisher was only a quarter step behind her in his stiff intervention. The quickness in becoming an over-protective father could be a natural response. Dylan didn't think so. His slightly bent knees, his shift of balance forward, and the balling of his fists told Dylan that he was a trained fighter, even if he wasn't a Hunter.

"Excuse me?" Samantha asked. A faint echo in her voice indicated that her microphone was on. This getting-hostile-exchange would be edited out of the footage aired on TV next week, but the snippet could just as easily wind up on social media ten seconds from now.

Abby's silhouette morphed from soft and fluffy society matron to sharp-edged Director of the International Guild of Demon and Vampire Hunters. "These people have not signed release forms. Save your questions for a formal interview."

"But we won't have the spontaneity of..."

"Do I need to call Mr. Thomas?"

Samantha deflated and lowered her microphone. It was still on and a red light blinked on the camera. The operator flashed Dylan a grin. He'd gotten it all. Dylan would study it later for clues into Abby and her relationship with the Siren's family.

A flicker of movement near the exit to the theater caught his attention. A vague silhouette and a near neon press pass suggested that Stevie, the werewolf tabloid reporter had returned, despite being banned from the studio.

He whirled to follow her.

Then the door to the backstage area burst open and Bryant Thomas emerged, flanked and followed by the full melee of the contestants avidly seeking their well-wishers.

No sign of Stevie.

Abby flashed a brief hand signal at the producer and backed away into invisible observer mode.

Dylan directed Samantha and the camera to the big man himself.

"How proud are you of the success of the first episode of your new show?" she asked.

He grabbed the mic from her and began babbling about numbers and market shares and encouraging viewers to call or text their votes in *right now*. The phone lines would remain open until ten tomorrow morning Pacific Time.

Dylan's phone buzzed. At first glance he saw only large numbers scrolling down the screen. Then the significance of those numbers registered in his mind.

"Sir." He caught Bryant's attention as he shoved the phone in front of him.

The producer's eyes widened, and his brows lifted. His big grin nearly split his face in two. "A record number of votes and the ratings are putting us number one in our time slot and in category. Ladies and gentlemen, your children have made the show a success. I congratulate you and the contestants. Every one of them is a winner tonight!" He gave the phone back to Dylan, and grabbed Celia Fisher, the nearest female contestant, in hold position (Dylan had learned that bit of dance vocabulary watching rehearsals) and quick stepped with her across the room.

The girl stumbled over her slower, less precise feet, then caught on and followed him competently. Brilliance would come later. At the last moment, Bryant spun her under his arm and landed her between her parents.

Laughing, they indulged in a giant family hug that included Celia's two sisters and Abby.

Dylan faded out of the room confident he'd get no more information tonight.

But he could look and listen for any other sign of Stevie.

"Dad, what's wrong?" I asked the moment Mom and my sisters broke the hug and went to talk to Aunt Abigail in the corner. As my godmother, Abigail FitzWarren felt closer than a blood relative, less dangerous than Mummy.

Dad glanced sideways at Mom, then at Bryant Thomas. The producer was edging toward the back exit and the trailers, a clear signal that this meet and greet with relatives and best friends should end soon. Dad grabbed my arm and pulled me toward the same exit where Mr. Thomas lingered.

"Your grandmother was in the audience," Dad said quietly in a tone that would not carry.

"I know. She came to see me before the show." I forced myself to engage Dad's gaze. We weren't telepathic but we knew each other so well, there were times we might as well be.

"She's planning something," Dad said, breaking eye contact. He nodded once to Mom. She returned the gesture before taking Aunt

Abigail's arm and leading her and my sisters toward the exit that opened to the front lobby.

"Something big," I replied to Dad. I aimed him out the back door toward my trailer. "She drowned two contestants while they were surfing the other day."

"I'm worried about you," Dad said once inside my private dressing room. He kept his voice hushed and his stance wary.

"Do I need to quit the show?" Disappointment grew into a great soggy lump in my gut.

"No. Oh, no, baby. You want this competition, a career in music among normals, so very much. And we want it for you too. The moment you called to tell us you made the cut, I called in some favors. You are protected."

"Aunt Abigail?"

"One of her operatives."

"Dad, is that wise? This is family business."

"Knowing the StormMother, the mate of Poseidon or Anshar, or whatever he calls himself these days, is lurking nearby, means your safety has grown well beyond a family concern."

"Why me? I have a mother and two sisters. Any one of us could become her tool in devastation."

Dad looked at his feet, then out the window into the growing darkness. As a last resort, rather than speak openly, he called up the weather report on his phone. In my family we call that self-defense. I had a radio in my hotel room that did nothing but scan for weather reports.

"What?" I asked.

He engaged the speaker function on the phone.

"Gale warnings have been raised along the Pacific coast from San Diego, California to Coos Bay, Oregon. A low-pressure area is organizing into a tropical storm along the equator. Meteorologists expect winds to grow to force one typhoon levels before midnight and increase to force five before landfall Wednesday in the early morning hours." He turned the device off.

I gulped. Force five was nothing to mess with. Lowland and coastal flooding was a certainty. "Mummy?" a.k.a. The StormMother.

"Unknown. This is tropical storm season, on both coasts." Age lines around his eyes and mouth grew longer and deeper. The flesh beneath his strong jaw sagged.

"Dad, talk to me. Why me, why now?"

He sank heavily onto the miniature sofa under the window facing the studio. A deep sigh deflated his chest as he expelled air. "Baby, your mother has lived away from saltwater for so long, she's lost a lot of her power. While her voice is still true, the siren magic is nearly gone."

"That's what you wanted, isn't it?" I took the bench behind the kitchenette table, careful not to bend any sequins from my costume.

"Yes. We knew when we married that most of our lives would consist of hiding from your grandmother. Lake Erie is fresh water, we are about as far from the ocean as we could find and still allow your mother to swim freely. She has to swim to maintain life in her body."

"What about my sisters..."

He held up a hand and gulped. Were those tears threatening to spill out of his eyes?

"Your mother and I weren't supposed to be able to have children. But we wanted babies so very badly that we went to a clinic and opted for artificial insemination. We have no idea who the donors were, probably not gods, kings, or heroes."

"So, Anemone's and Zinnia's magic is greatly diminished," I concluded for him. That explained why only I inherited his green eyes and blond hair.

"More like non-existent." He flashed a big grin. "Which was fine by us. We had washed our hands of your mother's heritage long before your sisters were born. Anemone and Zinnia have fine voices, and a great deal of beauty. But, no sailor would bother wrecking his ship to join with them."

"Then there's me," I said flatly.

"Yes, then there's you, and your two nieces." We both bowed our heads and mourned their loss. "Joycelyn and Brittney had wonderful voices and were much more beautiful than I."

"Don't sell yourself short, Celia." He reached across the narrow gap between us and squeezed my hand. "You are beautiful. You have both a voice and a face that men would wreck whole fleets in order to get to you."

"Was Helen of Troy a Siren?" I asked.

"I don't know. But you could give her a run for her money."

I blushed. "But you're my father, you have to say things like that."

This time his smile reached all the way to his eyes and stayed there.

"What happened that I am closer to Mummy than Mom or my sisters?"

"There was a storm. An epic storm."

I raised my eyebrows urging him to continue.

"Your grandmother raised that storm in an effort to drag your mother out into the open again." He never used Mummy's name. "The rapid air pressure changes, the wind and the waves, and driving rain threw your mother into a mating frenzy. She could no longer block her essential nature. Your sisters got caught in the same emotional storm. They sought out their high school sweethearts and let their hormones get the better of good judgement. Your mom caught me." He blushed this time. The joy emanating from him vanquished the tell-tale age lines.

"And you are a hero. Or are you a king in exile? Or maybe a forgotten god? That kind of status is required to generate magic in genealogy."

"In some circles I'm considered a hero because I rid the world of a few demons and vampires."

"I know that. You've always been my hero, king, and god because you are my dad."

We sat in companionable silence a moment.

"Look, Mom and I have to get back to Cleveland. It's still wedding season and the flower shop is inundated with orders. Your sisters can't manage it all alone. But Aunt Abigail has found airline tickets so at least one of us will be in the audience every week. In the meantime, trust that you are watched over by another hero. If the StormMother comes calling again, you won't be alone, but keep this medallion close by at all times. If it glows or grows warm, dial 0 0 0 on your phone. Help will not be far behind." He pressed a gold coin into my hand. It hung by a fine golden chain with a tiny but sturdy clasp.

Then he kissed my forehead and left before I could wish him farewell and safe travels.

When I finally examined the bit of jewelry, about the size of a fifty-cent piece, I found a Celtic cross engraved on one side. On the back a Star of David, a saber and quarter moon, a pentagram and the all-seeing-eye of Kali shared equal spaces. "Covering all our bases."

It felt warm and glowed against my hand, like the medallion Dylan had held up to the intrusive press woman at the recorded interviews.

CHAPTER 8

One did not need augmented hearing to listen to quiet conversations inside any one of the long line of trailers set up in the back lot of the studio. Dylan smiled to himself as he pushed away from Celia's cheap tin can of housing. Hollywood execs could learn a thing or two from FEMA about better temporary housing.

"All information is valuable," Dylan quoted Big Joe Jones his mentor/drill sergeant back at the Guild academy. Then the man had proceeded in drilling the class over and over how to compartmentalize his recently augmented brain in ways to catalog and retain odd bits of trivia.

And now he knew that Mike Fisher of Cleveland, Ohio was indeed a retired hunter and his wife Jeannie hailed from a long line of potentially deadly paranormals. What had changed her? Instead of luring sailors to their deaths she now hid from the StormMother, her mother or grandmother, someone so familiar to the family that they called her "Mummy".

He closed his tablet where he'd taken extensive notes about the conversation between Celia and her father. Now what should he do with this information? He certainly didn't want to report to Mrs. FitzWarren that he now knew about her secret family. Aunt Abigail could mean any one of a number of relationships, blood sister to Mike or Jeannie, godmother, or old family friend.

Unfortunately, even if he could get DNA samples, the test results would show scrambled, untraceable bits as a result of Guild augmentation. Abigail FitzWarren couldn't have risen to the position of director without having served as a Hunter. Therefore, she had endured augmentation like everyone else in the Guild; possibly multiple times since she'd been director for more years than he could trace. He'd seen her in Geneva after her most recent one. She looked fifty with a minimum of forty years in the Guild.

Along that track, how old was Fisher? In real years, not Guild reckoning.

Dylan had seen Celia's birth certificate (part of the documentation necessary for her to audition for the contest) at the start of this mission. It looked authentic and had matching records in Ohio bureau of vital statistics. Twenty-one years old and she looked fourteen. Dylan had searched further and found similar records for her sisters fourteen and sixteen years before that.

So, if Fisher had undergone only one augmentation, and assuming he joined the Guild in his early twenties he'd be in his early sixties. He looked forty-five at most, but his hair had begun to grey, and his skin had lost elasticity.

Dylan would have to go back into Guild records quite a way to find him, if he'd kept the same name.

But why didn't the records have any mention of one of the Guild's own retiring with a *siren?*

The records had been purged, of course. Probably by Abigail FitzWarren herself.

His back exploded in a wall of pain, as if a round Celtic shield with a bronze boss at the center, had slammed into him.

Air expelled from his lungs. His sense of up and down, right and left, twisted in a cyclone of disorientation.

He gasped. Nothing happened. His lungs refused to function.

He needed to chase down his own breath, get it back.

Then his mind clicked, and he knew that his lungs worked

perfectly well. His diaphragm was temporarily stunned. By force of will he punched himself from the front to neutralize the paralysis from the back.

New air rushed into him. His senses righted. The nanobots in his head shut up.

He swung around, knees bent, fists balled, and infrared vision engaged.

A short blonde termagant faced him, long-fingered hands wove an arcane pattern. In the uncertain light, with his augmented eyes, he clearly saw webs between each of her digits.

"Why didn't you fall flat on your face?" Celia stared up at him, her green eyes glowing like luminescent sea life.

"You're just the publicity guy. Aren't you?" I squeaked. Half-panicked I ran through the spell and the ritual to conjure enough air in a tightly focused cone to knock an ordinary man flat.

I reviewed it again like playing back an old black and white film. I'd heard the faint breathing and a footstep outside the back wall of my trailer. Dad had raised me to be paranoid. His days as a Hunter were over. So why was someone, anyone, eavesdropping on a private and very personal conversation?

My mind went immediately to Mummy.

I'd woven the spell correctly. There was enough force in my little tornado to flatten a small building.

So why was he still standing?

"You're a Hunter," I gasped.

That made him stop and relax his defensive pose. But his jaw firmed, and his eyes narrowed.

To his credit, he said nothing.

"Did Aunt Abigail send you?" *Damn him*, he remained silent.

"Oh, gods, this is too much. I don't need a babysitter. I really, really, really need you to go away and stay away." I turned and stomped back toward the front door of my trailer. Anger propelled me. My steps were less than graceful.

"You didn't follow your father out that door," he said.

I felt his eyes on my back.

He was observant. I'd give him that.

"I climbed out the bathroom window so you wouldn't see me."

He jerked his chin down once in acknowledgement.

Just as I was about to close the door on him, he spoke. "What am I supposed to protect you from?" He looked at his glowing medallion where it shone through the cloth of his dress shirt. The luminescence faded as we watched.

I checked my own talisman. It too lost brightness and color. Whatever had been out here had left the scene.

If I were still five years old, I'd say that Fred had paid a visit.

I paused with one foot halfway up to the final step into my dressing room. "I don't need protection. I can take care of myself." Or Fred would take care of me.

I remembered a day when second grade boys had chased me home. Somehow I'd gotten separated from Joycelyn and Brittney. The boys taunted and teased me because I'd spent too much time in the chlorinated pool and then sat in the sun until my blonde hair turned green. It matched my eyes and I thought it pretty.

The boys thought it weird and they were young enough to be frightened by weird. But because they were boys raised by macho fathers, they expressed fear and anger the same way.

I had to stop running. A stitch had grabbed my side and made breathing difficult. I could escape the boys if I had free water to swim in, or wade in. The nearest creek was more than two blocks away.

As I bent double, gasping for breath, a stone flew over my back. If I'd still been standing it would have hit my head and probably killed me.

A swarthy man stepped out from behind a tree and planted himself between me and the boys. With his feet spread and his hands on his hips, he glared at them from beneath a lowering brow, dark eyes taking on hints of red fire.

"Enough!" His commanding word echoed along the road and bounced against wooden fences and neat suburban houses.

The boys stopped in their tracks, mouths gaping, eyes wide with terror. As one they spun and retraced their steps, running faster than they'd chased me.

"You may return home in safety now," Fred said. "I've got your back."

I dragged in a big gulp of air, testing my side to see if it still grabbed in pain. No resistance to breathing. Another deep breath and I was nearly back to normal. I was just tired from unnatural running. "Thank you, Fred."

Joycelyn and Brittney rounded the corner in front of me, pelting toward me with alarm. "Celia, what happened? We thought you were right behind us. Are you okay?" they yelled from half a block away.

"I will protect you always, little Celia. Just call when you need me." With that he faded from my vision and my memory. I hadn't seen him more than twice since then. Until earlier this evening.

"Can you really protect me?" I sneered at the publicity guy. Hunter. He had skills. But did he have the strength, cunning, and guile to defeat the StormMother?

My mind reeled with the ferocity of the windstorm I had thrown at him. The memory of the roof ripping free of the sleazy night club in Las Vegas crashed through my being, bringing deep chills through all of my bones.

I doubled over and sobbed. I wished I could have gathered my sister's bright spirits into me when they died, regretting that if they managed to be reabsorbed by the universe, they'd go to Mummy. She'd use the power of their ghosts to complete her agenda, whatever that was.

If I willingly helped the StormMother, could I bring my sisters back?

Strong hands pulled me upright and rubbed my back.

I choked on my cries and gasped for air. I couldn't breathe.

"Easy, now. Slow down, deep breaths." The publicity guy lifted me into the trailer and onto the hard sofa. He sat me upright, back firmly against the cushions. Then he crouched in front of me, resting his big hands on my knees.

I stared at the point of contact, suddenly aware of the heat in his touch; heat that shot upward to my heart and brain and back down to my groin.

"Who am I protecting you from?" he asked again.

"Didn't Aunt Abigail tell you?"

"Abby is notorious for giving as little information as possible. Paranormal investigations rarely go in a single direction and implicate many innocents before we can discover the truth. She believes that minimal data keeps us from going into a mission with prejudice. Things go faster and smoother that way."

"Do they really?" I managed to gulp in air, bypassing the lump of tears clogging my throat. "Wait. You called my godmother Abby! No one does that. Not even Dad, her own brother!"

"Not to her face." He swallowed a bit of a grin. "She is formidable. We have to save some tiny bits of disrespect to combat her ferocity and maintain our sanity."

I couldn't help answering him with my own little grin. I loved Aunt Abigail with all my heart. But she scared me too—mostly because Mom and Dad gave her deference far beyond what I could see she'd earned.

"So, tell me, why did Abigail FitzWarren assign me to watch you?"

"You can't do anything." I slammed myself upward, forcing him to rock back on his heels. To his credit, he didn't lose his balance.

"People underestimate me. I can do a lot of things."

"I'll grant that you are strong and have super-fast reflexes. You've probably got enhanced vision and hearing—which is why you were able to eavesdrop on me and Dad. But you can't help against Mummy. No one can."

"Mummy? A family member?"

He stood up without bracing himself against any of the built-in furniture. He had more grace than I did on land. Briefly I wondered how graceful he'd be in the water.

Words dammed my throat. How did one explain the StormMother?

I went to the mini-fridge and grabbed a bottle of iced tea with lemon. I held it up to him in mute offering.

"No thank you. Caffeine and I don't get along this late in the day."

He moved up to crowd my back, keep me from escaping his probing questions. He acted like I'd been eyeing the door as a quick and easy escape route.

"Who's Mummy?" He reached over my head and retrieved two tall glasses from the cupboard over the sink. "I'll stick to water thank you."

I should too. Competition hours vied with Las Vegas hours and I hadn't made a clean transition yet.

"Look at the recordings of the audience from tonight's show. First balcony, directly across and above from where Mom and Dad and my sisters sat. Now get out and leave me alone. I'll deal with Mummy by myself."

"Mind if I escort you back to the residence? I'm headed there myself."

"I thought you'd have your own apartment since you are employed by the studio. Even if you are a Hunter."

"Nope. I'm temporary and therefore the studio put me up in that residence hotel complex. But don't tell anyone that. I need all the competitors and the staff to think of me as a studio employee assigned to be with all of you night and day to feed social media a steady diet of meaningless gossip."

I slumped, almost resigned to his constant presence in my life until I found a way to escape Mummy once again.

Stupid werewolf bitch. Stevie she calls herself. I wonder where that name came from. I've kept track of her since she tried to interfere with my Celia's interview. Shivers run through me like a cold current sneaking into tropical waters. She broke an ordinary thermometer and spilled the mercury across

the opening between Celia's hotel room and the pool deck. Doesn't she know how deadly that substance is to those of us born of the sea? Mercury will sicken most paranormals. It will kill descendants of the oceans. What does she hope she will accomplish?

Celia always runs barefoot from her room and then dives into the water without looking. One touch of the stuff on her bare toe and she will freeze in place, coated in liquid silver. Impervious to cleansing with ordinary water, by the time someone brought sea water to her, the mercury would turn her insides toxic.

No wonder this werewolf never made alpha bitch of her pack. She can't think through the consequences. She only knows that the mercury would tell her if Celia was a Siren, by freezing her, or a Mermaid by forcing her to grow a tail on land. She probably smelled the sea in her veins when she interrupted the recorded interview.

But how did she know to single out my Celia?

We'll see how she responds to... enhanced interrogation.

CHAPTER 9

Letting Dylan-the-publicity guy drive me back to the residence hotel was a relief. I didn't have enough energy left to call a cab or Uber or even find a bus. I'd have stayed in my trailer, but I knew the only way to restore me was a dip in the pool and a minimum of fifteen laps, followed by a soak in the hot tub enhanced with sea salt.

I did make a note of where Dylan parked his little electric sedan. He plugged it in as soon as we coasted into the parking structure of the hotel.

"Economy model provided by the studio. They have to save money somewhere to pay the big prizes." He shrugged as he pocketed the key and then swiped a card through the charging station.

I shrugged back. "Aunt Abigail is a champion penny scraper. So, by putting that expense on the studio she has money to pay for extras like forensics and clean up when things get messy."

"How did Abigail FitzWarren come to be your godmother if she's already your aunt?" He sounded like he really wanted to know. He'd already heard most of my family's dirty secrets.

"The story Mom tells is that she officiated at their wedding, some kind of special license in Italy. Abigail and Dad are half siblings, same mother different fathers. Abigail is older by six years. They've kept in touch even though Dad retired from the Guild and started a second career as a computer forensic analyst for the local police department —not the Guild. Aunt Abigail is also godmother to my two older sisters, and... and the two I lost."

"The two women with your parents in the audience tonight?"

"Yeah, they're fourteen and sixteen years older than me. They left home for college and marriage before I knew they were my sisters and not my aunts."

"And your parents raised their daughters along with you?"

Again, I shrugged. We'd made it as far as my door in the block of suites, each with two bedrooms with two beds and a bath apiece, and a kitchenette. I had three roommates, but that would end soon as two contestants a week were eliminated. Since we hadn't sent anyone home at the end of tonight's show, two singers and two dancers would go home at the end of next Sunday's show.

"Joycelyn and Brittney were born the same day as me. We considered ourselves triplets. Except they had no magic in their lovely voices. We had a trio act in Las Vegas until..." I choked and had to grab his elbow in order to remain upright.

"Until a freak storm ripped the roof off the night club where you performed and killed them with lightning and shrapnel," he finished for me, sliding his arm around my waist for additional support. "I read about it at the time. When I got this assignment, I did some more research. Am I right in presuming the StormMother conjured that storm?"

I could only nod, unable to speak while gulping back tears of grief and a knot a pain around my heart.

"Why do you keep her in your lives?" he asked. "Seems like she'd be a person you'd forbid to trespass at your home."

"I don't know. She's just always been there. Part of the family, not easily removed." I sagged against the wall outside my room.

"Get some sleep." He kissed my forehead like an uncle and nudged me to face my door.

"Sleep be damned. I need a swim." End of discussion. I closed the door on him a little too firmly.

Once inside, I discovered my three roommates had already hit the hot tub to soak away the muscle strain of performing. I stripped, and then remembered to don my most modest one-piece suit—it had virtually no back and dipped very low in front—before opening the sliding doors of our living room directly onto the pool deck.

The lights for the deck area were out. Only the dim underwater lights in the pool and the hot tub gave an indication of where the hazards lay.

I ran four long strides along the diving board, bounced once and jack-knifed in. Deep, I plunged, touched bottom, in a ritual that defined my swimming experience. Then I pushed off and up, seeking the surface.

Something solid drifted between me and the air above. I nudged it aside with an impatient hand.

I thought I had to pool to myself.

I surfaced, flung water out of my eyes and...

Screamed and screamed again, flailing for air and purchase and... anything but the drifting and soggy body of the intrusive press woman. She stared blankly at the sky. No breath stirred within her.

Dylan watched Celia dive into the pool from the board directly under his room on the third floor. He had no roommates, so he'd been assigned a single bedroom and bath with a mini kitchenette and sitting area by the sliding doors. Only the bath had a door other than the entry to the hallway. What the room lacked in amenities was made up for with a balcony designed for a single chair and round pedestal table big enough to hold a book and a drink, or his laptop.

He never went anywhere these days without his laptop with its own hot spot Wi-Fi and access to Guild databases. His tablet fed off the computer's access to anything except the Guild. He also had a Guild super battery that charged in less than an hour and stayed operational for twelve.

Celia dove deep then rose upward with a powerful kick. Her white suit barely covered the essentials and blended with her skin when wet so that he couldn't tell if she was nude or not.

The smell of chlorine dominated the pool area. Suddenly it took on the aroma of Ireland. Home. He drank in all of the fresh green things and a hint of salt.

He couldn't detect any of the California desert dry or pollution.

Celia's scream pierced his brain. Panic choked him. And then his augmentation kicked in. He ran out the door, around one corner to the emergency fire exit. The balls of his feet barely touched down even as he kicked off his shoes. He took the landings in flying leaps, one hand on the rail to guide his turns.

He crashed through the exit door onto the pool deck before Celia's second scream split the air like a lightning bolt followed by gigantic crash of thunder. From three paces back he executed a long shallow dive, skimming through the upper level of water.

Instinctively he wrapped his arm around her neck and shoulders, tugging her onto her back while he stroked toward the side of the pool.

She flailed and fought his grip. "Lemme go!" she cried.

"It's okay. I'm saving you," he replied.

"Saving me from what?" She stopped fighting him and took over kicking them toward the side of the pool. Her voice sounded mighty strong for someone in peril.

"You were drowning. Now I'm saving you."

"I'm not drowning. But she did."

His grip slackened in surprise.

With a powerful kick she bent double and pushed away from him.

Dylan switched his attention to the dark form floating nearby. Adrenaline still pumping, he swam over to the cause of Celia's panic.

She swam circles around him, the current she created pushed them together.

"Stevie," he said, treading water. Still in full protective mode, he lassoed the form with his arm, easier than Celia, and pulled her back to the shallow end.

With his feet firmly planted on cement, he paused long enough to access the situation. "Stevie," he said again, recognizing the heavy eyebrows, pointed nose, and prominent jaw.

"Celia, call your Aunt Abigail," he said on a sigh. The energy and clarity of augmentation began to fade. He needed to pass off this situation soon, before his head exploded.

"I should call 911." Somehow Celia had managed to run inside and retrieve her phone.

Meanwhile other residents began to gather, gasping, and taking photos with their phones.

Dylan ducked his head as if examining Stevie closely for signs of how she died. "Celia, please tell Abby to make it look like police and EMTs," he murmured.

She raised an eyebrow in question even as she punched numbers into her phone.

"What I need to know is how do you drown a werewolf two nights before the full moon?"

His medallion beneath his dress shirt lost its glow and warmth. It sat there, inert but weighing heavily on his senses.

And he was pretty sure he'd ruined his suit by diving into the pool without thinking beyond saving Celia.

So this was what living like a Hunter was like. I'd always known that Dad had retired from the Guild a long time ago, about the time he married Mom, almost forty years ago. But he still had the instincts. And the enemies. And Aunt Abigail frequently wanted his help with some paranormal computer problem.

But the dozens of helpers in pseudo police and fire department uniforms—really good imitations, just some alterations to the patches and badges—swarming around the residence hotel and congregating around the pool was beyond my experience. They made a point of interviewing all of the residents, just like the police on television shows. The victim, "Stevie" Dylan had called her, had been dead only a short time before I found her.

A guy in a police uniform allowed me back into my room long enough to find a cover-up after I broke out in goosebumps and my teeth chattered with the chill of evening air and shock.

When the roommates had given their statements—they claimed they saw and heard nothing—they were allowed to go to bed. I had to stay up and answer questions from three more people. In all that time Aunt Abigail and her minions kept Dylan on the other side of the pool from me.

When the shock wore off and exhaustion took over, I fell asleep on one of the lounge chairs outside the reach of the pole lights around the pool. I think I mumbled something when I felt Aunt Abigail cover me with a blanket. But then I forgot the episode as I tumbled back into a dreamless sleep.

Dawn was just beginning to relieve the darkness of its nighttime duties when a weight shifted the curves of the flimsy lounge chair.

I opened one eye reluctantly to see who disturbed me.

"Mr. Thomas!" I struggled to pull myself upright. The producer and judge of the show had no business being here, least of all confronting me at the butt crack of dawn in a pool lounge chair.

"Easy, my dear," he said quietly.

People still bustled around the pool, but they emitted less frantic energy than the night before. The firefighter and EMT uniforms had disappeared and only three police remained. Aunt Abigail and Dylan still conferred at an umbrella table across the way.

The pool no longer held water, only a couple of people in pale blue coveralls crawling around the bottom with tiny brushes and tweezers. I guessed they looked for evidence. Another person in the same blue protective gear picked at a filter.

Yet another in red coveralls, crawled in front of the sliding glass door to my room. He/she picked at the cement where it met the metal slider.

I gasped, not certain what evidence might reside there.

"What?" I asked, still a bit confused. The sensation of bumping into Stevie's dead body in the pool made me shiver all over again.

"I know this has been horrible for you, Celia," Mr. Thomas said. "But I need to know what you know about Stevie."

"Was that her real name?" I yawned and stretched my arms over my head. My legs twitched, but I was hesitant to move them and touch the august personage sitting so intimately beside me.

"Stephanie Wollencek. Yes, she was a journalist working for a legitimate weekly news rag of dubious reputation. She's been there for years, and a pain in the ass to minor celebrities. She can't get near big name people. I know she interfered with your recorded interview a few days ago. Have you seen her on the studio lot before or after?"

His voice was gentle and soothing. I had no reason to fear him.

Then I broke eye contact. My trust in him evaporated. "Guild tricks," I muttered.

He threw his head back and laughed. "Your father taught you well, my dear. But I still need to know everything you know about Stevie."

I wiggled myself higher on the chair to sit upright. This time I didn't bother with sensibilities and bumped him.

He immediately stood and dragged a deck chair over. He placed it sideways so he could sit close to my lounge and face me. I knew his Guild reactions would grab me before I even thought about running away from him, after I untangled myself from the blanket.

"I saw her at the interview. She tried to rearrange my hair after the dresser spent an hour or more trying to get it to behave the way she wanted it."

"I heard about that."

I closed my eyes and tried to review my interactions with people for the past few days. "I don't remember seeing her around, even on the periphery. I've been pretty focused on rehearsals and fittings and interviews, you know, all the stuff required to put on the show."

"Yes, of course." He looked down and away. Then he patted my hand. "Get as much sleep as you can. I've rearranged your schedule so you don't have to be at rehearsal until noon." Then he rose and turned to the remaining minions. With a lift of his hand he summoned Aunt Abigail. She hurried over as if she truly were his administrative assistant rather than the Director of the Guild.

"See if there is anything we can do about the vaccination welt. It shouldn't stand out like that nine months after the inoculation," he whispered to her as they passed shoulders.

"What did Dylan mean when he asked, 'How do you drown a werewolf?' I didn't know werewolves really existed," I asked the moment Aunt Abigail was within hearing distance.

Mr. Thomas went still, halfway to standing. "Did he now? I'll look into it."

I sensed layers and layers of deception. My mind refused to delve into it any deeper right now.

"Into the shower with you now, Celia," Aunt Abigail said, bustling me and my blanket out of the lounge and back toward my room.

"Careful here at the door, you need to take a very long step over the area we just cleaned. It's very hard to get mercury out of the cracks and crevices."

Mercury! I stopped a full yard away from the safety of my room. "Did Stevie spread it?"

"We think so. Now step long and careful. A normal person won't be affected by it."

I closed my eyes and took that last step. Nothing happened so I guessed I was safe.

Lisa stood at the counter between the kitchenette and the sitting space practicing her point, plié, raise up on tip toe warm up exercises. She had almost as much trouble with her dance routines as I did. She gave me a little wave as I shuffled toward the bedroom we shared.

I stumbled over my own feet as Aunt Abigail shoved me into a hot shower.

I let the water sluice over me in soothing waves until the kinks left my muscles and my knees turned to rubber.

Aunt Abigail must have sensed the moment when I'd passed my ability to stand on my own. She had me wrapped in a huge towel and into my bed only seconds before I succumbed to fatigue. I fell asleep still wondering how to drown a werewolf and how said werewolf knew how poisonous mercury was to my kind.

CHAPTER 10

Bryant Thomas handed Dylan a double shot of whiskey, straight up.

Dylan took it with a hand that was a lot less steady than he'd like.

"Don't be squeamish. It's decent Irish and shouldn't make you blind, but it will knock the sharp edges off whatever is bothering you," the producer said, then took a seat by the window of Dylan's room.

Dylan had watched Abby bundle Celia off to her room and figured he didn't need to worry about the girl. For now.

"A little early in the day," Dylan replied, staring into the glass of clear liquid. But he did take a long sip. The lovely gift from the gods burned all the way down. He gasped and experienced backwash of the flowery under taste with just a hint of the bogs of Ireland beneath that.

Heat began flowing through his veins and relaxed his muscles.

Then his mind clicked in and he realized he still wore his waterlogged and stained slacks and shirt. He vaguely remembered discarding his jacket and shoes in the stairwell on the way down.

"Thank you, sir. I needed that." Dylan rose and headed for his closet, thinking only of a hot shower and clean clothes.

"What did you mean when you asked 'How do you drown a werewolf'?"

That stopped Dylan in his tracks. He bent to tug off his socks while he thought. "Reaction. I smelled the wolf in her and my medallion glowed when I first encountered her. We found her dead in the pool without an obvious wound or burn scar. I presumed she drowned. How could that happen? We're only two days away from the full moon. She should have been at her strongest and most alert. Who has the strength to overcome that?"

He tossed his socks into a corner and reached for clean underwear in the top dresser drawer.

"Who indeed?" Bryant Thomas raised an eyebrow in question. "I've tried to stay away from Guild business. But now it is overlapping my show. Bring me up to date."

Dylan looked at the open door of the bathroom with longing. Damp chills crept up from his bare feet and threatened to take over his gut. He needed more whiskey if he couldn't get into the shower right away. "Can this wait twenty minutes?"

Thomas looked him up and down and frowned slightly. "Of course. Forgive me for invading your privacy. You've reported to Abby. Report to me in my office when you've cleaned up, eaten and had enough coffee to get you through the day." He set down his own empty glass and exited, back straight, long legs stretching their limit. He closed the door quietly behind him.

"So how does one drown a werewolf? And why?" Dylan muttered as he prepared the shower. "The StormMother of course. She's the only one with enough command over the elements to not bother with standard execution methods. No silver bullet. No pyre. No beheading. Just water. Lots and lots of water, enough to overcome a paranormal predator."

"You have got to be kidding me!" I threw a pair of dancing shoes with three-inch spike heels at Paul. He ducked, covering his head with his arms.

"It's standard!" he shouted back at me.

"No, it's not." I wiggled my bare toes, trying to bond with the Earth. The wooden floor remained inert.

I still had a blister on my heel from a misplaced sequin on the tap shoes from last night's performance.

Last night. Oh gods! I'd found a dead body in the pool last night.

I could not dwell on that right now. I had an argument to win. "Last week you said two-inch block heels," I protested. Already I knew this was a losing battle. But I had one more trick up my sleeve. My phone provided an internet link to the catalog of the shoe store the studio used to custom create footwear for all the dancers. They used a 3D printer and casts of my feet. I shoved the phone under his nose.

"See! Character shoes suitable for ballroom or Broadway style dancing. Nude elastic across the instep, available in a variety of colors, will dye to match a specific costume, and two-inch block heels for better balance and leverage. See, see, see, that is the standard."

"You'll have to take it up with Millie. And with Mr. Thomas," Paul said, straightening up from his cringing pose. "And they need a week to make and deliver."

"Only if we have them dyed to match the costume. If we go with basic black, beige, or white, I can have them delivered by tonight!"

The camera woman who followed us everywhere grinned from ear to ear. I knew that little bit of temper tantrum would make next week's show.

"Please, Celia, just try the shoes on. You'll get used to them really quickly," Paul pleaded.

I typed in an order for my preferred shoes, one pair in each of the basic colors, charged them to the studio account and hit *Submit*. I was sure I'd need them if I stayed more than just this week. I already knew that a group number was planned for the opening with white and gold costumes and our performance number was red and black.

"I will try on those torture devices, but if I fall and break my neck it's on your head." I pouted.

"Thank you, Mei Mei. Once through the dance and you'll love them. I'm sure." Paul brought me the offending shoes and knelt to slide them onto my feet.

CONFESSIONS OF A SIREN SINGER

"Have you ever worn heels?" I asked, not willing to admit that the left shoe not only fit perfectly, it didn't rub or bind my toes.

"Yes, I have," he replied, fitting the other shoe for me.

"When?" I asked in disbelief as I circled each foot in turn and found I could sorta point my toes like he'd drilled into me over the weeks of rehearsals and eliminations.

"I had a drag number in *Guys and Dolls*."

"That must have been fun." Oooooh, I liked being almost as tall as him with the addition of the heels. Talk about leverage in the lifts!

"That entire musical was a blast. We extended the road show for two months before heading back to Broadway. Best revival I've been in yet. Now, from the beginning of the dance, five, six, seven, eight."

He took my hand and swung me under his arm as I sang in a soothing tone, "I Believe in You," from *How to Succeed in Business Without Really Trying*. We'd recast the number to a duet with dance. Not exactly faithful to the original play but suitable for the competition.

I'd started learning the steps over a week ago, as soon as I had the first dance under reasonable control, because no one was eliminated the first night. From now on we'd only have one week to learn and perfect our numbers.

If we survived past the fifth week, I'd get to do solos plus a duet with Paul. The final weeks I'd have to perform the duets with male competitors who had survived that long. At that time, Paul and the other pros would perform exhibition numbers without contestants.

I wasn't ready to trust another partner, pro or not. I liked Paul and had no problem throwing myself into the first lift.

I ran three steps and jumped. He caught me around the waist with both hands and lifted me with his upstage hand until I had enough height to strike a pose with one leg bent, the other stretched out behind me and my arms in a circle above my head, back arched.

But then I had to get down and land on that spindly little heel…

My balance wobbled.

"Focus, Mei Mei. Focus on your spot. Align everything you've got on your spot. His second hand came up and steadied me.

My body crept back in alignment.

Amazingly, Paul did not drop me. He guided me deftly back to the floor with both hands.

I let my arms circle his neck for greater security and fetched up with my face within inches of his.

A spark of electricity wound around us, anchoring us together. Our eyes met, our mouths reached for each other.

And he pulled away.

"Continue," he gulped as he spun me again out to the full stretch of both our arms.

Somehow, I managed to complete the dance. Ninety seconds of relying on muscle memory while I thought about that almost kiss.

Did we dare pursue that moment of impending intimacy?

The camera caught it all.

"Can you get into Abby's office?" Dylan asked Bryant Thomas during their morning briefing.

"Why?" Bryant had his head lowered as he scanned spreadsheets on his desktop monitor.

"I'd like to remotely listen in at the press room, see what the other reporters have to say about Stevie."

"So far the media have only reported an unnamed drowning victim in an unnamed hotel pool," Bryant replied.

"I sent out a carefully worded press release late last night. Didn't register with the tabloids, and legitimate media had an armed robbery of three liquor stores with a lethal shooting of the perp and the clerk at the last one. Stevie wasn't important enough to top that."

"If they only knew." Bryant cracked a smile. Then he pulled a key from his center desk drawer and tossed it to Dylan.

He caught it easily.

"Bottom left cupboard." He pointed across the room. "You'll find what you need for listening without going through Abby. I'd like to know what the press has to say in the backrooms. Any ideas on what could drown a werewolf?" Bryant lifted his focus from the monitor to Dylan.

"The StormMother," he said succinctly.

"A myth."

"Werewolves are classed as myths too, but we've both taken down a few of them."

"Expand." Bryant's gaze drifted back to the computer.

"That's the first time anyone has asked for that on this case. Abby knows what we're dealing with so assumes I do too."

That got Bryant's attention. "What do you know?"

"You aren't Guild anymore." Dylan clamped his teeth together in order to suppress a smile. Bryant might have retired from active duty and let his augmentations fade, but once in the Guild, always in the Guild.

That meant that Mike Fisher was also involved, more than just to protect his daughter. He'd have to remember that.

"You ever work with Mike Fisher?" Dylan asked.

Bryant shrugged. "Once or twice. We went through the academy together. He had another name back then. So did I. Then I spent more time in the far east while he worked the middle east."

"Ever meet his wife?"

"I heard he retired and married."

"He married a Siren."

"Celia Fisher is a Siren. Their daughter? Of course, I met them at the meet and greet after the show. Didn't recognize him. It's been almost forty years since I've seen him."

"Sirens are the daughters of sea nymphs paired with a god, king, or hero. Hunters are classed as heroes if you extend the myths into modern times." Dylan pulled a mini parabolic dish, earphones, and power pack from the cupboard. "And sea nymphs come from a mating of Poseidon and the StormMother," he added.

Bryant blew out a long low whistle.

"Glad I bought a bungalow in the hills. My old beachfront condo might be under water the next time she throws a temper tantrum."

"Good thinking. Now if you will excuse me, I have some gossip to listen to."

"Wait, does Celia need more protection?"

"Unknown. I need to know more about the family dynamic. Did you know that the Fishers refer to the StormMother as 'Mummy'?"

"That does not sound good. Family feuds are never pretty." He turned away. "Estranged family members bring out the worst in us."

"Something I should know, sir?"

"No. But I think I have a long overdue phone call to make."

"I'll get out of your way. When do you need this equipment back?" Dylan stood up shaking his knees to release the kinks from kneeling.

"What's wrong?" Bryant asked, half rising from his chair.

"Nothing. Just some muscle stiffness."

"Shouldn't happen until ten years after an augmentation. Your joints should be loose and well-lubricated."

Dylan shrugged.

"What's wrong?" Bryant insisted.

"I've requested a review of my last augmentation," Dylan said softly, humiliated that he had to admit it. But for his own sanity he needed to say the words aloud.

"Abby know about this?"

"She says she's contacted the clinic in Geneva."

"I'll follow up on that. Abby does still listen to me upon occasion. You go find out what you can about Stevie and why she's dead."

"Plan on it." Dylan ducked out of the office and through the reception area. Halfway to the door he stopped short and whirled to face the woman at the desk.

"Abby?" he choked.

"Do. Not. Call. Me. That," She spat between gritted teeth.

"Of course, Mrs. FitzWarren. I'm just surprised to see you here."

"Officially I am Mr. Thomas's executive administrative assistant."

And your offices occupy the entire fifth floor of the building; a floor that was added three months ago.

"Yes, ma'am."

"You've lost most of your accent, Dylan."

"Aye, missus." He dropped into his native lilt without thinking. "That's one o' m' talents, ma'am." This time he laid on a thick western drawl.

"West Texas," Abby said flatly.

Dylan made a mock finger gun and pointed at her, then raised his finger quickly and blew on it, as if blowing a gun barrel free of smoke.

She tipped an imaginary bonnet at him. Then she wrote something on a sticky note and handed it to him.

He read a series of ten digits, then raised an eyebrow in question.

"Override code for Elevator B. You need anything, and I mean anything, you come to me first. I take care of my Hunters. I'm not trying to blow you off. I'm just busy."

"Aye, missus." He tried to cover his surprise by tugging his forelock.

"I am not your bloody landlord in a feudal kingdom." Her words sounded stern with a hint of upper crust London under the flat American tones. But she smiled. "I heard what you want that listening equipment for. Go use it. I too find the puzzle of who could drown a werewolf most intriguing. And next time your brain goes gaga, the override code is also my private cell number. Don't abuse it."

CHAPTER 11

"Cross and heel and cross, open. Behind, side, front, open pivot left, and step," Paul called as I mangled the tricky footwork and trickier timing. One and two and three, four. And the next eight counts were a bridge with a slow one, two three four....

I could sing it perfectly, but my feet wouldn't catch up.

I ended up facing the wrong wall with my weight on the wrong foot and wobbling for balance. My eyes crossed along with my feet.

Paul caught my arm and held me upright until I planted both feet on the ground. I still wobbled, so I kicked off the offending high-heeled shoes.

"What's wrong, Mei Mei? You did it fine in flats yesterday," he said in a soothing tone while he rubbed my lower back with one hand and still clung to my arm with a firm grip.

Only that grip had gentled as his hand slid down to entwine our fingers. I leaned my head on his shoulder in defeat.

"I didn't do it fine yesterday. I ended up on the right foot facing the proper direction once. *Once* in three hours of working on nothing else. I'll never get it. I might as well give up now and save the judges having to eliminate me."

"Not yet. We still have three days. Let's take it to the pool."

"We tried that yesterday." I eyed the three shoe boxes lined up against the mirror near the music station. We'd tried this combination with all three pairs of the low-heeled character shoes and the high heels. I'd tried it in tennis shoes and barefoot. Visualization during meditation—Paul was big on this trick while training—hadn't helped. Last night I dreamed this combination, ending by falling flat on my face in a pool of water on stage and I couldn't get up.

I woke up choking and scaring Lisa into a full-blown panic attack.

"Okay, okay. I know you aren't a natural dancer and I'm not a natural singer. So, I guess I have to compromise. It's nearly noon. Go eat lunch in the canteen, practice singing this section, take a walk. Take a nap. Let me work on this and see if I can find a better combination that fits the music."

"Thanks." I kissed his cheek, which was all too close, and slid away from him, until only our fingertips touched. Then I had to leave. Had to, or I'd end up running back to him for a fierce hug and a hungry kiss. My gut felt empty the moment I lost contact.

So I turned my back on him and picked up my flimsy flats.

"No fraternization clause in the contract," he muttered.

I kept walking, not wanting to remember that I'd signed a contract with the same clause. We had to wait for six months after the last show before we could date or follow through with our instincts.

Who was it who said that dancing is the vertical expression of what we wanted to do horizontally?

Maybe there was a good reason for that clause.

Musing on that, I wandered over to the canteen for a bowl of New England clam chowder and crackers. I took a single table and let the creamy, salty goodness slide down my throat. All around me, stars and bit players from a dozen shows being filmed at this studio ate and studied lines, or zoned out waiting for their next call. I watched groups of contestants from *Here I Come, World* mingle and talk and nibble. Excitement burbled out of them. They talked and giggled and mostly ignored me. That's what happens when you take a small table with no extra chairs. I'd removed the invitation to visit.

Thinking of my own sore feet, and wishing I'd kept the second chair to prop them up, I noticed many of the contestants had shed shoes in favor of bandages on blister points. The men frequently massaged the soles and insteps of their partners. They all draped arms around the shoulders of their partners and sat close, touching thighs or arms.

But it was all easy camaraderie in a very touchy-feely group. At no point did any of them gaze longingly into each other's eyes, hold hands, or kiss. If a deeper relationship was in the offing, none showed it.

Was the tug of attraction and wish for fulfilment I felt for Paul special? Or my first adult gush of lust?

I made my way back to my trailer and slept a bit, then read a book, an archeology text about ancient Babylon I'd found in the hotel suite. It was signed as a gift to me, but the name was encoded in odd symbols, so I kind of thought Mummy as the donor. I might as well read it since I hadn't thought to put any new books on my phone.

Close to five o'clock on the west coast. That made it seven in the evening in Cleveland. Mom and my sisters should have closed the flower shop by now, and Dad would be home from work, cooking dinner. Friday night: fish and chips with coleslaw. Dad wielded the deep fryer with the expertise of an accomplished chef.

A wave of homesickness made me curl in on myself on the couch. Tears of loneliness pricked my eyes. I dialed the first number on my contacts list.

"Mom," I said on a long sigh of relief when she picked up the home landline.

"What's wrong?" she asked. I guessed she picked up on my tone. I didn't call home every day.

"I need to talk to you." That was our code. I didn't want an audience, just a sounding board.

"Okay, I'm in your father's den and he's in the kitchen at a crucial stage. The whole family is due here in a few minutes. But I have time for you, Celia."

I heard the background noise diminish when she closed the door. That was one thing about our family that I loved. We respected closed doors and privacy. Curiosity had no place in the family when a door closed. The rest of the time we shared everything.

"Mom, how do you know when you're in love, or it's just... attraction?"

"You know so deep in your heart that if anything—*anything*—were to separate you that half of yourself goes with him."

I had to think about that. I loved working with Paul, and when we weren't together, I missed his guidance and friendship, his jokes and his gentle encouragement. And we were together so much during the day.

But right now, when he was working out problems with our dance, I respected his need for solitude.

"Is that how you felt when you met Dad? Or did you grow into it?"

"We grew into it. I helped him subdue a malicious Kraken. Mummy aided us with calm seas and entangling kelp. Then she tried to take over my life again. I fled. Your dad followed me. I really resented his intrusion into my place of solitude when I needed to be alone, to get away from Mummy and her demands. But then your father and I worked out ways to reduce Mummy's influence on me and I was *very grateful*, if you know what I mean."

We both chuckled. Growing up, accepting that Mom and Dad had a very active love life and the door to their bedroom was closed often, even in the middle of the day, was just a part of life.

I expected to find the same delight when I met *the one*.

"Thanks, Mom. I guess I'm not there yet. But it is growing on me." I thought that would end the conversation.

"Celandine." Mom's voice held the stern command I remembered from childhood that meant I *really* needed to stop and listen.

"We've talked about this before, when you were in high school and the football players *expected* the cheerleaders to fall into bed with them."

Gulp. Dad had weighed in on that one too. They were frank and honest about what drove the boys and why it was important to not let hormones override my morals and common sense.

"You are not normal," Mom reminded me. "You have paranormal

strengths and talents. For multiple millennia you were bred to lure men to their deaths. When lust overcomes your sensibilities, that tiny core inside you, no matter how hard you try to suppress it, will demand that you overpower your partner and murder him. A normal man cannot survive a tryst with you."

Double gulp. She had never had to say this to me in such blunt terms.

"Your partner, Paul, may have been kissed by Terpsichore. But she is only a Muse, not a goddess. He does not have a paranormal aura. If you do love him, you may not have the strength to keep him alive."

"Thanks, Mom. I needed the reality check." Casual camaraderie it would have to be.

"Good. Have you eaten yet?"

"Yes, Mom. Paul takes care of me and reminds me to eat. But I miss home cooking. I can almost smell Dad's catfish frying."

"Plain old cod tonight, but the potatoes and cabbage are fresh and local. I'm flying out to L.A. Sunday morning and taking the red-eye back that night, so I'll have time to take you out for fish and chips after the show. Dad will come next week."

"And if I'm eliminated Sunday night?" If I totally flubbed the dance, that could happen.

Mom laughed. "Don't doubt yourself so much, Celia. I'll see you Sunday."

Three seconds after we hung up, my phone beeped with an incoming text from Paul.

Got the fix. 2 more clls to make then we're good to make changes. CU 7 sharp RH3b

---

Changes? Oh my. I think I needed more clam chowder before seven tonight when I met him in rehearsal hall 3b. That hall was tiny. No one wanted to practice there knowing every gesture and move would have to be exaggerated by a factor of ten to fill the stage with movement during the performance. But it was open and available all night.

I'd be lucky to get two hours of sleep tonight.

Five days of nothing. Five effing days of listening to the press corps and not one of them acknowledged Stevie's passing, or that she had been one of them. Entertainment news was dominated by females and driven by fashion. You'd think at least one of them could have said something about Stevie's horrible taste in clothes, hair and makeup.

All they did was acknowledge a new guy, named Anshar with a Middle Eastern accent. Something bothered Dylan about the name. It didn't jibe with any modern ethnicity that he could think of.

Was it worth running the name of a tabloid press reporter through the Guild database? Dylan didn't think so.

He wrenched off the headset and stowed it in his backpack along with his mini dish and power packs.

"Bloody waste of time," he muttered. "You'd think Stevie never existed."

That thought made him pause. Maybe, just maybe, she didn't exist elsewhere. Press passes were easy enough to forge for all but the most secure venues with political VIPs.

He returned to his office—a tiny alcove on the same floor of the admin building near Bryant Thomas's office. It had a lockable door designed by the Guild and a secure desktop computer. If stolen or used by someone else, the entire contraption would freeze, send the contents of the hard drive to the London office and then blow up. All in a matter of fifteen seconds, before a potential hacker could even start to type a fifteen-character alphanumeric, symbolic password that he changed twice a day.

Yeah, the Guild was paranoid. With paranormal enemies, it needed to be.

He logged in, counted to twenty and logged in again using a different password. That got him into a surface level data base. Stevie had mundane ID, therefore she had to be in somebody's system. He started with California driver licenses. Yep, she was there, with an address. No need for corrective lenses. Height and weight seemed accurate enough based upon his observations.

She had AP credentials but no listed employer, therefore she was freelance, selling her photos and stories to whichever rag was willing to pay.

Now to go deeper. Where had she come from?

Landlords did background checks, so did mortgage companies.

She didn't live alone. Twelve registered residents, all with the Wollencek surname, in a big old house in a part of Beverly Hills that had been the hot spot to live during the silent movie era. Updating the houses had become too expensive and time consuming. Celebrities moved higher into the hills and further out of town. Wolfpack Ltd, Inc. now owned the property. The mortgage was down to about twenty percent of the market value. They'd been there a while. And could the name of the corporation be any more clichéd?

He switched over to a more extensive database of all known werewolves, in the world.

Stephanie Wollencek and crew were way, *way*, down the list. Wolfpack Ltd, Inc. didn't register at all.

First, he emailed a correction to the minions who maintained the database, and then called Abby on her normal landline. It went to voicemail after only one ring, "Damnit, Abby, pick up, I've got new info you need."

Then he hung up, cursing himself. He should never have called her Abby.

Maybe he could chalk it up to the faulty nanos in his brain. "I should just pack and be on the next plane to Geneva." He buried his face in his hands and thought some more.

Just to amuse himself he entered the name Anshar into the database and let it churn.

"I could take down a pack of werewolves who are trying to stay under the radar and not causing much harm to normals."

Not the best use of his time or talents.

But he needed to know why Stevie had targeted Celia with her anti-male, anti-Hollywood producer attitude.

He needed a different database; one he didn't have the clearance to access. The Guild's British intelligence bureau MI8 kept track of all conspiracies, large and small, theory and fact based. Why would werewolves, and low-level ones at that, target a Siren?

Only Abby could get him into that website. Was this important enough to "abuse" her private number?

An impish smile crept across his face. Family legend said that he had a Leprechaun or three in his lineage. He knew how to get that information through the back door of another site. "I don't care if it is considered a disorganized wingnut chat room. They are usually more accurate than the official lists."

The computer screen flashed. "Unknown name. Please check spelling." Anshar didn't exist either.

CHAPTER 12

Something stirs on a wayward wind. The paranormal creatures, created from the old gods mating with humans, prowl the night without regard to the cycle of the moon that rules them.

The werewolf knew of this. She felt compelled to seek out other paranormals to discover why their cycles are disrupted and their hungers unabated. She smelled the sea in Celia's blood and sought her out. Stevie's pack has stayed together, unnoticed for over one hundred years. They pay their taxes, work at day jobs, and stock up on raw meat from a butcher shop for their hunts. Then they run the hills all night to burn off their blood lust.

No more. They are now driven to hunt humans at the dark of the moon as well as the full moon.

Did Anshar kill the werewolf in order to protect Celia?

Dryads and naiads, sylphs and nymphs wander in broad daylight amongst people, no longer wary of discovery. Few notice them in Los Angeles, Portland, Las Vegas, or Austin. Those cities embrace the weird.

Even witches dance nude under the full moon in public parks.

Soon the dead will rise.

Anshar now knows the dangers to our Celia. He should join with me now as he did before when he helped to thwart the spell that would confine me and *keep me from maintaining a balance between the chaos of storm and the calm needed to continue humanity.*

Humanity ignores us. Humanity is killing our world.

I hear the words Climate Change *more and more often; spoken on a note of dread. Humans must be eliminated in order to heal our world. These others sense it. I know it.*

I can turn these confused paranormals into allies. But I still need Celia's power to save our world. If she will not join me, then she must be eliminated, because she has the magic and the strength to thwart me.

"Ooooh, I like it!" I crooned as Paul wheeled the ornate wooden frame of a full-length mirror around the floor. The glass had been removed from the frame.

"We'll be dressed alike, mirror images of each other. Only you'll be blonde, dressed in black and I'm brunette dressed in white," he explained.

"I've seen that done in contemporary dance pieces, but never in Broadway," I countered as I stepped to the other side of the frame from him and set about smoothing my hair as if looking into a real mirror. Instinctively, I combed my bangs back and tucked the sides behind my ears imitating his hairstyle.

"But it really fits the play. The character is singing encouragement to pump himself up with confidence."

"I believe in you," I sang the chorus. "You know this will work even better if I take the load of the singing and you the dancing..."

"Exactly. You still have to dance some. And I have to sing some. But we'll be playing to each other's strengths."

"Mr. Thomas will notice." My heart sank to my gut. The head judge literally had the power of life and death over this contest. His disapproval influenced not only the other judges but the audiences as well.

"Oh, he'll notice. But he'll also reward creativity when we work together at the end, in perfect synchronization and harmony."

I looked at him a little skeptically. "You're going to have to work on your vocals. You have a tendency to go flat when I reach for the high notes."

"Yeah, I know. But I'm working on it and I do it less often when I sing *with* you. Your pitch is so very perfect you drag me up and out of my mistakes."

He gave me that wide grin I found so endearing and reached to give me a big hug of approval. I had to fight hard not to melt into him. Mom's words burned in the back of my mind.

I tripped over my big toe on the industrial carpet that ran down the middle of the corridor outside my room. Paul caught me around the waist. I giggled with fatigue.

"No more late-night rehearsals," I begged, suddenly sober as my big toe began to burn from the stumble. My open sandals protected my soles while walking across superheated pavement, but not much else.

"This week, Mei Mei, we've got this number in the bag." Gently he kissed my cheek and nudged me toward the door.

I passed my key card over the light sensor. It buzzed and flashed green. The telltale click of the lock disengaging remained silent. I stared dumbly at the mechanism, too tired to figure out why I couldn't hear the lock open.

"You really are tired, Mei Mei," Paul muttered. "It's only midnight. Get some sleep, love. And make sure you eat something in the morning. We have an eight o'clock call for group opening number rehearsal. Carmen is a genius choreographer, but she loves to challenge you to overcome your weaknesses and take your strengths to new levels."

"Ugh," I moaned. I felt like he'd been doing that to me for the last four hours.

He reached around me and opened the door for me. "Sleep, Celia." Another gentle kiss to my check and he disappeared into the shadows in the direction of his room.

One foot in front of the other, I shuffled through my usual nightly routine and collapsed into bed, not caring that Lisa had left the AC unit on high. It was easier to pull up the quilted bedspread and snuggle into its warmth than to summon enough strength to get up again and flick the temperature control.

~

The annoying buzz of Dylan's phone vibrating against the nightstand woke him from deep sleep. His eyes remained blurry and his limbs slack for too many long breaths until he realized that he was awake and needed to react. He touched the screen of his phone to awaken it.

"Dylan, I need you to disable your traps and open your door," Abby said, clearly, succinctly, and patiently.

The oxymoron of his boss being patient jolted him out of his bemusement. His reflexes engaged and he obeyed.

First, he removed the hairbrush tied to a thread that spanned the door from its precarious perch on the edge of a lamp table to the light switch. Anyone opening the door would break the thread and send the brush clattering to the floor. Then he brushed aside the talcum powder laying in a thin streak right where a person would step when entering. The unwary would find it slick and lose balance. Finally, he used his terrycloth robe to insulate his fingers as he unclipped a wire attached to a 9-volt battery from the metal door latch.

"Took you long enough," Abby said as she burst through the door followed by two androgynous figures in scrubs and surgical masks.

Abby gazed briefly at the residue of each of the three traps. "Simple but effective." Her lip curled up in a not-quite-sneer. "Presuming anything this simple and low tech would wake you."

He watched her step over the residue of talc on the tile entry.

The anonymous Greek Chorus stayed by the door.

"Mrs. Fitzwarren, how can I help you, at this..." he checked the digital display on the bedside table, "this early hour."

"Four in the morning here is one in the afternoon in Geneva." She continued inward, aiming for the window-side table and chair.

"Geneva?" He plunked down into the chair opposite her, pulling the robe closer around his body.

He looked to the extra people, amazed that they remained so still and silent even when he gestured for them to perch on the side of the bed.

"Yes, Geneva." Abby smoothed her flared gray skirt behind her legs and sat gracefully.

"Have the medicos found a cure for my deteriorating augmentation?" That might identify the anonymous ones by the door.

"Possibly." Her hand patted the side seam of her skirt, but did not delve into the pocket.

"Mrs. FitzWarren, can you administer it, or do I need to find a medical doctor?" Excitement cleared the foggy remnants of his too-deep sleep.

The people wearing scrubs and face masks suddenly made sense.

"I have an injection of nanobots for you. They need to go into your carotid artery so that they travel directly into your brain within moments. They are new, prototypes, and have a very short lifespan outside cerebral fluid."

"Prototypes?" Dylan gulped. Something vital clicked off in his brain, sending the existing nanos into gibbering panic. His hands shook and his teeth chattered. Suddenly the air conditioning felt like it went into overdrive, chilling the air and him well beyond his comfort zone.

"Will they negate the defective augmentations in my brain?" Speaking helped him control his chattering teeth. "It's too cold in here." He wrapped his arms around himself.

He needed to turn the AC unit off. But he'd have to stand and reach across Abby to the unit's manual control. His fears, and hopes, kept him anchored to his chair.

As if reading his mind, Abby bent from her waist and stretched one hand to touch the screen control of the AC.

Dylan's chill did not abate but the air immediately felt stifling, unbreathable and laden with toxins.

"For as long as I've lived in California, I still do not like air conditioning. Natural atmosphere is so much better." With another twist Abby pushed open the sliding door behind her.

Dylan drew in a deep breath and then exhaled slowly as if singing a long series of low notes. When he was out of breath, he captured more air on the same rhythm Celia used when warming up her vocal cords.

"Better?" Abby asked. "Concentrate on your breathing. In on three counts, hold three, out on another three. Repeat. Relax into the rhythm of life." Her voice took on a soft lilt as if guiding a meditation exercise. "That's it, Dylan. Breathe in, hold, breathe out, hold."

Near hypnotized by her voice, Dylan had no choice but to obey. His eyes drifted to half-mast and the lull of sleep crept through him. He sensed movement off to the side but could not yank his attention away from Abby's compelling words and mesmerizing eyes.

"What will the new nanos do to my brain?"

"They will help you control your augmentations until we finish this case and can ship you back to Geneva for a more thorough evaluation."

PAIN! A sharp stab erupted from his neck as if a bee with a foot-long stinger had sought him out directly. Immediately he slapped the jab and encountered a restraining hand.

"A moment more. They've injected half the nanos," Abby whispered, leaning forward. She captured both his hands with her own and held them firmly on the tabletop. "Give my medics just a moment more."

"Grrrrr," Dylan disagreed with her. "I don't need any more..."

A heavy hand landed on each shoulder and held him in place on the suddenly uncomfortable chair.

"Sorry my nurses are so clumsy. They don't usually use this big a syringe." Abby's grip on his fingers tightened, punishing his bones for trying to interfere.

His spine arched with the need to escape while holding still.

"Abby, they can't be doing this right!" he squeaked.

"Just this once I'll let you get away with calling me 'Abby.' Once you get the full injection and Nurse Mathilde removes that bloody big syringe, we'll be back to normal Mr. McQuilleran. And you will feel a lot better with all your synapses firing in sequence again."

A warm gush followed the needle outward, taking the pain with it. Dylan pressed his fingers against the wound. Unsurprisingly he felt warm, thick, wetness that dripped alarmingly down to stain the white terrycloth collar of his robe.

"I think you'd better take me to Urgent Care, Mrs. Fitzwarren."

CHAPTER 13

I must have slept. The next thing I knew, a note I had not summoned buzzed in the back of my throat. I blinked and the digital clock shone four in the morning. My T-shirt was hiked up to my breasts and I lay on my back, not the position I'd started my slumber in. Somehow I'd managed to kick off my shoes and remove my capris.

Now a strongly acidic stench burned my nose.

The vibration I found myself humming grew stronger but didn't banish the smell.

My first thought was of an overdose of chlorine in the pool outside.

But the doors had been closed and the AC turned up when I came home. I must have turned it off when I shucked my excess clothing.

Not chlorine. Something more metallic than chemical.

Copper! I sat bolt upright in my bed.

The events of the night in Las Vegas when Mummy attacked the night club replayed in my mind in vivid and gory detail. I smelled again the blood that gushed from Bethany's mouth. It tasted just like a copper penny I'd sucked on when I was ten because a television show said that blood smelled like copper tasted.

"Who's bleeding?" I asked aloud.

In the other bed beside me, Lisa grunted and rolled over. "Three and four, five, six, and seven, eight," she mumbled.

I'd had a few of those dreams these last few weeks.

In the dim light reflected from the full moon shining onto pool deck I could see just enough to know that my roommate wasn't hurt.

Who then?

I slid out of bed, stuffing my feet into my fuzzy slippers, and walked carefully toward the central sitting area. My nose worked with every step, seeking the source of the blood that must be pouring out of someone.

The smell and the compulsion to follow it grew stronger toward the sliding doors. I pushed them open, heedless of the noise they made.

The odor slammed into my senses the moment I stepped out onto the pool deck.

Quickly I spun right and left. The smell remained the same. I looked down, my nose stopped burning and the insistent note grew stronger yet.

With my head tilted back, I had to shut my eyes to avoid the metallic irritant.

My nose led me around the corner and up the open stairs. My leg muscles protested the climb to the fourth floor at the top of the building. Instincts I didn't know I had dragged me upward, ever upward.

The hum burst into a pure tone that matched a vibration I had yet to comprehend.

I had to protect and save whoever lost their lifeblood in copious quantities.

The door nearest the stairs glowed in the moonlight. My eyes squinted and brought the grain of the wood into sharp focus. The reek of spilling blood seared painful memories into my mind.

A migraine pounded at my temples.

I had to run away.

I couldn't.

Someone needed me.

I resorted to the one thing that always solved my problems. I sang high E sharp. The door panels began to quiver in sympathetic vibrations with me. The latch clicked open, loud and clear, unlike my own door earlier. Why bother with a key when on the night of a full moon my voice eased every chore and opened every path.

As if in a dream I touched the portal and it swung open. Automatically my voice dropped to a simple A above middle C easier to hold true than almost any other. An orchestra could tune to that note, A880.

The center of the universe.

That single note kept me awake and aware. Dylan sat by the open balcony window, his face lying awkwardly on the table while two EMTs pressed white bandages to his neck. The gauze quickly stained red.

Aunt Abigail was on her phone, spitting commands at someone on the other end.

I couldn't interpret her words and didn't care to.

Dylan McQuilleran commanded all of my attention.

In the back of my mind Mummy laughed. She pushed me to throw the medicos aside and let the man bleed to death.

I flung out my hand to remove the person who held the syringe in the wrong position. She flew across the room and landed against the far wall with a thud.

"NO!" I screamed at the StormMother, pulling the note up a notch, then another and another.

Something within me attached that note to the wound in Dylan's neck. The invisible cord drew me closer, ever closer until my hand replaced that of the first person in blue surgical scrubs. I matched his pressure against the wound.

The pulse of blood flow lessened, became a sluggish puddle.

The single binding note became a lullaby that reminded me of low tide swishing against the sand. A gentle breeze wafted in from the west, soothing his racing heart and twining the music between us.

His panic and fear of death skittered from his mind to mine. "Hush," I sang to him.

"But… but…but…" he protested, atonal and sliding away from harmonizing with me.

"Hush now, love. I will take care of you. Always."

Sleep my child and I will tend thee
   All through the night.
   Guardian angels God will lend thee
   All through the night

He drifted off to sleep. His wound finished closing, no longer leaking blood. The remaining nurse hooked him up to a transfusion and IV nutrients. The one I'd flung against the wall was gone.

My knees wobbled.

Aunt Abigail pushed a chair behind my knees and let me collapse into it.

I fell asleep, my fingers still pressing against Dylan's neck and the siren song within me half finished.

A sweet note lingered in the air, surrounding Dylan with comfort, like a cocoon, or a womb.

He drifted on the gentle waves of a tropical sea above white sands that sparkled in the morning sunshine.

He smelled salt.

Was this a rebirth? The time when we were no longer part of the ocean, alien to it.

He was going to drown…

"Don't thrash," Bryant Thomas said quietly from beside him. Dylan's left side. He thought.

He couldn't thrash if he wanted to with the great weight across his chest. Restraints?

The producer's hand on his shoulder settled him. The rasp of sheets below and on top of his body told him he was safe on land. For now.

He felt every thread of the weave of whatever shroud that confined him.

"Where am I?" The place didn't smell like a hospital room; nor did it feel like his own room in the loft above his Mam's cottage on the northwest coast of Ireland.

"You are safe in your hotel room in Los Angeles," Bryant said.

Safe?

"I remember Abby and two medical people, and… and…"

"A horse syringe full of nanos to stabilize your last augmentation. Abby informs me that your last scan shows them working overtime to merge with your brain and correct the faulty ones. Oh yes, your last augmentation was faulty. The newest batch of microscopic robots had a flawed update. She's recalled two other agents who got treated from the same batch."

"Why did Abby allow someone so inept to puncture one of her very valuable agents with that over-sized needle? Or am I no longer of value to her, since my second augmentation failed?"

"You are still very valuable to her, to all of the Guild." Bryant sounded reassuring. "I banished her from your room, though she wanted to hover like a mother hen."

"Abby doesn't care enough about anything but the Guild. She doesn't hover."

Bryant laughed out loud, then quickly stifled the sound. But he continued smiling. "Abby cares a great deal about every one of her employees and agents. We are the Guild she adores. We are the children she never had."

Dylan wanted to snort in derision. The weight across his chest stirred.

He woke up enough to open his eyes and discovered a pale and slender arm holding him down. Fingers still pressed against his wound, a caress now rather than pressure to keep his blood from leaking out.

He reached up with his right hand to caress that arm, knowing instinctively that Celia owned it. Celia had sung the hole closed.

And an IV attached to the back of his left wrist returned blood to him along with a drip of a colorless solution.

"You needed three units of transfusion," Bryant said. "That's done now. The IV is to keep up the liquid volume in your veins. You probably won't need either by the time the Guild doctor comes back."

Dylan let his right hand stroke Celia's hair.

"How did Abby allow an inept nurse to wield the syringe?" That was the question that burned in the back of his mind, urging him to get moving and solve that puzzle right now.

"We don't know for sure. In the confusion of Celia throwing her against the wall with a single swipe of her arm, and then binding herself to you with some kind of seaweed glue that oozed from her body to close your wound, one of the nurses escaped. We found her at the foot of the stairs with her neck broken. Her body temp suggested that she died before she climbed the stairs with her companion. Someone else took her place and tried to kill you."

"Mummy," Celia whispered from where she'd planted her face against Dylan's bed while she bound herself to him and then collapsed in exhaustion. "Mummy exists as sea mist most of the time. She can coalesce into human form for a few hours at a time."

"If she's sea mist, then she can take on any face or form," Dylan completed the explanation.

"The StormMother tried to kill you," Bryant said flatly. He pulled out his phone and rapidly typed a text. "Why?" he looked up from his intense concentration on the phone.

Celia shrugged, then tried to sit up. But she had to remove her hand from Dylan's neck in order to do so. She yanked at her hand twice. Her fingers gripped the wound even tighter.

Bryant inserted his own fingers beneath hers and pried them loose. A stiffening gel ripped free of Dylan's skin. He felt a brief warm trickle that solidified within seconds.

"What is that stuff?" he asked as the scent of seaweed washed ashore and baking in the sun engulfed his senses.

"I don't know but I'm going to take a sample," Bryant replied. He pulled a baggie and wooden spatula from his shirt pocket. "Orders from Abby," he explained.

"I didn't know I could heal," Celia said. She stared at her splayed fingers where the amber colored goo still dripped—the color of kelp bulbs. "All the legends and family lore say I can only slay with my voice."

"Something new to add to the literature," Dylan mused. He examined the story in Coptic and ancient Egyptian in his head. Neither language had the lyrical quality needed to describe what had happened to him, and to Celia. Maybe he should examine the oldest versions of Irish Celtic, a people and their language tied to the sea that ringed their island. They were edging toward civilization about the same time the Greeks were, but along a different path.

"I wonder..." Bryant Thomas said quietly. He pushed aside the sleeve of Celia's long T-shirt. "The welt left over from your plague vaccination is gone now. I wonder if that has anything to do with your sudden ability to heal."

"I don't suppose you or the StormMother speaks Sumerian?" Dylan asked, oblivious to Bryant Thomas's statement. He wrapped his free arm around her shoulders and drew her back down so she could rest her head against his shoulder.

Where she belonged.

When had that happened?

"Sumerian?" His mind wandered again. As long as Celia stayed beside him, he could let the nanos in his brain seek connections no one else saw.

The name the Guild database spat out as inaccurate, *Anshar*. Babylonian, ancestor of the gods.

Which museums had collected the most literature and artifacts of the ancient empire?

"I think I need to go to Turkey."

"Not today, my love," Celia whispered.

"Aunt Abigail," Celia whispered into her phone. She'd just stepped out of the shower and couldn't take the time to towel off. She had to share her newest inspiration with her godmother. Keeping the phone on audio only was probably a good idea. One never knew who was meeting with Abby at six thirty in the morning.

"Yes, dear. How do you feel? Do I need to have Mr. Thomas rearrange your schedule again? Switch to video, please. I need to see the color and texture of your skin to make sure you are okay."

"No. I'm fine, really. I slept deeply for the first time since I came to L.A. I think I purged some of my anger against Mummy last night by thwarting her. I'm rejuvenated." That was the only word to describe the bouncing energy that had returned to my body as the hot water sluiced away my fatigue and worry.

Early this morning when I clamped my hand on Dylan's wound and created a sea weed based glue to close the gaping edges of the gash that should have been only a pin point hole, I'd bound myself to him, mind and body. Paul was just a pale imitation of... of I don't know what. Any lingering attraction to him had faded to a shadow of friendship.

My life and my heart now belonged to the Hunter.

That's what truly gave me new energy and put a bounce in my step.

"Then how can I help you, Celia?"

"Aunt Abby, I think I know why the StormMother tried to kill Dylan last night." Oops! I'd called my favorite relative by her forbidden nickname. Dylan's and Mr. Thomas's use of the semi-affectionate name was addictive.

"Oh?" She didn't sound like she'd noted what I'd called her.

I didn't need to see her to know she reached for something to take notes with. A pen and paper? A computer keyboard? It didn't matter. She and I both knew that she'd make a backup of what her prodigious mind recorded.

"Dylan is a linguist. His primary goal in life is to hear Sumerian spoken." How did I know that? The thought snuggled into my heart as true as if I shared the same ambition.

"The older the language, the more fascinated he is," Aunt Abby confirmed.

"The spell the ancients used to block Mummy's power of chaos over burgeoning civilization was in their own language, the oldest language ever recorded: Sumerian. Thousands of years have passed, the spell broke down long ago and released her to wreak havoc among humans again. She must be doing so, partially in revenge for restraining her and partially something else, something new that irritates her."

The memory of her reaction to fresh chlorine bothered me. Chemicals.

The cleanser didn't bother me or Mom. We were generations removed from Mummy's primal spirit. I couldn't put my finger on it.

"Are you saying that a new spell to disrupt or contain her power has to be in the same language?" Aunt Abby asked.

"Yes. And Dylan is the only one who has the knowledge and resources to find it."

He'd said he needed to go to Turkey.

"But he also has to learn the language."

"He already reads it. Now he just has to learn to speak it."

"There is no one left alive who speaks Sumerian. It's been dead for thousands of years."

"Mummy knows it." And maybe Fred.

"But we can't allow Dylan to get close enough to her to hear her speak it."

CHAPTER 14

"Miss Fisher, what do you call that foot?" Carmen, the choreographer from hell demanded. She stood in front of Paul and me, hands on hips and toe tapping in impatience.

I was in the ignominious position of one foot planted and turned out, the other up at the level of my shoulder, my butt two inches off the ground and Paul supporting me with his hands in my arm pits.

And I needed to apply pressure to the back of my left hand. A phantom slice of pain followed by a lingering ache took my mind back to Dylan's hotel room. Somehow, I knew that a doctor, a real doctor not Mummy in the guise of one, withdrew a long IV needle from his arm.

I tried not to wince in sympathy. Or was it empathy?

"Um..."

Paul lifted me up so I could stand and face my torturer.

"Um what?" Carmen's voice rose toward an atonal shriek.

I resisted the urge to cover my ears with my hands. In my peripheral vision I knew that other singers winced.

"You said flexed foot," I defended myself. I'd been very careful not to point my toes, having already been reprimanded for that. Paul had drilled me so often and so long about the importance of a pointed foot, it almost, *almost*, seemed natural.

"I said, *flexed*, not dangling. You must be in control of every inch of your body every second you are on stage. Now show me again, from the turn into the drop."

I swallowed my angry retort as the back of my right hand burned when Dylan had the second IV needle removed and clamped with a pressure bandage.

He/I felt immediate relief that plastic tubing no longer connected him/me to life-giving fluids.

Keeping these flashes of insight silent, I took my place to Paul's left and held out my right hand. Before I could think about what I was doing, he pulled me into a full spin and a half in front of him. Then as he released my hand I dropped backward, trusting him to catch me. The moment I felt his fingers supporting me I flicked my upstage (right) leg up to nearly touch his nose, heel out, toes back.

"That's it!" Carmen cried, clapping her hands together once. "I knew you had it in you if you'd just concentrate on the dance and not whatever has sent your eyes glazing all morning." She turned away to stand with her back to the big mirror in the rehearsal hall. "Now all of you, from the beginning, no stops, not even if you fall flat on your face. Keep going just as if this were a live performance.

We shuffled to our marks, little Xs of hot pink tape scattered about the floor. I took a deep breath and smiled as if I truly were on stage.

"That's it, Mei Mei. Dance like you sing with all your heart and your mind. Whatever is bothering you will wait until we are done."

I wasn't so sure about that.

Something worried Dylan and therefore me. Something we both needed to deal with sooner rather than later.

Somehow I endured another half hour of rehearsal, then sagged against the wall beside my rehearsal bag full of shoes, street clothes, more rehearsal clothes—the current set was soaked with sweat—and snacks. Paul reached in and found a bottle of water, uncapped it, and placed it in my hand, curling my fingers around the plastic.

"Drink," he said.

I obeyed.

"Now tell me what is going on in your head. I feel like you have gone to live somewhere else and only your body remains here with me."

"Family dispute. My grandmother." If he only knew the *whole* truth.

~

Dylan plopped into his desk chair in a cubicle down the hall from Bryant Thomas's suite of offices. This close to the second episode of *Here I Come, World* he had far too much to do to sit poolside all day, dreaming of Celia and her magic seaweed and let his new nanos feast on his brain. He knew from experience that the best way to deal with the dreaded robots was to stay busy, let them do their job, and ignore them during the process.

Not an easy task.

Easier than forgetting the tangible bond Celia had created between them. She had magically glued them together.

At this moment he knew that she rubbed analgesic gel into her freshly washed feet while trying to relax in her trailer.

He was on his feet and headed toward the rows of portable dressing rooms before he'd even opened his laptop.

"Going anywhere interesting?" Bryant Thomas asked, suddenly blocking his exit from the rows of offices.

Dylan had to stop and think about that. "Sir, have you had that amber goo that smells of seaweed—kelp bulbs to be exact—analyzed yet?"

"The results are not yet in. Why do you ask?" The producer didn't relax his posture. His fist tightened on a flash drive. Probably data he wanted incorporated into the next round of press releases and social media leaks.

"I... I think..." Best to just spit it out. "I think there is more than just an herbal bandage in it."

"Like the corpsmen discovering superglue as a way of closing wounds on the battlefield in Viet Nam?"

"More."

"As in...?"

"I think the glue stuck me to Celia and her to me. I know where she is and what she's doing all the time. I just have to think about her and I *know*."

"Can you block her out?"

Dylan shrugged. "Haven't tried. Haven't wanted to try. She's a really sweet girl with only my best interests at heart." That barely covered his feelings, and certain knowledge that the bond he shared with Celia was life-long, and deep. Truly deep and important.

Bryant groaned and pinched the bridge of his nose as if warding off a migraine. He did that a lot. "Do something with this." He handed over the flash drive. "I need to talk to Abby."

"And I need... I need..."

You need to get out of my head and go back to work so I can get to my next rehearsal on time. Celia's words sang in his mind.

Smiling, he complied as best he could. But his hand kept reaching for his wound as if he could still feel the pressure of her fingers restoring his life blood to him.

Push your heel down and your toe up.

Instinctively I obeyed the quiet voice in the back of my head. My calf muscle stretched to comply, and my foot flexed properly and completely. How did Dylan know I had a little more to give to the weird position?

"Remember how that feels, Mei Mei," Paul whispered into my ear as he raised me up by my shoulders and into the next combination of steps.

We had decided to run through the opening number one more time at the end of our practice session of the mirror piece.

"Dance requires you to push each position into completion."

"I thought you said this opening routine doesn't count for our scores," I said, sliding to the side while tugging him to follow. The steps were becoming automatic, I didn't have to think, "Do this, then this, then this." I just did it.

"No scores, but an overall impression for the judges. They take note of each tiny improvement." Paul guided me around in a circle. We faced the same direction, his right hand at my right waist, my left hand across his body to hold his left hand.

Being this close to him felt natural, but not intimate like it had yesterday. Since my psychic healing episode with Dylan, any attraction, or lust for Paul had dissolved.

How could that happen so quickly?

I needed to talk to Mom.

Later. Meet me at your trailer. We have to talk.

I loved having Dylan in my head!

I looked at the digital clock on the shelf by the music station. We were five minutes past our allotted time. I could sense movement and heard the shuffle of feet on the other side of the door.

We finished the last ten seconds of the dance, and I landed in a wide stance, arms stretched, fingertips just barely touching Paul's. This time I stretched arms and legs out, and my torso up until I almost had to rise onto tip toe to fulfill the movement.

"Good girl!" Paul chortled and gave me a high five.

I gave him a smile, barely noting his look of perplexity that I didn't linger as usual and talk to him casually. My mind was already circling around my trailer, pacing with Dylan as he waited for me.

He wasn't in sight when I unlocked the flimsy door of my personal dressing room. The size and privacy of the trailer still felt like an amazing luxury. His gentle hand on my shoulder didn't surprise me. Nothing he did, ever again, would surprise me; we were that tightly linked.

"There's iced tea and lemonade in the fridge," I said, not daring to turn around and into his arms.

He took the decision away from me once we were fully inside and the door closed. His big hands cupped my face and he bent his head to mine.

We paused and stared at each other, stretching the moment, teasing us with anticipation.

And then we could wait no longer. He devoured my mouth with his own. My hands ran up and down his lean back, relishing the taut muscles.

I knew his eagerness to rip off my clothes.

As I hesitated, he withdrew a fraction—not so far away as to end our chance at intimacy but far enough to dampen our ardor. A little.

"Not yet," I whispered.

"Tell me why. Put it into words not just vague and disjointed feelings." He kept his hands on my face as our foreheads touched.

"We... I need to know that this is real and not just the temporary backlash of magic."

"It certainly feels real to me," he sighed.

"Me too. I've... never experienced anything like this. All I know is that Mummy is a master manipulator and I want *this*, this thing between us to be real and not the product of her convoluted plans."

He straightened and dropped his hands to my shoulders. "There's no storm brewing, so this isn't like the time she sent your parents and your sisters into a mating frenzy."

"My parents loved each other before then, and long afterwards. We barely know each other."

"You're holding something back. We can't lie to each other or even withhold the truth any longer."

"I know." I could just think what he needed to know, and he would. Speaking it aloud gave it more reality, something tangible we both needed to deal with.

A big gulp of air fortified my resolve. "Just before I touched you, applied pressure to your wound." My fingers found the slight thickening of his skin where the jagged puncture still healed. "The StormMother told me to let you die. I defied her."

"Did you know that touching me like that would bind us together?"

"No. I was acting on instinct."

"You needed to heal me." A big grin split his face and brought light to his hazel eyes. "That instinct tells me that we shared something special before that moment."

"Are you sure? I could just have easily killed you. My kind is hardwired to seduce mortal men with song and drag them beneath the waves to their deaths."

"But you didn't." He dropped his mouth to mine once more.

Pressure built within me as my lips softened and parted. He probed delicately with his tongue. We explored each other in a lovely prelude.

He drew back first. The heat between us cooled enough to let me think.

"You are right. We need to wait and test the ground." He breathed heavily. "We hardly know each other and we both need to concentrate on our day jobs."

I drew in a long breath and banished the fog of lust in my brain. "How did you know to tell me to push my heel out when I thought I'd flexed my foot just fine?"

"I felt the little bit of slack in your calf." He laughed. "I can also feel your stomach growling. Let's go find some dinner—off site so we can talk and get to know each other for real."

CHAPTER 15

Dylan sat on his balcony, arms crossed along the railing. The pool deck was empty except for Celia. He watched and listened to her talk to her mom.

Feeling the closeness and love between them brought tears to his eyes. He hadn't been with his mother when she died twenty-five years ago. It wouldn't have mattered to her because of the dementia. She didn't know him, barely knew herself. She didn't notice that after his first augmentation he looked like he had in upper sixth form. That was the summer before he'd had to put her in a home with full time care. He'd been twenty-seven and near the end of his first doctorate in linguistics.

Even through the tough years of her memory loss, he missed her. A stab of jealousy for the relationship Celia maintained with her parents must have leaked through him, into her. She looked up from her poolside lounge chair and waved to him.

His envy faded, replaced by gratitude that she had a happy family life.

That blessed link between them brought the rather intimate conversation into his mind. He blinked and thought deeply about the nano robots that still gnawed at his brain. They'd calmed down in the last twenty-four hours, but not gone away. He had the ability to tap into them and block that bond. But he cherished it too much to let it go completely.

For now, he'd live with it.

"Mom, are you and Dad telepathic?" Celia asked on a whisper.

"Um... what happened?"

Dylan had to chuckle at that. His mother had known the first time he'd kissed a girl, his first crush back when he was fifteen and randy as all get out. That was a mom's job.

"Mummy attacked Dylan McQuilleran."

"Who?"

Dylan sensed the mother's alarm.

"The publicity guy for the studio. You may have met him last week. I don't know for sure. He works for Mr. Thomas, but he's really a Hunter. Aunt Abigail assigned him to protect me."

"Why would Mummy attack him if he's assigned to protect you?"

"I'm not sure, but... but I knew when he started bleeding out. A note came into my head and I had to sing it out loud until I found him. I *had* to. And then I knocked the StormMother out of the way and clamped my hands over the wound, singing something strange, like a lullaby in a language I didn't know. I thought it was pure instinct, but it might have been something I heard long ago."

She left the name Fred unsaid. But the image in her mind was the middle eastern man Dylan had seen at the front gate; the man reminiscent of a dozen ancient coins.

That made Dylan sit up straight and listen intently rather than just let the conversation float through him.

He tried to force his memory to replay those awful moments when he knew he was dying and could do nothing about it. Abby must have been hypnotized into oblivion while the StormMother attempted murder. He narrowed his focus to Celia. What had she sung? He'd heard it but couldn't bring the precise tones into focus. It was like a radio signal two blocks away, melodic noise without the definition of lyrics.

"Did an amber glue ooze out of your fingertips?" Mom asked.

"Yeah, it was the color of a kelp bulb on the beach before it turns brown in the sun. Mom, how do I know that? I've never been to a saltwater beach, not even here in L.A when the coast is only a couple of miles away."

"You know it from racial memory." Mom's voice sounded flat.

Dylan interpreted the tones just like Celia did.

"The amber glue, what was it?"

"Something magical. Mummy doesn't like to admit it because it interferes with her agenda. Old folklore about Sirens doesn't like to admit it because the ancient Greeks wanted to paint us as evil. We can heal as well as kill."

"The wound closed, and he stopped bleeding within seconds. One more minute and I'd have been too late."

"There must have been something special between you before that."

"Maybe. How do you know that?"

"Because your father suffered a stab wound soon after I met him. I liked him. I was attracted to him. Then before I woke up from the exhaustion of working magic, we were bound together for all time. We can't lie to each other. We can't keep secrets. And we know where the other is and how they feel at any given moment."

Celia looked up from her place by the pool and engaged Dylan's gaze. He couldn't look away, knowing how special their link was to both of them.

He almost missed the shadow that crept out of the pool and crawled toward her.

He'd seen that sideways waddled and swish of tail in Mexico.

A crocodile! An Australian saltwater variety if he had any guess.

From its intent trajectory, Dylan knew the creature was not ordinary. It had to be a shape changer.

He engaged his augmented speed and flew down the stairs, freeing his belt as he ran. Panic surged up from his belly like three-day-old bile. He had to get to Celia before the croc did. He burst through the doorway from the stairwell with a metal bending slap to the center panel. Then three strides to the fifteen-foot monster and he leaped upon its back, looping the fine leather strap around its top jaw, cinching tight, and hauled its head back.

Thank God for late night documentaries while he recovered from his first and second augmentation.

~

I didn't have time to scream. Even as Dylan wrestled him the giant croc started a death roll, trying to force Dylan off its back and free the restraint on it jaw.

How could he hang on?

I didn't know so I did the only thing I could think of. I jumped upright, forgetting my still open call to my mom, and sang. I called soothing darkness upon the reptile's vision. Something I'd heard, long ago in my distant past but barely remembered. The words meant nothing to me, only my intent to lull the monster to sleep. Not too different from what I'd sung to heal Dylan, more than instinct, less than a memory.

When I ran low on air, I stretched upright and drew in deep, controlled breaths, making each exhale a sleeping dart that penetrated the feeble mind of the crocodile.

Slowly, ever so slowly, I watched tension flow out of the beast's muscles. It stopped fighting the belt.

When the great head dropped onto the pool deck, Dylan jumped free, wrapped and buckled his belt around the full jaw, and studied it.

I kept singing, afraid that if I gave in to the urge to let the music rest, the croc would wake up and resume its mindless quest to kill me.

"It's okay, Celia. You can release it," Dylan said quietly, touching my arm to draw my attention back to reality.

"Where did it go?" Instead of the giant amphibian, a tall, heavily muscled, bald man lay sprawled across the cement at the edge of the pool.

"A shape changer," Dylan said. He pulled out his phone and dialed someone with a single stroke.

"Aunt Abigail," I said. I didn't need to see her number on his screen to know who he called at ten in the evening.

Then the screaming at the other end of my phone captured my attention. I hadn't severed my phone call to Mom. But it was Dad demanding I explain.

"The danger is over, sir," Dylan explained for me. "I have a feeling Abby is going to ask you to research crocodilian shape shifters and why the StormMother might compel one to kill your daughter. And I hope you had the sense to record what Celia sang. She probably isn't aware of it, but I think, from the cadence and grouping of words, the lyrics were in ancient Sumerian. I need to study it."

CHAPTER 16

"By St. Bridget and St. Patrick and all the leprechauns in Ireland, Abigail, I need my books!" Dylan pounded the desk in his boss's office.

He'd sat for the last two hours with headphones and a portable oscilloscope examining the recording of Celia's soothing song. Every note caressed him like a warm blanket on a cold night. Now he understood why an aggressive and predatory shape changer had fallen asleep rather than follow the compulsion imposed upon him by the StormMother.

Dylan wanted nothing more than to curl up and sleep the clock around. Hunters didn't need as much sleep as mere mortals. But they needed some, and he hadn't had any. Here it was seven o'clock in the morning and he was still awake, comparing the length of words and the phrasing of Celia's voice to every example of Sumerian, in cuneiform, hieroglyphs, and text approximations he could find in his own digitized library and the Guild's. Nothing matched.

He suppressed a yawn.

"If the paper books you seek are so important, you should have digitized them long ago." The director of the Guild presided over his research while dealing with her own paperwork. Her eyes looked bruised and age lines sagged around them. Little comfort to him that she'd had no more sleep than he had.

Just like her to avoid dealing with a problem by pointing out his shortcomings rather than coming up with a solution.

He thought about releasing a stream of curses. She'd just reprimand him and send him packing without a copy of the recording.

Good morning, Celia greeted him.

His attitude brightened. At least she'd had some sleep after Abby's minions had hauled away the big Werecrocodile for interrogation.

What's your day look like? he asked.

More of the same, rehearsals, costume fittings, staff meetings. I see an interview has been canceled. Your doing?

Yeah, I'm tied up with Abby.

Good luck. She withdrew from direct contact with him.

Still he shared her satisfaction of eating a bowl of cornflakes with fresh strawberries and skim milk. Her cup of black coffee dispersed his craving for sleep but left a bitter taste in his mouth. Why couldn't she drink tea like a proper person?

He caught himself on that thought. She was a proper person, just not a Brit raised as he had been where tea cured everything.

Two rapid swallows banished the taste of coffee on his tongue. He reached for the mug of tea he'd left cooling on the desk. It had gone cold and stewed. The microwave would restore it but not refresh it.

He'd been sitting too long as it was, so he stood and stretched, yanked off the headphones and took the mug across the room to the nook in a wall unit that held the beverage service stuff.

"Would you set the kettle to boiling, please," Abby asked, not moving from her own massive chair.

A please and a pleasant voice from Abby? Was the world coming to an end?

Like the well-trained minion he was, and because she had asked nicely, he complied by making fresh tea for them both. The electric kettle must be another Guild designed gadget for it boiled within a minute. He barely had time to prepare a porcelain pot with two measures of loose tea leaves.

While the tea steeped, he loaded a tray with two clean mugs (tea cups just weren't big enough to satisfy Hunter cravings) a sugar bowl, a milk pitcher and silver spoons, only the best for the Director of the International Guild of Demon and Vampire Hunters. At the last second, he retrieved a plate of fresh lemon slices from the mini fridge. Right now he wanted the brightness of citrus rather than mellow milk.

"Shall I pour?" he asked politely when he'd placed the laden tray on Abby's desk. Of course she'd cleared a space on one corner the perfect size for his burden.

"Yes, please. Now where are the books you need?" She looked up and smiled sweetly.

"My cubicle in the Belfast office. Top shelf to the left of my desk." He poured two mugs of tea and allowed her to embellish her own. She took a lemon slice and two lumps of sugar. Too sweet for his taste. He settled for one lump and two slices.

Celia nudged his mind to let him know she was joining her roommates in the studio limo that would deliver them to their appointments at various buildings.

That allowed him to settle back into his own armchair and contemplate what he was missing from the recording.

"The office manager has the books in hand. Do you know which pages he can scan and send to you, or can you wait twelve hours for express delivery?"

"Have him scan chapter thirteen of the Bierenbach and chapters seven and nine of the Champsuissé." The tea slid down his throat in civilized refreshment. "Then have him forward all five books on the express flight."

"As advanced as our computers are, this will take approximately ten minutes. You will use that time to review the interrogation recordings of our crocodilian friend." She turned her computer monitor so that he could watch the images along with her from his chair at the other end of her desk.

He didn't have the clearance to call up the recording on his laptop which she had graciously allowed him to place on the credenza behind her and to her right. More so she could monitor him than to keep him close.

His job was hunting. Interrogation belonged to other experts. The Were creature hadn't needed much prodding. A dry atmosphere in a very cold room made him spew words after only two minutes of repetitive questions.

"The girl blocks the StormMother from cleansing the earth. The StormMother who created us all gave me the honor of assisting her. I failed because of the Hunter. Now I must die." With that he folded his arms across the metal table, rested his head atop them and closed his eyes.

"Did he die?" Dylan asked as soon as he swallowed a choking mouthful of tea.

"No, dear. We are not so cruel. We locked him up in a warm and moist cell, close to his natural environment, until we know more about the whole situation. Ah, the first chapter you requested is ready for your review." She tapped his laptop where the screen had changed from the bouncing line of the oscilloscope to a selection of pages, fifteen in all. With a touch he enlarged the first page and began reading.

After rehearsing the group number on the stage, I checked my link to Dylan. All I got was scrambled images of lines and dots. My voice singing something no more comprehensible than the lines and dots filled his head. So that's what happened when a linguistic genius concentrated really, really hard on something that fascinated him.

I guessed I would be eating lunch in the canteen with Paul and the other contestants.

For a moment I sagged in relief. I loved that Dylan and I were together, in more, and better, ways than normal, but on the other, keeping up with his mind, in at least six different languages at any given time, was exhausting. I had enough trouble keeping up with where and who I was!

I carried my tray of fish and chips to the table where my roommate Lisa and her partner Alex were already sitting, close with shoulders touching and long, lingering glances between them. Paul sat across from them. He looked up, hopefully, his almond eyes moist like a lost puppy.

Damn.

I liked the guy. I admired and respected him as a partner and as a friend. But the momentary crush I'd had on him was just that, momentary and a crush. He couldn't compare to Dylan in any way, shape, or form. Except for dancing. I had no idea if Dylan could dance. And I was learning to love dancing, when it was simple enough that I could keep my feet straight.

In my limited experience, I thought that language nerds would be socially inept.

Do you dance?

Some. My mum insisted I take ballroom dance classes when I was young and clumsy. Haven't done much since.

That's good enough for me.

I smiled at the people gathering around the big table in the center of the cafeteria and took a seat beside Paul but made certain that several inches separated my chair from his and I did not accidentally bump his shoulder as I lowered myself into the hard plastic that did not invite someone to linger longer than needed to scarf down a meal.

Talk to him. Let him down easy. Remind him of the no fraternization clause in your contracts.

So Dylan wasn't so absorbed in his work that my tumbling emotions slid off of him.

What about us? Aren't we bound by the same contracts?

I'll have to check. But I think it's primarily between contestants and pro partners. The intensity of the competition tends to create false emotions. And I'll be very careful to make certain I don't favor you more than anyone else in my publicity releases.

Another sag of relief.

Paul grabbed my hand and held it between both of his beneath the table. "Talk to me, Mei Mei," he whispered.

I withdrew my hand from his. "Sorry, it can't work," I whispered. "Contracts."

He jerked his chin down once in acknowledgement and turned his attention back to the group where a wild discussion of the proper amount of mustard in the coleslaw was hotly debated.

I couldn't taste a thing.

The rest of the week continued in much the same vein. Paul and I rehearsed in the studio and on stage, but now that I had learned the routine, we didn't need the pool. The group rehearsed on the stage so Carmen could get the placement of each couple on various levels of risers and platforms just right. Bryant Thomas wandered in and out of the practice session, taking notes on his tablet. I'd love to see what he recorded, but knew I never would. Dylan and I ate dinner together every night in quiet, out-of-the-way restaurants where we wouldn't be interrupted.

And every evening Dylan delivered me to the door of my suite, kissed my cheek politely and withdrew. When I sought refuge against my aching muscles and surging hormones in the pool or hot tub, I knew that he watched me from his balcony. I shared with him my joy in swimming.

He never joined me physically, but I knew he welcomed the stretch of my muscles and the soothing warmth of the watery environment.

He never mentioned the shape changer who'd crawled out of the pool. I knew Abby's minions had hauled him away, stoic and silent. The Guild would take care of him. That's all I needed to know despite my curiosity.

I talked to Mom or Dad every day. They watched the national weather programs closely, seeking patterns indicative of Mummy's interference.

Then came the Sunday night show. Dad was in the audience, not

Mom. No sign of Mummy, either in person or visible on camera. But the sky was gray with moisture rather than pollution—the stock for creating a soupy storm.

Hurricane season had another few weeks to churn the air into something stronger. I heard about a monster storm zooming across the Atlantic from Africa toward the east coast of the U.S. It zig-zagged an unpredictable path, keeping weather critters guessing its eventual landfall.

Another smaller storm hovered off the coast of Mexico, taking its time deciding when or if it would strengthen into something significant and which direction it would head.

That made me more nervous than knowing Mummy was in the audience, criticizing my every move.

I just wished I understood her agenda. The werecrocaile had said I interfered with her purpose. Nothing more or less.

The Mexican storm was in position to answer her command. I didn't know if she needed to take her misty form to the center of the storm to unleash it, or if she could direct it by remote control.

"Good job, Celia. No mistakes," Paul said slapping my back as we exited the stage at the end of the opening number and introductions.

He'd stopped calling me "Mei Mei." I didn't know if I was disappointed or relieved. The moment we hit the Green Room, I checked the monitors that swept the audience while the hosts explained the basic rules. I found Dad in one of the front row seats reserved for friends and family. Dylan flashed a big smile and held up a hand in greeting as the camera swept past him. He knew I was watching him.

I knew where he was even without looking. I also knew that he fiddled with his phone and tablet, texting to social media about the show. His ever-present laptop was in his backpack at his feet.

You still need to push yourself to complete the movement. If there hadn't been a mental chuckle at the end of Dylan's comment I might have blasted him with every curse word I'd ever heard.

"Your thighs were slack on the lift," Paul said. "The judges noticed." Then he guided me back to my trailer to change for our number.

Okay, I'd heard it from two sources, I needed to pull my leg muscles up to my nose, as the metaphor went. I think I understood the meaning. I had to make my entire body act as a single unit.

Last week we'd been ninth in the lineup. Tonight we were fourth.

The first three performances passed by too quickly. I spent most of that time concentrating on not throwing up. I'd never been so nervous in my life. If I flubbed so much as leading with my heel instead of my toe, I'd be out of the competition and on my way home. Maybe that was for the best. If I returned to Cleveland, far away from saltwater, Mummy would have less power to disrupt my life. For the health and safety of all the friends I'd made in Los Angeles I should leave. The sooner the better.

Not yet! Dylan pleaded with me. *I can't lose you.*

Time and distance can't break this link. I need you whole and hale to complete me.

Then go out there and dance your heart out. Prove to the judges, the audience, and to me that you are living up to your full potential. That's what I need to stay whole and hale, you beside me. You, singing the life back into me.

I couldn't argue with that.

Nor could I ignore the stage manager beckoning Paul and me to our starting marks on stage.

The package of publicity material finished playing on the big screens to the side of the long projecting stage. The lights came up. A single note played on the grand piano.

Paul sang, weakly, as he was supposed to. I sang back at him full and strong. We danced together and apart. We spun the mirror frame and reversed position until we were indistinguishable.

And I pushed my thighs and calves and toes and heels as far as I could, stretching each movement to full completion, as I never had before. No slacking off.

And then, near the three-quarter mark I stumbled, as planned. The audience gasped. Paul raised me up and showed me the correct movement. The audience, and better yet, the judges laughed when they caught the joke that it was all part of the choreography.

Dylan's smile warmed my mind and my core until I knew that I had nailed the number.

Looking back through the mirror frame, Paul and I sang the last notes in unison, the lowest of my register, the top of his, so that most listeners couldn't tell the difference between our voices.

The audience rose to their feet with applause. And so did the judges. Paul's grin buoyed me up to face the critiques and get our scores.

"You almost caught me," Bryant Thomas chuckled. "I was ready to mark you down a point for the stumble, then you recovered as if it was part of the number. I don't know if it was or not, but you made it work. Kudos for the acting in this performance. That's as important as the singing and dancing in musical theater. Kudos on the dancing and singing too. The two of you worked together, neither shone brighter than the other even though you let your native talents shine when needed. Good job."

Paul's arm around my waist kept me upright after that. My knees were weak with relief. As we passed Dylan in the audience on our way to the Green Room, he gave me a wink and a thumbs up. I gave him the wink back and straightened my spine to get the scores.

All of the monitors in the Green Room flashed straight eights from the judges. Then the average from the live audience, eight point five. I felt as light a sea mist with sunshine sparkling with magic. A song of triumph burned in the back of my throat. As much as I wanted to burst forth with the "Hallelujah Chorus" I kept it all inside, sharing only with Dylan.

Then the twirling bubbles inside me faded as we watched the rest of the contestants perform. Good scores where we expected, bad scores where we didn't.

When the last couple took their bows and received their scores on stage, we all filed out to pre-arranged markings. The tension inside me ramped up. All sense of glory vanished. The next few minutes would inform the world if I stayed or went home.

I wasn't ready for defeat. I owed it to Paul and Dylan and my family and my dead sisters to continue.

One couple after another was deemed safe until four dancers and four singers were left. I was among the singers, along with my roommate Lisa.

Two singers and two dancers would go home tonight.

I was back to fighting my stomach's rebellion.

"Easy, Mei Mei," Paul whispered. "They just said that some of us were chosen at random and not by lowest scores."

Trust him, Dylan added.

He didn't seem particularly worried. Was he in a position to know the outcome ahead of time? I hoped so. He did have to get out the press releases in less than a minute after the final results.

The hosts made a big deal out of dragging out their announcements while a single cello in the orchestra drew out a long note that didn't seem to me to be in tune with anything. It set my hands to shaking and my insides quaking. A headache gnawed at my temples...

"Paul and Celia are... SAFE!" Miss Bouncy proclaimed.

CHAPTER 17

Dylan clicked the appropriate files for each contestant and hit send while confetti fell from the ceiling and the remaining sixteen contestants hugged the unfortunate four, two from each category, who were eliminated. The judges and hosts joined the onstage party in a "spontaneous" bump and grind celebration to the show's theme song.

He'd dutifully prepared win and loss press releases for each contestant to go out to social media as well as hometown news outlets.

He didn't need to see Celia commiserating with Lisa to know her regret at seeing a friend leave the contest as well as her secret joy at having survived the first elimination. Still, he needed to watch her, absorb every nuance of her expressions, and feel a bit of jealousy as Paul swung her around in a hug.

His laptop beeped that the files had made their way into the internet. Nothing more he needed to do right now to keep the publicity mill rolling forward.

On his way toward backstage, he slapped Mike Fisher on the back in congratulations and received a blank and wary look in return. "I'm

Dylan McQuilleran," he introduced himself. "We've talked on the phone and Mrs. FitzWarren gave me your dossier," Dylan said quietly.

The man was Celia's father, but Dylan didn't share any ties with him. His emotions and thoughts were carefully guarded. As they should be, given his Hunter background.

"Ah yes, you gave me directions to elevator B last week."

"May I escort you backstage? I know the way and have the credentials to bypass security," Dylan offered.

"That would be splendid."

Together they shouldered and elbowed their way through the milling crowd that half-heartedly flowed in the opposite direction toward the exits.

"I don't like the weather forecasts," Mike subvocalized the moment they were clear of the lingering audience in the official backstage area.

"I saw small craft advisories go up about three this afternoon. Still it should take a few hours for the storm center to move north and inland."

"It's the peripheral winds that we need to hunker down for," Mike replied. He spotted Celia headed toward the backstage door with Paul and the two singers who had come up with the lowest scores. The young man was almost as strong a vocalist as Celia, but even more awkward on the dance floor.

Celia raised her hand in greeting, gesturing outside. Dylan knew she wanted him and her father to meet her at her trailer. He hoped that Mike understood the wiggle of fingers.

Bryant Thomas led the judges in the same direction. The stage should be clear of all but technicians closing down equipment for the night.

The back door opened to release the first eddy of contestants.

A crack of thunder filled the entire building with ominous sound.

Blue-white lightning blinded Dylan right on top of the thunder.

The lights went out with chain reaction pops and sizzles from one end to the other.

"Duck!" Dylan screamed as he ran toward Celia, knocking her to the ground and covering her with his own body, heedless of the sparks raining down on them.

〜

"Damnit! I just had this place rewired," Bryant Thomas said, loudly enough to penetrate the silence that spelled doom in my mind.

I had to keep my eyes clamped shut for fear of the blinding, blue white light dancing along the wires and blowing the lights.

But the crackle and sizzle of electricity unleashed had died down. No more popping lightbulbs either.

Dylan's gibbering panic that I might be hurt, or he'd lose me broke through my own panic. "I'm okay, Dylan. I'm okay," I muttered. At least I thought so. Nothing hurt or burned beyond the reassuring weight of him across my back.

"You sure?" His hands ran the length of my arms and along my nape. His touch was too brisk to consider it a caress, but it certainly wasn't an impartial assessment when his mouth followed his hands to kiss my neck. "Just checking for bleeding," he whispered.

Slowly I opened my eyes as I heard the crowd of people beginning to stir. At first the area around me appeared pitch black. No window to let in any lingering autumnal light. Then gradually the battery-operated exit signs made sense to me.

"Okay people, time to get outside. Clear the area." Mr. Thomas's precise, theater-trained voice dominated the whimpers and chatter. "Is anybody hurt?" he called more loudly.

I shook my head in denial before I realized even a Hunter couldn't see much in this gloom.

The clatter of the pressure bar on the backdoor opening alerted me to the onslaught of slanted light. In comparison to the previous darkness, the twilight outside seemed like blazing noon. I clamped my eyes shut again, not wanting to deal with reality, just absorb the feeling of being cherished by Dylan.

"The storm has passed. It's safe to go back to your trailers," Mr. Thomas called.

All around us people picked themselves up or helped others to their feet.

"We're clear," Dylan whispered to me. He heaved himself upward and I missed his reassuring weight and warmth.

Light filtered through my eyelids at an undemanding level. Finally, I had to open my eyes. A lot of confused people milled around. They gravitated toward Mr. Thomas's commanding figure. He gestured them outdoors in ones and twos. He nodded to everyone, whispering reassurance to each. "Check your group to see if anyone is missing," he said over and over.

I noticed Dylan held out his hand to me. I grasped it tightly as I got my knees under me and then found enough balance to come upright. Paul stumbled over to me from not far away. His eyes looked glazed and a trickle of blood marred his face. I slid my arms around him to make sure he didn't fall. Broken glass lay scattered about in odd patterns.

"Medic!" Dylan called as he too got a shoulder under Paul's arm.

Aunt Abigail appeared beside me in a heartbeat. "You okay, Celia?" Somehow, she had a first aid kit the size of Dad's tackle box in her hand.

"It's Paul."

Without a moment's hesitation she gave my partner a visual assessment then escorted Paul, with Dylan's help, over to a chair that rested against the wall by the exit. Usually a security person sat there, checking people in and out against a list that Mr. Thomas updated daily.

Aunt Abigail spread open the first aid kit and began swabbing a small gash on Paul's temple with antiseptic. "Does it feel as if there is any glass still embedded in the wound?" she asked gently.

Dylan found a stash of bottled water near the stage entrance, opened a bottle and pressed it into Paul's hands. "Just sip it," he ordered. "Don't guzzle, and don't bother that it isn't chilled. Right now you don't need cold to shock your system any further."

I backed away. Clearly these two professional crisis managers didn't need me.

And there was my dad, right behind me, ready to hold me up or escort me out, whatever I needed. I leaned into his comforting presence and just breathed.

Paul winced beneath Aunt Abigail's tender touch.

I gasped and reached to comfort him.

Dad's arms tightened around me, guiding me toward the door.

"Mei Mei, don't leave," Paul pleaded. One glance at his blood-streaked face and my heart melted.

"Not good," Dad muttered.

"Dad, I have to stay with him. He needs me."

"Not good," he replied again.

Dylan stood and backed away from Paul to stand on my other side. His mind threw up barriers between us. The emptiness where our link used to be left me gasping for air. I looked up to him, pleading with my eyes, trying to understand what he'd just done.

"Go to him." He wheeled and left the building. Outside I could hear his calm voice asking questions, organizing frightened people, and ignoring my mental fists beating at his mind barriers.

"Easy, Dylan," Mike Fisher said quietly outside the confines of the buildings. He acted like he wanted to squeeze Dylan's shoulder in comfort but refrained at the last minute.

"It's early days yet."

"Feels like years." Dylan had to think hard to remember the last time he'd felt so alone, so empty and couldn't. Before Celia came into his life and his mind he hadn't known just how lonely life as a Hunter was.

"Jeannie told me about her conversation with Celia. Did you know that my wife and I share a similar bond to what you and my daughter have just discovered?"

"I thought our link was unique." Shocked, Dylan paused in his trek toward a middle-aged woman who picked at her hands like she was trying to dislodge tiny thorns. Probably glass.

"Rare among the normal populace. My research into obscure folklore suggests that among paranormals, you and I and other augmented Hunters border on that classification, a telepathic link with a loved one is quite common."

He sounded so calm and matter of fact, while Dylan's insides quaked with emptiness. "I can't talk about it right now."

"Less than a week of being joined at every thought is not a lifetime. You still have time to forge new and stronger bonds." Mike suppressed a chuckle. "Even people who love each other fight occasionally. Jeannie and I have had some whoppers over the years."

Dylan could well imagine the fights he and Celia might have over little things, like him leaving the toilet seat up, or not scrubbing the pots and pans properly, then making up with slow delicious love. Love, not sex. True love.

"We both know that Paul is clinging to false hope any way he can. Celia will get over feeling guilty. In the meantime…"

"I'll keep busy and start by calling for more EMTs. Looks like we have quite a few cuts from flying glass. It might put a crimp into Paul's pleas for sympathy when Celia realizes he's not the only one caught in the backlash of Mummy's temper tantrum." He could almost smile as he made his way over to the woman scrubbing her hands raw in an effort to dislodge fine shards of glass.

A bit of his emptiness filled with affection when he realized his headache was from Celia trying to batter down his mental barriers and not his nanos going berserk.

Then he noticed the hawk-like profile of an EMT entering the building. It looked like the same man who had lingered outside the gate when security exiled Stevie from the studio.

A face that had graced ancient coins for a thousand years or more.

I sat with Paul in the ER. No concussion. No stitches. They patched him up with butterfly strips and sent us back to the residence hotel. Mr. Thomas sent a car to retrieve us. I guessed that if the driver wasn't a Hunter, he was at least employed by the Guild and knew how to take care of any paranormals that might come after me.

The pros who needed temporary lodging during the show lived in a separate wing from the contestants. They didn't have any contract obligations against fraternization with each other, and many of them were couples or even married before the show. Paul's roommate, Ivan (pronounced Eevahn) wasn't in when we returned. Paul thought he might be staying with Eve or Kathi down the hall. Apparently, he often did.

They had a single bedroom suite on the second floor facing the freeway.

So I stayed with Paul, offering him only a few minutes.

"Don't go," he pleaded, clinging to my hand.

"You need a shower and a good night's sleep," I said firmly. "So do I." For once the pool did not entice me. I knew what had crawled out of it the other night, even if it wasn't common knowledge among the cast and crew living here.

"Please, Mei Mei." He pouted and turned his big brown eyes on me in the best puppy dog imitation I'd seen yet.

"Paul, besides the no-fraternization clause in our contracts, you and I both know this won't work."

He stiffened and turned his back on me. "We can make it work. Especially if we win. Then we are both Broadway bound."

I thought about that for a long heart-pounding moment.

"The contract has our best interest in mind. Working together as closely as we do creates a sense of intimacy. Sometimes a false sense. If it lasts six months after the show concludes, then maybe it's for real. I don't think it is."

"I think we share something special."

"In the rehearsal hall. But look at us in our down time. You go out for sushi. I prefer British style fish and chips."

He made a disgusted face. "Too much fat, even if they are both fish."

"You like to play pool with the guys. I prefer to play in the pool by myself. Our only common ground is when we work together."

His slender shoulders slumped. In that moment of vulnerability, I realized that for all of his bouncy brightness and confidence on stage —he'd performed with road companies for four years—he was only two years older than I. Someone had to be the adult in this relationship.

The knot of guilt worked through my gut, then slowly dissolved. "We are friends, though. And I hope we remain friends when this is all over."

"But we will never be lovers," he said sadly. Then he heaved a sigh and stiffened his spine. "On stage we have to pretend though. I got a heads up from the main office that next week we have a tango from *Evita*. It's supposed to be rather steamy. The gossip peddlers want to play that up."

"On stage and in the rehearsal hall."

"You can run back to that publicity guy now." He held the door open for me.

Dylan. The publicity guy who wanted Paul and I to play up the steamy side of the dance. If he wanted too hot to handle on stage, he'd get it. But for the time being I'd let him think it continued off stage too. Serve him right for slamming the door on our mental and emotional link because he was jealous of a needy and clingy boy. I stopped battering at his mental shields. For now.

CHAPTER 18

Lisa sat in the darkened living room of our suite, mesmerized by the news channel. "We weren't the only ones hit by freak thunderstorms," she gasped as soon as I entered.

"You're supposed to be packing," I said calmly, wondering if I was disappointed that an almost friend was going home, or delighted that I'd have more space to spread out and be the natural born slob I was.

As infants and toddlers, Joycelyn, Brittney, and I shared the same cradles, crib, and bedroom. Frequently we'd all crawl into the same bed in the middle of the night, no matter that Mom and Dad tucked us in separately. Gradually we all demanded our own room. Even then we still tended to migrate together. I was the first one to stay in my own bed, in my own room because I sprawled, arms and legs flung wide. Mom had to threaten to dynamite my room to get me to pick up my toys, clothes, and leftover snacks along with their dirty dishes.

Containing myself and my things while rooming with Lisa left me often unsettled and irritable. That was only one of the reasons I spent so much time in the pool where I could sprawl my body if not my things.

You could say that I reveled in chaos. And that thought gave me pause.

"I packed this morning," Lisa said, never taking her eyes off the TV.

Sure enough her two big, royal blue, rolling suitcases stood by the door along with her matching shoulder bag designed for a laptop and overnight essentials.

"You've got to see this. The flooding in Venice is so sad, all that priceless art lost to rising ocean levels."

That grabbed my attention and wouldn't let go. I had to sit in the chair that faced the screen squarely.

I wanted to cry at the pictures of people wading through murky water that covered the steps and half the doorways of the famous buildings I'd seen in photos and news clips all my life.

"That's what they get for defying Mother Nature," Lisa said with only a hint of remorse in her voice.

"Wh—what do you mean?" I was shaken enough by the devastation wrecked by the StormMother.

"Well, the city was built on a scattering of islands in a big inlet. They kept adding dirt from the mainland so they could build. They've been defying storms and high tides for centuries. Now they are succumbing. All their artificial barriers overwhelmed." She shook her head and continued to watch.

Then the images changed from rain and rising tides to a dust storm in Arizona. The camera caught the wind-driven wall of sand racing toward Phoenix. The newscaster called it an Haboob. The next scene showed winter blizzards around the Great Lakes with frozen waves making dazzling patterns around docks projecting into the water.

"It's only mid-October," I gasped. "Still two months from winter."

"Yeah, and look at those rainfall projections for southern California," Lisa said, pointing at a weather map with the remote. "This is supposed to be a dry state!"

"Three to six inches of rain ahead of the main storm center approaching from the southwest."

"With temps in the low sixties. That's positively freezing for L.A."

Chills ran up and down my body raising goose bumps on my arms.

My phone buzzed and rang in my sweater pocket. One look at the number made me pause. Dylan didn't have to call me. If he was over his snit of jealousy he could just ping my mind.

I answered the phone. He wouldn't call unless it was important.

"Are you watching the news?" he asked without preamble.

"Yes. Global weather devastation."

"And more." He sounded worried. Not just sounded, but felt very worried. His emotions were leaking around his barriers. He was a Hunter, trained against a psychic attack. He should have better control. I could have slipped in and reestablished our link. I didn't. Not just yet.

"What?"

"The flooding in Venice has demolished cemeteries and tombs. Not only are skeletons and bone dust floating about in the sewage that won't drain, but some nasty and bitter ghosts and ghouls came out with them. I've battled more than a few of those creatures. Ireland is full of t'em." His accent came back full force, thick and lyrical. He must be upset for that to happen.

I rose from my chair and went into the bedroom, closing the door tightly, before I spoke again. "Is there a Hunter in the area?"

"Yeah, a new guy who is proving very talented. Archie. Rumor has it he's dating Margot Tremayne, our music director."

My mind didn't want to probe that connection. The few times I'd had to work directly with Ms Tremayne I'd found her sweet and understanding, but also no-nonsense when it came to music. Paul could request variations of tempo or rearrangement of the musical phrases to fit the dance and the ninety-second time frame. That didn't mean he got what he requested if it compromised her vision of what the music should be. I usually agreed with her more often than with Paul. Trying to envision her with a Hunter was beyond my imagination.

"What else?" I asked.

"Clouds from superstorms means no sunlight, vampires are also out in force."

"What about creatures aligned with moon phases?" The death of a werewolf and the presence of a werecroc came to mind.

"So far, no reports of undue activity. The moon's gravitational pull hasn't changed, just its visibility."

"Is the StormMother behind all this?" I asked, new chills blossomed on top of the old ones. I grabbed the decorative throw at the foot of my bed and wrapped it around my shoulders. My teeth chattered and I couldn't control them. He had to hear my fear.

"Celia, I'm sorry I shut you out. Will you please let me back in?"

"You are in control of our link this time. Your choice. But I need to face you to know that you mean it this time." Forcing myself to keep my voice neutral eased some of my chill. Knowing he was as shaken as I by our separation and the news brought warmth into my belly. I let it spread until I barely needed the blanket around my shoulders.

"I'm on my way."

"Meet me on the pool deck, in that dark corner by the staircase. Lisa is still here, and my other roommates should be back any minute. I think they went out for pizza and beer after recovering from the power outage and exploding light bulbs."

"Good idea."

I stepped out onto the deck from the sliding glass doors in the bedroom. By the time I'd stepped into the shadows between the light spilling out from my suite and the pool lights and reached the stairs, Dylan was waiting for me.

I barely had time to pocket my phone before he swept me into his arms and delivered a searing kiss that melted my bones and gave me the courage to face any wrath Mummy might throw at us.

"I've missed you so much!" Dylan said between kisses to her chin, her cheeks, her brow, and that special place below her left ear that made her wriggle in delight.

"It's only been a few hours," she murmured, matching him caress for caress, with mouth and hands and melding her body up against his.

"Too long. I felt empty and alone. I never want to feel that way again."

"Then don't let your territorial testosterone get in the way of good sense." She giggled.

And he knew he was forgiven.

The next evening, I was looking forward to resuming my dinner ritual with Dylan, quiet time away from the noise and bustle of the studio and contestants.

I knew the moment he got a call from Aunt Abigail.

"I have never heard of a Bubble Gum Demon before," Dylan said blandly.

From the confines of my trailer, where I soaked my feet, I tried hard not to chuckle. No one was around to hear me, so I could have let loose with a belly laugh.

"Neither had I," Aunt Abigail said. She sounded acerbic in Dylan's mind. I could envision that peculiar frown of hers when she disapproved of something, usually the cleavage showing above Brittney's or Joycelyn's prom gown.

"What is it doing and where did it come from?" Dylan sounded sober, but his mirth rippled across my abdomen.

"Best guess is it escaped from some stupid children's computer game and got into the software that controls traffic lights. There's been at least three five car pileups and gridlock for twenty miles on I 5."

Aunt Abigail sounded blank. I knew her well enough to know she was working hard to suppress her emotions.

"T'is L.A., me darlin'. What d' ye expect fer rush hour on a Monday?" Dylan replied. His lilting accent in full play.

"Pink goo oozing out of red lights and dripping into hot engines, constipating them into solid masses of metal that won't move under any circumstances. Stop laughing, Dylan, and go find the beastie before it gets any worse."

So much for our dinner date, love, he sent to me privately.

As soon as Aunt Abigail gave Dylan a location for the traffic control central computer and signed off, I called her. Her private number and her office number went right to voicemail. No doubt she had important Guild matters occupying her phone lines.

Then Dad showed up at my door. He let himself in before I could call out. I was sprawled on the bed with my feet dangling over the side in a basin of warm water with Epson salts.

"Hard day at rehearsal?" he asked as he bent to kiss my cheek.

"I thought dancing in heels was bad. Barefoot is worse, even with those toeless, elastic quarter socks that cover the balls of my feet so I can spin without tearing up the skin," I complained.

"What number are you doing?" He sat on the edge of the bed, grabbed one wet foot and began massaging it.

Heaven! If only Dylan was the one curing me, I might never get off this bed again.

"The number I'm doing with Paul isn't the problem. We've got the tango from *Evita.* It's the big production number for the opening that's the problem. Contemporary dance to some antique music that's got me tangled in knots. I'm not cut out for this, Dad. Give me something to sing, *anything,* and I'll bring the house down. But dancing is beyond my comprehension. It just doesn't make sense on dry land." Tears burned the back of my eyes.

"I understand. If your mom can learn to waltz for our wedding, then you can learn to do this, Celia. You are naturally graceful. You just have to train your feet to do something new and different." He began working on the other foot.

"It's my brain that needs retraining. I can't picture the steps in my head. All I see is music scores when I close my eyes."

"What you need is food. I'm buying. What's your tummy hankering for?"

"Pizza and beer, but not the pizza they serve in the canteen. The crust is too thin and crunchy. I want chewy. But that's got too many calories, fat and carbs. I won't be able to fit into my costumes..."

"You are working hard, burning more calories than you take in, Celia. You've lost a full dress size since entering the competition. Your mom noticed it during the show last night. Medium thick crust pizza coming up. With sausage and green peppers, and extra cheese. And craft beer with real flavor not just hops making it too flowery." He grabbed my hand and pulled me to a sitting position.

"Mushrooms and black olives, too," I insisted as I scrambled to find my sandals. "And fresh tomatoes on top."

"Sounds like a winner."

"Um... Dad, I hear that the streets are one huge traffic jam. Can you find your way along back roads?"

"I can. Where did you hear that?" He paused and didn't look me in the eye.

"My link to Dylan is back." I couldn't help but smile. "And I eavesdropped on a call from Aunt Abigail. Have you ever heard of a Bubble Gum Demon?"

"Um... maybe." A Hunter not admitting to anything until he had to. I stared him down.

He ducked his head. "I spent the afternoon diagnosing the problem, at double my usual consulting fee. It's Dylan's job to deal with it."

"I'm guessing that Hunters are spread pretty thin right now," I said quietly. We traversed the parking lot to find his rental car, a little hybrid the same model as the one he drove at home. For some reason the air and the pavement didn't seem as hot as yesterday. Maybe the perpetual summer of southern California was finally fading into autumn.

About time, Dylan mumbled.

"Yeah. More paranormals wandering around than there are Hunters to deal with them. I made it clear to your Aunt Abigail that I am no longer a Hunter," Dad said. "I'm not up to the rigors of the job. Computers are the extent of my assistance."

"Why? I mean why are there more paranormals running amok than usual, not why are you limiting yourself."

"I'm not certain of the connection, but I suspect the StormMother's temper tantrums have stirred them up and broken spells that seal the demons in places where they can do no harm."

"You mean the Bubble Gum Demon." I couldn't contain it any longer. Pressure built in my mind and my gut. I had to laugh. Just imagining the pink goo sloshing around traffic lights brought on another bought of guffaws until I doubled over.

Dad wasn't much help. He lost it too. We stood there clinging to each other laughing like maniacs in the vast parking lot filled with row upon row of cars.

It isn't funny! Dylan protested in the back of my mind.

That sobered me.

Ask your father if the demon existed before the game, and if a Hunter sealed it into pixels to contain it.

I relayed the question to my father. He straightened up and braced his hands on the top of the car. "Yes. The game is the seal that keeps the demon out of our reality. I wrote the code for the game. I was part of the team that devised the spell to get it in there in the first place. I don't know why the seal is breaking down."

"Does that mean that the millions of people playing that game will suddenly have it explode and freeze their computers and phones and tablets?" I asked them both.

They both cursed volubly and creatively; in English and in Gaelic.

CHAPTER 19

Dylan stared at the bank of computer monitors at traffic control central. Half of the screens showed the blue strobe of death. The other half blinked and swirled in asymmetrical patterns that were worse than English as a polyglot mongrel of a language.

All of the people who normally worked this office had fled, leaving him alone with the Bubble Gum Demon.

On top of that, pink goo splattered the walls, the keyboards, the manual switches and the live feed screens.

"I need help," he said.

"Get Mike Fisher on the line," Abigail FitzWarren said. Her voice over his mobile was calm and reassuring. The Director of the Guild personified.

"Set him up in conference mode," Dylan said sotto voce. His gaze flitted from one side of the vast room to the other, seeking a pattern, or rather a break in the chaos of pixels gone berserk.

"Done. I've sent out a digital version of an Amber Alert to all media forms."

"Don't forget Twitter."

"She did that." Mike's voice came through the speaker on the phone more clearly than Abby's had. "I'm not a Hunter anymore, Dylan. I don't have the speed or strength to wrestle with this guy."

"I can wrestle him back behind a barrier. But I need to know every detail about the magic involved." Dylan scooped up a glob of oozing harem pink goo on one finger. It sat there, surprisingly inert for the moment. No new demon ooze filled in the spot he'd wiped clean.

So, it had limits. Detached from the main body of the demon substance it had no initiative or momentum.

"I didn't perform the spell. I just wrote the code." Mike sounded exasperated.

I learned just enough code in high school to be dangerous, Celia said through their link. *Let me know what help you need.*

Immediately, Dylan felt more confident, just knowing she was still a part of him.

"Mike, do you remember the code?" It must be complex, beyond even a Hunter's ability to remember.

"Of course, I remember. Code is in my blood, just like languages are in yours. Think about computer code as another language and learn to translate it. It will make more sense that way," Mike coaxed. "You'd better write this down." Then he recited a long string of numbers and letters and odd symbols. But he put them into word length sections and paused at a logical sentence break. When he reached the end of a paragraph, he drew a deep breath.

In the background he heard Celia repeating the phrases with a musical rhythm.

"Is computer code an offshoot of Sumerian? No, no, it's more like Dogon which is a living remnant of Egyptian hieroglyph." He tapped notes into his phone.

The pink stuff took on the sickly sweet smell of rotting corpses and stopped moving.

Ah, it recognized its previous prison. Did the goo stall in place?

He hoped it wasn't gathering energy for a new surge into the working parts of the massive computer system. Los Angeles had a lot of traffic lights and controls.

He shuddered at the thought of a million people trapped in their cars going nowhere in miles and miles and miles of gridlock.

"Celia, sing it all backward," he suggested.

"What?" Her voice screeched over the phone in the most unmusical tones he'd ever heard come out of her mouth. She must be with her father. At least she was safe, unless the two of them were also caught in the traffic snarl.

The second he mentioned singing the code something in the pattern of words and phrases caught his attention. An old song... more than that, a hymn. Not a favorite of his mother's Anglican faith, but still viable.

Did he dare?

"Please, Celia, sing it with me."

"But... but... I don't know the music. The words are still gibberish for me."

Dead silence on the line.

Dylan gathered his courage and flashed his thoughts to her.

"Oh! We have to recite the spell backward to reverse... whatever is going on."

"Mike, I'm guessing there was a German, or at least a Lutheran on your team?"

"Two Germans and four Americans. We didn't discuss religion," he said after a moment's pause.

"Good enough to take the chance. Let's do it, Celia."

She hummed a note. He caught it and adjusted downward to match his own light baritone. All those years of singing acapella in the boys' choir finally paid off. He'd had to drop out when his voice changed and had never gone back. He just had to hope he'd outgrown the awkwardness of surging hormones. His voice wasn't nearly as fine, or as trained as Celia's. He had to push himself to harmonize with her.

Was this the test they needed to know if they could be more together than a mental and emotional bond?

"Failing never bulwark; God our is fortress mighty a," they sang out together. He wavered on the notes, but he had the words correct to reverse and repair the spell. She had the notes correct in awesome power, not compressed or distorted by digital distance. He expected nothing less.

The mass of pink shrank in on itself and dried into a stiffer consistency.

"Again, Celia," he whispered.

He felt her take a deep breath, so he did too.

This time the Bubble Gum Demon coalesced into a single entity, pulling tendrils of itself out of the computer circuits. It took up most of one wall of the city block sized room, and looked like a giant wad of gum pressed on the underside of a restaurant table in that hideous shade halfway between pastel and blood red.

It gathered itself and darkened.

If this guy was like most demons, he was preparing for a new assault. It slid forward, no visible feet, just that mass of stinking gel. Dylan could suffocate if it managed to cover his face.

He needed the power of Celia's voice to guide him, but he had to be physically present to make the spell work.

"Now sing it right ways around, from the top!"

"*A Mighty fortress is our God, a bulwark never failing,*" Celia belted the triumphant hymn with all the surety of a full choir with organ and trumpets accompanying her.

Dylan could only limp in her wake and hope it worked.

The demon froze in place, the region resembling a head thrust slightly forward, entranced and ensorcelled by the voice of a siren.

Numbly, Dylan opened the internet on his phone and touched the app for the silly children's game.

The demon reared back, resisting the lure of the magnificent voice.

Dylan turned up the volume on the device and turned it so the screen faced Big Pink.

Celia intensified the power of her song. Me mumbled along with her, getting most of the notes right, even if they were weak.

Big Pink, like any male, had to follow that voice to its doom.

Sweat broke out on Dylan's face and back, but he kept singing. The stench of his own testosterone on his skin overwhelmed the rotting corpse stink of the demon. He had to resist the urge to liquify himself and follow that alluring voice into the phone. He had to stay resilient. He had to invoke all his Hunter training to remain himself, one entity, separate, and unaffected by a siren.

He needed to plunge into her in a glorious and magnificent act of procreation, to merge his personality with hers. To become one body, one mind with her.

She threw up a barrier between them. Their link shattered once more.

But Big Pink was no more.

~

"You can stop throwing up now, Celia," my father said from the other side of Aunt Abigail's private restroom attached to her office.

"No, I can't!" I sobbed. Bile burned the back of my throat and my stomach spasmed once more. I coughed and gagged. My system was empty.

I didn't dare lift my head above the rim of the toilet, absolutely certain that movement would set off a new round of the heaves.

Shifting feet, multiple feet, told me that something changed back in the office. I didn't care. The cold porcelain on my forehead eased my woes a little. A very little.

"Celia?" Dylan asked gently from right beside me.

I hadn't heard him come in or the door open or anything.

He ran water in the sink and then pressed a wet washcloth on my face. With tender care he wiped my mouth clean of the remnants of my violent upset. Thank goodness I hadn't eaten anything. The pizza Dad had promised me would have burned holes in my throat on the way back up.

I lifted my head a little bit. Dylan pressed a second cloth against my forehead. I sagged onto the floor, no longer dependent upon the throne to receive my involuntary offerings.

He threw the first washcloth into the sink and somehow produced a glass of water that he pushed against my mouth.

I sipped delicately, afraid that even this simple remedy would set my tummy into rebellion again. Surprisingly, the water was tepid and slid down my ravaged throat easily. Before I could grab the glass and gulp more, Dylan pulled it away from me.

"Easy, just a sip."

His voice washed over me, soothing my chills and my fears.

"We got the demon, Celia," he said. "Big Pink will not bother us again."

"I used magic to kill a living, sentient being!" I sobbed. My stomach clenched but did not try to turn itself inside out. "I killed it with magic."

He paled a bit and looked away. Then he sank to the floor to sit cross-legged in front of me. "I wouldn't call a demon with the power to paralyze modern society a sentient being. Others are. This guy wasn't. He's the kind that reacts on instinct alone. All Big Pink knew was how to invade electronics and coat them with goo."

I swallowed back my revulsion. In that moment I could decide if I feared the lethal aspect of my magic more than the effect of the demon.

How different would our lives be without computers, and cell phones, and... and digital anything?

"You didn't kill it," Dylan said after several moments of silence. "*We* contained it behind a mighty fortress; a bulwark never failing."

That brought me up out of my doldrums with a glimmer of hope. "The words of the hymn. We enclosed it in a magical seal."

"That's right. You can use your magic for good, not just the traditional luring of sailors to their death on rocky shores. You healed me. Then you helped me quell a demon that threatened us all. Magic doesn't have to be evil."

"I... my mom and dad walked away from the realm of sirens and sea nymphs and the StormMother and never looked back. They severed their ability to work magic."

"So, you've had no training on how to control your powers?"

I shook my head and settled into a more comfortable position sitting on the tile floor, one arm still resting on the rim of the toilet bowl. My stomach was still chancy enough to keep me wary of leaving. "I am never playing that stupid computer game again, that's for certain."

"We made a good team this afternoon, Celia, and not just because the link between us was wide open and functional," he said. He studied the pattern of hexagonal tiles on the floor. "I'd like you to reopen the link so we can continue working together, even after the competition finishes and we figure out how the StormMother wants to use you, alive or dead. Together, hopefully, we can stop her temper tantrums and harmful antics."

"Quell the StormMother," I said numbly. "As much as I dislike Mummy's agenda, she has been an important part of my life, my entire life."

"Your parents allowed her to interfere in your lives?"

I had to shrug. "Mom and Dad never told me why we had to accept her coming and going in our lives, but we had to stay strong and not let her manipulate us."

"But she did manipulate you. When?"

Tears burned hotly behind my eyes. Grief still invaded my system and took over my conscious thoughts. All I could see was the falling girders in a cheap nightclub in Las Vegas as a thunderstorm spawned tornados. I heard again my nieces' lovely voices turning to shrieks of fear and pain. I watched again in choking despair as their life spirits fled broken bodies no longer able to support them.

"Celia!" Dylan grabbed my shoulder and shook me back to reality.

I felt him battering at the barrier I'd erected between us. Reopening our bond didn't feel right yet. I'd worked magically and freely without a thought to the consequences because he shared part of the responsibility. A huge part of my sense of self had gone behind the mighty fortress along with Big Pink. I had to find myself again, without him before we could join again on such an intimate level of emotion

Through will power alone, I regained my sense of the here and now with a gasp and a new resolve.

"Can we contain Mummy like we did Big Pink? Can we keep her from ever again taking innocent lives with no greater motivation than because she can?" *Or forcing me to use magic again.*

CHAPTER 20

The world continued to spin. Life went on. Familiar patterns controlled my actions. But my mind and heart were no longer fixed upon the competition.

Dylan continued to churn out publicity for both traditional and social media. Aunt Abigail told me that he spent a lot of time in her offices studying ancient texts and trying to fit a recording of my instinctive soothing of the Were Crocodile to the symbols he barely understood.

I did my best to ignore the gnawing emptiness in my gut created by my severance of our link. I had to come to terms with my use of magic before I could risk letting Dylan into my mind and my churning emotions.

Without Dylan's constant presence, I should have had more mental energy to apply to the next dance routine. Should have. The only way I could get through the number was to imagine his tall and lithe body in my arms guiding me through the sexy tango.

Sunday night came and at the end of the show I wasn't in jeopardy. My scores with Paul anchored us in dead center of the pack. I didn't know well either the singer or the dancer who were eliminated. But our numbers decreased, and we all felt the pressure.

Then came the announcement from Bryant Thomas. Supposedly he spoke directly into the camera, but I felt his eyes on me. "Next week, the contestants who find themselves in jeopardy will be asked to remind us all why they made the cut to appear in this contest. You will perform your primary talent solo. No special costumes, no dramatic lighting, no props or support from a partner. Just sixty seconds of your best performance. No one yet stands out as a true leader in this competition. All of you are vulnerable and must be prepared. I expect nothing less than brilliance from each of you."

That was a surprise.

"What will you sing?" Paul whispered to me as soon as the sound system silenced and the cameras closed down. "Sixty seconds can feel like an eternity."

"In the dance world, maybe. For a singer, that's barely enough time to build any dynamics into it."

"So, it has to be something powerful that shows off the full range of your voice."

"Operatic aria," I muttered. Lots of those around. But I had to choose something familiar to general audiences but still a serious challenge. My life in the competition relied on me impressing the judges.

Just throw in a little of your magic. Not enough to lure them to their deaths, but to entrance them.

"Shut up, Mummy!" I muttered.

I didn't realize I'd spoken out loud until Paul looked at me strangely. "What did you say?"

"Nothing. Just muttering grumbles."

He looked at me askance. He didn't believe me for one moment.

You need to practice singing with magic if we are ever to prevail over humanity and save the Earth from blatant abuse.

I needed to call Dylan right away. That was the most information Mummy had given me, that I comprehended, in her mad quest and manipulation of me.

Use your link, Sweetie Pie, she taunted me.

163

Not yet. I wasn't ready to open that door yet. The call and the decision of what to sing would wait until I had privacy in my trailer.

"What will you sing if you land in jeopardy next week?" Dylan asked from inside my trailer the moment I opened the door.

"What the hell are you doing in my trailer?" Celia yelled at Dylan.

He braced himself for more verbal abuse.

Instead, she did worse. She ignored him, marched into the bedroom and slid the folding door closed and flipped the latch.

"Celia?" he asked meekly. This last week without her in his head or in his arms, had been horrible. Loneliness and homesickness for the wild coast of north east Ireland had flooded every waking moment.

A stray beastie in his brain began to vibrate waves of panic.

He clamped down on it. There were other wee critters in there that were supposed to keep those demons at bay and let him think clearly and logically.

"Celia, please talk to me." He stood at the closed door, head bowed, knees weak, and wanting to weep with loneliness.

Damnit! He was a Hunter, augmented twice. He'd survived. He'd contained or banished countless demons and turned an equal number of vampires back into dust. No tears or remorse for any of that.

How could one mere slip of a girl with a voice that could quell angels leave him in such miserable state of vulnerability.

"I… I can't," she whispered, just loud enough for him to hear with his ears, but not his mind.

The link between them remained turned off but still he sensed her standing on the other side of the flimsy plastic fabric door, with one palm pressed flat on the barrier.

He lifted his own hand to match her position. So little separating them, so much more keeping them from coming closer.

"Tell me why, Celia. Tell me you don't love me, or need me, or want me at your side."

"You are too dangerous."

"I know that. I'm a Hunter. I'll give it all up if you will just talk to me."

"You'd slay Aunt Abigail if you left the Guild right now. She needs you."

"Madame has backups to her backups. I need you more than Abby needs me."

He heard the slight shuffle of her feet.

"She's short of active Hunters right now." At least she was thinking beyond her own narrow loop of self-containment.

"I know."

"You... you can't understand my dilemma."

"Try me. I've been inside your mind. And you've been inside mine. We belong together. We work better together than alone. I need you to find a way to counter the StormMother."

"That's just it. We work too well together," she wailed.

Something about the episode with Big Pink had frightened her deeply. Containing Big Pink threatened her.

"Then tell me how that is wrong. I can adapt." Being a Hunter meant he had to think on his feet and find new solutions when tried and true didn't work, because there was very little about dealing with paranormal villains that remained tried and true.

It was dealing with normal everyday people that was the problem.

Or dealing with a vulnerable Siren.

"I... can't."

"Celia. I know you are frightened. I can smell your fear even without our link. It's more than a link. It is a bond. There's an emotional superglue between us. I can't help you if you don't tell me what is wrong."

A long moment of hesitation nearly broke his sanity. And his heart.

Then he heard the hook of the latch flip and he had to step back to let her open the blasted barrier.

She kept her gaze on her feet and her hands clenched at her sides.

He reached to lift her chin so he could see her eyes. At the last second he closed his fingers and dropped his hand back to his sides.

"When we sang that triumphant hymn, our magic doubled and redoubled. Neither one of us could have banished that demon on our own. But together... we not only banished it, we sealed the fortress more tightly and more completely than the original." She paused to take a deep breath. "We damned near sealed everyone listening behind that bulwark. Innocents as well as demons. We brought my dad to his knees. He nearly passed out. And he was a Hunter."

"But he got back up again and took care of you." At least that was what Mike had said when explaining why Celia had to spill her guts in Abby's toilet.

The words "Collateral Damage" were on his lips, but he could not bring himself to say them. He'd *never* believed in that concept of war. Hunters were supposed to protect normals. All of them. He'd always planned his spells and prowess to avoid collateral damage and he mourned deeply any time an innocent got caught in the backlash.

"What happens when we direct our joined magic on a wide broadcast that engulfs a lot more people? And when we confront the StormMother we will have to broadcast our spell far and wide to encircle the storm she will unleash against *ALL* humanity."

Dylan had to back away from her. "You are right. We all need to think about that." He turned and left the trailer, not knowing what to do, or where to go.

I had to put aside my loneliness and depression over the loss of Dylan in my mind and my heart. All I had was the competition. One step at a time, one foot in front of the other. I danced and practiced and repeated every step until my mind as well as my body knew what to do. I worked on keeping Paul in my peripheral vision and moving with him while not following him.

I still wound up in jeopardy the following Sunday, and I didn't really care. I'd prepared for that with the same single-minded determination as I did all the rest to keep from running back to Dylan, or back to Cleveland to drown myself in Lake Erie.

I wouldn't give Mummy the satisfaction of giving myself up to her home in salt water.

By the luck of the draw, I ended up performing last, the position I needed. The judges who made this final determination would leave the studio with only my voice in their memory.

Still wearing the poodle skirt and short sweater with tennis shoes I'd worn for the swing number from *Grease*, I transformed my mind to a subservient Asian woman in full kimono and heavy headdress.

"What will you sing for us tonight?" Bryant Thomas asked, looking directly at me and not the camera as he was supposed to do.

"'Un bel di, Vedremo' from *Madama Butterfly*, by Puccini," I said simply and sent a quick glance to Margot Tremayne the conductor. She had chosen to play the accompaniment to the familiar tune solo on the grand piano.

I heard a gasp from the operatic judge. Many opera singers and aficionados considered this aria one of the most challenging ever written for soprano voice, not because of the musical technicalities, but the emotions. I had to *act* as well as sing.

Mr. Thomas smiled and nodded. "Not Broadway style, but still musical theater."

One note to give me the pitch. I held it in the back of my throat for one heartbeat, nodded again and sang the first note soaring upward in joy and wonder. As I'd learned from watching countless hours of videos since I was six. I kept my eyes opened and engaged the audience in the second balcony as if they sat directly in front of me. I begged them to join me in the wonder of true love, couched in regret of a forbidden romance.

I coaxed the audience into my heart with whispered joy, then brought them to a peak of exaltation with climbing emotions only to plunge back down in a roller coaster ride of my voice, their feelings, and the wondrous music.

I didn't need magic to draw them in to my story. I needed only my empathy, my acting, and my need to share with them my own emotional roller coaster with Dylan.

No one stopped me at sixty seconds. I continued to the end of the phrase at seventy-two seconds. The last note lingered in the air, a ghost of the audience sharing this experience with me.

Silence. Stunned silence.

Then as one, the audience, the judges, the musicians, and my fellow contestants rose to their feet slamming their hands together in thunderous applause.

Dylan joined them. My heart swelled at his response. He was the only one that mattered.

But then I had to take a bow and listen as the judges awarded the next round of competition to me.

By the time the lights dimmed, and the audience exited, I'd lost track of Dylan. Somehow, I knew he would not await me in my trailer.

Doing his best to banish the heart sick loneliness of life without Celia in his mind every waking moment, Dylan returned to his room. He didn't want to talk to anyone. But he needed to move, needed to keep Celia close by; needed to watch her.

So, he stood on his balcony with the lights off behind him. *I'm just one more shadow among the gloom. An ever-present phantom in her life.*

But he wanted more, ever so much more.

Right on schedule, the contestants erupted from their rooms and either dove into the pool or sank into the hot tub. Predictably, Celia was the first one to claim the diving board. One bounce and she cut a clean arc of a jackknife dive, touching her toes with her fingertips. Then she flicked her legs back as she plunged into the water with barely a ripple, let alone a splash. If he didn't know better, he'd think she wore a mermaid's tail as she swam from one end of the pool to the other.

Unable to endure his aloneness any longer, he changed to swim trunks and headed downward, leaving his electronics behind. He needed to swim with Celia, and then laugh with the other contestants in the hot tub. Time he made friends with them to better fill the gossip mill called publicity. No more lurking at a side table beneath an umbrella while he watched them.

As long as Celia stayed in the competition, he had to protect all of the contestants as they would certainly be caught up in the backlash of a confrontation with the StormMother.

He'd given up on help from the Guild. The august organization had no record of or references available about the entity Celia and her family offhandedly called "Mummy," other than the most ancient of ancient legends that explained natural weather changes as the temper tantrums of a vengeful goddess. Tiamat, goddess of creation and chaos; the tumultuous mingling of salt and fresh water.

The linguist in him wondered if the StormMother spoke ancient Sumerian fluently, or just used time-honored hymns to augment her power.

After hearing Celia sing the syllables and phrases of her lulling spell, he almost had a grip on the pronunciation, but not the grammar and vocabulary.

The nanobots in his brains began to gibber incoherently again, trying to make synaptic connections that did not exist.

He collapsed on the bottom stair with his head between his knees, fingers pressed against his temples. His knees had less substance than the pool water he sought.

"How long?" Abigail FitzWarren asked.

Where had she come from?

More important, how long had he been out of touch with reality? The pool deck was quiet and dim. The table and lounge chair area at the side by the slatted ten-foot-high fence were just visible from his position.

"I called her, in case you're wondering," Celia said. She'd wrapped a brightly striped towel around herself and her short hair was still wet, the soft curls straightened by the water.

"How long have these spells been back? They went away after the shot of replacement nanobots," Abby demanded. She whipped out a miniature medical scanner from the folds of her casual skirt. He'd last seen her dressed in formal wear, as stylish as any society matron. Now she appeared the frumpy administrative assistant to Thomas Bryant, producer. Her number was in the packet of information given the contestants as the person to contact in an emergency.

She was also Celia's godmother.

"A week, maybe more. They never truly went away, even with the shot. Not this bad since before the shot," Dylan murmured. He had to swallow a couple of times to get his words above a cracked whisper. Too soon, he had to stop speaking just to keep the stabbing pain in his brain from blinding him.

"Only half of your mechanical augmentations are firing. Help me get him up to his room, Celia. Then I'll call Geneva. Midnight here means it's nine in the morning there. Our surgeon should be awake."

Dylan barely noted her words as four hands pulled him upright and then two feminine shoulders inserted themselves beneath his armpits. Abby's presence faded into insubstantiality. All he could really sense was Celia's surprising strength and the scent of home in her natural perfume.

CHAPTER 21

"There are no other agents available," an anonymous voice came from Aunt Abigail's phone. She had it on speaker, so my eavesdropping wasn't totally an invasion of her privacy.

No one had told me to leave Dylan's room, though I knew I should. Sometimes Dad got called on Guild business and he always cleared the room. Sometimes Mom got to stay. Sometimes.

This concerned me. So I stayed, keeping quietly to the armchair that looked out onto the tiny balcony above the pool.

"I will not put my Goddaughter in danger by removing her bodyguard to the clinic."

Dylan groaned at that statement. He was awake and his eyes had lost some of the glaze of pain, but he still hurt. I could tell by the tightness of the lines around his eyes.

"I am sorry, Ma'am," the voice on the phone said. I thought it was a man, probably a highly placed assistant or possible deputy director. "There has been unusually heavy paranormal activity worldwide. Every agent in the Guild on active status is currently deployed."

"What about reserves?" Aunt Abigail barked into the phone.

Dylan winced again at her tone.

"Are you sure you want to call them in, Ma'am?"

"I've got two retirees here in town. Start the paperwork to make them active again. And where's Archie Driscoll? Margot Tremayne is in town so he might be here too."

Margot Tremayne? She was the music director of the competition. And I knew that Dad was in town until tomorrow morning when he was due to fly back to Cleveland.

"Mr. Driscoll is currently in Vienna chasing a swarm of ghouls terrorizing the opera."

Aunt Abigail spat a string of curses the likes of which I'd never heard from her, or anyone else outside of drunken gamblers in Las Vegas who'd just lost their plane tickets home, their Rolex watches, and their silk shirts.

That seemed to rouse Dylan a little. He struggled to sit up against the headboard of the king-sized bed. He kind of filled the mattress with his long legs and big feet, not to mention his well-defined chest with only a fair sprinkling of dark auburn hair arrowing downward.

I rushed to help him up and rearrange a multitude of pillows behind him. He flashed me a soundless thank you before settling back and closing his eyes again.

"Don't take me off the job, Abby."

My godmother sneered at him. "I'll let you get away with that horrible nickname this once because I know you are sick and in pain. But, never, ever again will you call me that."

He waved a half salute at her in agreement. "Please don't take me off this job, Mrs. FitzWarren. I do better with something to concentrate on. Just like when I went through augmentation. I translated cuneiform script into Egyptian hieroglyphs and then into Greek and lastly into Roman Latin. In my head. From memory. It's the only way I got through it, and the only way I can get through this."

"All Archie Driscoll did was memorize every note of music J.S. Bach wrote and figure out the mathematical algorithm that predicted the next note of every damn piece," Aunt Abigail returned, a bit spitefully.

I was impressed. With both men. Dad's genius was limited to

172

computer programming and ferreting out lost bank accounts from hard drives owned by Chicago gangsters. A lot of people could do that without augmentation. Dad did it faster, instinctively, and more thoroughly.

"Celia, do you have your phone with you?" Aunt Abigail asked. She took her phone off speaker and put it to her ear. "I need to stay on line to consult Dylan's surgeon."

I pulled my phone out of the bra of my swimsuit, where I'd stashed it the moment I knew I'd need both hands to help Dylan.

"Call your father. Tell him I'll make it good with the police commissioner in Cleveland."

"What about Mom?"

"I don't think I need her yet. Not until we know more about the StormMother and what she wants."

"Laptop," Dylan croaked, waving limply toward the computer on the lamp table across the room.

"In the morning," Aunt Abigail said, staying his hand. "I'm surprised you can even see, let alone read a screen."

Too easily Dylan flopped his head back against the pillows and closed his eyes.

"Call Dad," I told my phone. Instantly I heard the clicks and beeps of modern technologies connecting us.

"What's wrong?" Dad asked, quite loudly. Of course, he'd think my world had collapsed for me to call him at one in the morning.

I stepped into the bathroom to separate my conversation from Aunt Abigail's.

"The Guild is reactivating your status," I said.

Another loud string of curses, almost as creative as my godmother's.

When he calmed down, I related the string of events since I'd found Dylan huddled on the stairs near the pool deck. His pale, clammy skin, and incoherence had scared me.

"You should have called me then," Dad said.

"You're retired and have been for thirty-five years. Aunt Abigail is still active and has authority."

"When did you get so smart and practical?" he sounded resigned. In the background I heard him rustling about, probably dressing.

"I learned from you how to act calmly and rationally in an emergency and not fall into hysterics until it was over."

"Something your sisters and nieces never figured out."

"Come quickly, Daddy. I'm feeling the need to scream and sob, but not in front of Aunt Abigail or Dylan."

"Is Dylan likely to relapse or spring into full Hunter mode if you have hysterics right now?" I heard a door close and footsteps along a cement walkway. Dad was already on his way. Just as I knew he would be.

"I don't know. But Aunt Abigail would probably just slap me and order me back to my room. I kinda feel like I should stay until you get here."

"Good girl." A car engine started up, masking his voice. "I'm putting you on Bluetooth while I drive, so keep talking. It's the best way to stay calm."

"I have rehearsal first thing in the morning. Paul and I are doing a jazz number. I'll have to wear heels and a full skirt. We're doing *Holiday Inn*. Every couple has a different holiday. We drew "Easter Parade" in the lottery. The song is well within my range, but the dance is more demanding. I'd really like to learn the steps in the pool. That helps."

"Get the steps into your muscle memory first. Then let the water teach you to how to make them flow together. That's what made tonight's number so memorable," he said.

I couldn't tell how close he was yet, at this time of night, even in Los Angeles traffic calmed down to near nothing. But the engine of his rental car purred like he'd stopped for a light.

Hurry, Daddy. You can run the stop light.

"Good thing I stopped for the light," he chuckled. "There's a cop car right behind me." Had he heard my thoughts? More likely he knew me well enough to sense the panic behind my prattling words.

"Celia," Aunt Abigail called. "Get Bryant Thomas over here, now.

I'm re-activating him too. And tell him to marshal all of his paranormal friends as well."

Mr. Thomas! In a weird way that made sense. Why else would Aunt Abby masquerade as the executive assistant to the producer of this competition? He had to be a retired Hunter for her to stick so close to him rather than maintain her offices in London or Geneva.

"Aunt Abigail needs me. I have to go now, Daddy. Please, hurry." We hung up.

I sat on the bathroom floor and made the call, resigned to being Aunt Abby's administrative assistant for the night. Now who would Bryant Thomas call in from his paranormal associates? I'd heard rumors about Janet Drycr from a previous season of *Dance From The Heart.* He was married or engaged to his pregnant wife back then. Now he was a widower, having lost his young wife to the plague. I'd find out if the rumors were true or not very shortly.

Dylan has discovered my true name, though he doesn't realize it yet. He now has power over me. Curse him and his entire family. I curse him to a loveless life and the same loneliness I have suffered for millennia.

If only Anshar would join me. Together we made beautiful music and beautiful babies. But he has locked himself away from me. I must work alone until I can bring Celia back to me.

Dylan must never learn the language of my original tormentors. Those Magi came from different parts of the globe. They each spoke different languages, but used a common one for their spell. So the spell was imperfect since they did not understand all of it. Their symmetry was misaligned, closer to chaos than order. I embody chaos and merely absorbed their spell rather than let it control me.

No one speaks that language anymore. A few fragments of script survive, mostly accounting and laws, no literature or poetry. If I destroy the last remnants of ancient Sumerian and the translations of the spell, I have a chance to retain my power over the elements and the paranormals, those descended from a mating between a god and a human.

I have a chance.

But I must absent myself from the center of activity while I seek out those remaining fragments of a forgotten language. I must keep my search secret from Anshar, for he knows how to thwart me. I will search all the dimensions for the ghosts of Celia's nieces. Since I authored their demise; they should respond to me. It has been less than a year since their deaths. They will come when I call.

With Brittney and Joycelyn beside me, Celia will have no choice but to align her voice with theirs and do my bidding.

I will sweep away all of cursed humanity and let the beloved Earth recover from their tyranny. When we are clean once more, then my girls, my sirens and almost sirens will spawn a new race of people who will respect their planet.

They will respect ME!

~

"Tiamat," Dylan said. He wasn't sure if he spoke aloud or only thought the word. The noise in his head tried to drown out everything else. "Tiamat is the key." He knew that for certain whether he said it or not.

If only the nanobots would shut up for two seconds he could make sense of... something.

"My books. I've got to find my books." With one mighty heave he lifted his upper body so he could sit.

A firm hand on his chest pushed him back. He hadn't the will or the strength to resist the restraint.

"Stay," Abby commanded.

He tried to salute her. No one brooked Abby when she used that tone of voice. He might as well be a trained dog to her.

"What did he say?" Was that Celia speaking? How'd she get to wherever they were?

He tried to figure out where here was. Blanks. His eyes didn't want to open and he smelled nothing unusual. Only a slight susurration of someone shuffling bare feet on the fake hardwood floors of his suite.

"Tiamat," Dylan repeated. If he could only make someone understand. Maybe if he gave them more information. "Books."

His mind flew to the digital pages he'd studied so intently looking for clues to the language Celia had sung to lull the Werecrocodile to sleep.

He'd missed something. Or the translations of the original cuneiform were incomplete.

Concentrating on the images of the tiny indentations on clay tablets gave him half of a moment of clarity. One string of untranslated syllables stood out in his mind. What if... what if...

"Laptop!" he shouted as loud as he could. The nanobots silenced in reaction to his violent explosion of sound. It still sounded like he said "Tiamat," but his pointing finger at the machine on the table by the window should get the message across.

Then the bots roared to life again, more insistent than ever.

But for that one brief moment of silence he had the will to open his eyes. That was all he needed to confirm he was still on his bed, Abby sat in a chair beside him, keeping one hand on his chest while she manipulated her phone with the other, and Celia paced from the windows to the corridor door and back relentlessly. Her feet pounded out a rhythm that reminded him of something. Some Broadway song or another.

"If the laptop will keep him quiet, get it for him," Abby said.

A moment later he felt Celia place the portable computer on his belly.

He opened it, caressing the frame gently. His old friend and companion through the worst of augmentation and depressing battles of wits with demons and vampires alike. His fingers found the keyboard and the power button. Tiny vibrations and new warmth from the base of the computer told him he'd managed to wake it up. The last items he'd worked with should still be on the screen.

If only he could keep his eyes open and focused.

"What do you see?" he ground out.

"It looks like book pages, but I can't understand the text," Celia said.

"Link. Please?"

She did not reply.

Movement to his left. Abby shifted her position.

A jostle to his left. Celia perched on the edge of his bed, careful not to let any part of her body touch his.

He knew that, sensed her hesitation.

Then her hand dropped atop his where he rested them on the keyboard.

The world opened up to him through her eyes. His heart skipped a beat and came back stronger, steadier.

"What am I looking at?" she asked softy.

His mind, if not his eyes focused on the ancient text and the crude translation beside it. "Start bottom right, work left, at the end of the line move up and work to the right."

She nodded and followed his directions.

Slowly they worked through the first page, one letter at a time. He shared the meaning of each scratch with her. "Oh," she gasped when words, phrases, sentences and paragraphs started to make sense to her. Sacks of grain, jugs of wine, loads of fresh fish from a war-depleted fleet... an account ledger that told anthropologists a lot about the ancient culture.

They finished the first page and he scrolled to the next, and the next, picking up speed with each new bit of comprehension.

The nanobots in his head calmed down as he focused on the meaning of the text. Through Celia, he felt Abby nod, as she made note of his well-being on the scanner in her phone.

"Allocate fifteen cestaurs, is that the right word for their currency?" Celia paused in their reading.

"Close enough. Fifteen coins will do for now. What are they allocated for?"

"Allocate fifteen coins for the services of twelve... twelve Magi?... for the suppression of... of Tiamat!"

"Yes!" Why had he missed it before?

"Accounts are boring," Celia giggled. Her grip on his hand

tightened. She was enjoying the wonder of translating the ancient puzzle as much he. "So what kind of monster is a Tiamat?"

"Mummy," he sighed. "The Magi turned the goddess of chaos and creation—creation out of chaos if you will—into a tamed and almost manageable StormMother.

"Oh."

He treasured the quiet while she thought that through. He could, should, follow her process, but at the moment it was too much work to concentrate on anything but the text.

"How did they do it?" Abby prodded, fingers on his wrist pulse point.

"Read further. There should be an account of what the fifteen coins bought. Our ancient scribe was a meticulous bookkeeper."

"Sounds like we need Archie to decipher it."

"Archie?" Celia asked.

"Archibald Driscoll, before he became a Hunter with an amazing musical talent, he was my forensic bookkeeper," Abby said. "I'll give him twelve hours to finish his Phantom of the Opera gig in Vienna, then he's coming here to help us subdue the StormMother."

CHAPTER 22

Dad took me back to my room in the wee small hours of the morning. "I can sleep perfectly well in Dylan's armchair," I protested as I fished for my keycard.

"Not tonight. His neurosurgeon is on his way from the airport. Must have flown by private jet to get here from Geneva before dawn," Dad replied.

"So? I'll know everything that goes on whether I'm in the room or not." Somehow severing our link again seemed wrong. I'd spent the last hour meditating on how to decrease the intensity of our bond. It had kind of worked. I knew that Dylan slept, but I did not share his dreams. Or were they nightmares?

"But you won't be one more body to trip over." Dad dropped a kiss on top of my head. "Get some sleep, CeeCee." He hadn't called me that since I was six and had insisted I was grown up enough to have full name. Yeah, I'd been a brat about it.

"I need to be with Dylan..."

"You will be, in your mind. But we have to present a face of normality to the rest of the world. That's the first law of the Guild. Right now, normality is you getting enough sleep to rehearse. We're counting on you to keep the attention of the world on you and not on Mummy's temper tantrums."

"If people had paid attention to climate change thirty years ago and done something about it then, Mummy wouldn't be throwing storms and natural disasters right, left, and sideways."

"Maybe, Maybe not. But she's out of control now and we are the only ones who can calm her down. That includes Dylan, and you have to do all that you can to continue with the contest as if there is nothing wrong." He swiped my key card for me and pushed the door open.

I hesitated. "Nothing will ever be right for me if something happens to Dylan."

"He may have to return to Geneva for a while, but as long as you are linked he'll be all right. Trust me, I know what's happening to both of you. And as much as I want to be an overprotective father and keep every man away from my baby girl, I recognize that some things are inevitable. Love him with my blessing. Now get some sleep." He pushed me inward and closed the door firmly behind me.

"As if I can sleep..."

I fell across the bed on top of the covers, fully clothed, if you call a swimsuit and a towel clothes, and didn't stir until around four. My gut churned for a moment as a doctor did something to Dylan... something similar to the injection Mummy had used to try to kill him.

Dylan's fear became my fear that lasted for almost half an hour. To keep from running back to his room and getting underfoot, I showered and changed to night clothes. By the time I fell back into bed again, Dylan slept deeply, dreamlessly. Restoratively.

And so did I until the alarm woke me at six-thirty. Time for another day of rehearsals. This time I complained about the cartwheel of a hat the wardrobe department wanted me to wear.

"That is not an Easter bonnet. It's a beach umbrella!" I screamed at anyone and everyone who bothered to listen.

"I agree," Bryant Thomas said from the other side of a clothes rack in the warehouse of a room reserved for costumes. "I want to see her face from the second balcony." He jerked his chin down once, turned

181

on his heel and returned to whatever it was that executive producers did. That one brief gesture told me more than the seamstress needed to hear. Dylan was okay, medically at least.

I knew that.

His mental state was a different matter. He clung to my mind as if his life, and his sanity, depended upon me and me alone.

Dylan shifted back and forth between the armchair by the sliding glass doors and the straight chair on the balcony. He kept the laptop with him, even when he went to the bathroom and paused long enough to down a nutrition shake handed him by Abby's assistant. Marci? Was that her name? She worked for Mrs. FitzWarren, the director of the Guild, not Abigail the administrative assistant to Bryant Thomas.

She'd taken over nursing duties at dawn when Abby took her pet surgeon to breakfast and they both stayed away long enough for him to get some sleep.

"I've got those publicity releases ready for Mr. Thomas," Dylan said when Marci poked her nose onto the balcony to check on him, as she did every fifteen minutes. She followed Abby's orders precisely, as if she knew how vulnerable he was, both physically and mentally.

She held out her hand for Dylan's flash drive. "You didn't take very long to finish these," she said, sounding too much like Abby.

"Routine mid-week stuff. I can do it in my sleep." He turned his attention back to his computer, but not the folders reserved for *Here I Come, World*. The clay tablets in a museum in Ankara pulled at him with every breath.

He had more to discover about them, more than he could find from digital scans of a decades old photograph.

"Marci?" he called, barely more than a whisper. He knew she wouldn't go far and had probably called a messenger to deal with the flash drive.

"Yes, Mr. McQuilleran?" She stood on the other side of the glass door, which she'd left open.

"Call Abby and tell her I need to go to Turkey. Today."

"No one calls her Abby," she replied on a disapproving sniff.

"Old joke you are too young to remember."

"I'll have you know that I have received a third-class augmentation. I am older than I look."

"Third-class?" That must be new since his first treatment. Back then he had the choice of full Hunter or a brainwash to make him forget that he'd helped slay a dozen vampires in a remote Mexican mountain village.

"Vision, and hearing. Authorized to carry a weapon and read classified material."

"That makes sense, considering who you work for."

"I turned forty last month."

"And you look twenty-two. I get it. You still aren't in the exclusive clique that gives Her Majesty a nickname she hates as a way of staying sane while dealing with her." He turned his full attention back to the screen and enlarged the picture of the tablet, zeroing in on a section that looked like it might have been printed upon, then wiped clean while the clay was still damp and malleable.

What had the ancient scribe erased?

"And tell Abby I need a psychometric assistant!"

Sorry Celia, I have to do this without you. You need to stay here and keep Mummy's attention away from me.

Dylan stood at the back entry of the *Anadolu Medeniyetleri Muzesi* antiquities museum in Ankara, Turkey. He had his credentials in hand. At least his academic degrees and publications were authentic, even if the Guild had fudged the dates. He looked too young to have received his first degree in the early 1990s.

What he really wanted to do was hightail it to the nearest Suk where he could stand on a street corner and just listen to a dozen different languages and dialects flow over him. Celia would appreciate the musicality of some of those languages. And then there was the ritual call to prayer from the top of mosque towers five times a day. He detected slight differences in accent from neighborhood to neighborhood. Ankara, an ancient city and even more ancient crossroads delighted all of his senses.

But here he stood, waiting for the museum guard to rise from his prayer rug, roll the bit of tapestry into a neat bundle and unlock the door. Dylan respected the man's faithfulness, no matter how inconvenient.

"I'm probably the only person alive who appreciates the tightness of our timeline," he muttered.

"I do. I need to get back to those flooded cemeteries in Venice and figure out which ghost belongs in which grave," the mousey man beside Dylan complained. Ignacio Bocella looked the epitome of a linguistics scholar, short, wiry, nearsighted, and stooped shouldered. Instead he was the Guild's most highly rated psychometric. He could touch any solid object and instantly know who had made it and for what purpose.

"Trust me, if you can figure out what I need to know about one particular clay tablet, most of those ghosts and ghouls will go back to where they belong on their own."

Dylan looked up from his study of the abstract, blue and white tiles surrounding the door. The sound of keys jangling in the lock on the inside lightened some of his apprehension.

Seconds later he presented his passport to the robust guard. His uniform shirt strained across his shoulders, making him look more like a pro-wrestler than a rent-a-cop. He also topped Dylan by almost half a foot. The weapon on his hip gave him authenticity as well as authority. This one man could make or break the mission.

"I'd like to have this guy with me next time I venture down a dark alley," Ignacio muttered in Italian. "Even the Djinn would be afraid of him."

Dylan smiled and said, in perfect Arabic, "We have an appointment with the Director."

The guard grunted a reply in a rural dialect Dylan had to think about translating. It didn't flow like it should.

He had to quash a glimmer of excitement that his guard might hail from a province that retained remnants of an ancient Anatolian dialect.

You don't have time for that, Celia reminded him. His mind filled with warmth, comfort, and purpose. He was constantly amazed at how easily they had slid back into easy telepathic communication, not always agreement, but... rapport.

Don't make me endure this production number alone!

The sharp stab of a cramp in her calf when she pushed too hard to reach the desired "line" nearly sent him to his knees. He had to be there with her to massage away the knotted muscle.

Coming home to you as soon as I can. The link with her faded to semblance of a piece of soft cashmere yarn, barely visible or felt until one of them strengthened it with deliberate communication.

He wasn't certain how they'd learned to manage their bond so efficiently, but after the ups and downs of the past weeks, he now felt totally comfortable with her in the back of his mind.

Miraculously the guard only glanced at their passports and waved them through. "Upstairs, last door on your left." Again that enticing accent.

Dylan yanked his attention back to their mission.

"Damn but there's a lot of stuff demanding my attention," Ignacio said as they passed a double door locked with two chains and padlocks.

"Later. I promise that the clay tablet in question will challenge even your talent."

The little man raised his eyebrows and peered over the top of his thick glasses.

"First we have to get past the director and probably at least two forensic archeologists. Cuneiform tablets are rare enough that not just anyone can waltz in and inspect them."

"I suppose touching them is an even greater challenge. I'll need to take off my gloves..."

"When the time comes, I'll try to set up a distraction."

"Hunters are good at that. Glad I don't have to do the fancy talking and footwork."

~

"Do the Turkish men do *anything* but drink coffee?" I asked Dylan on one of his rare phone calls. Mostly we didn't need digital devices because of our link. But it was nice to actually hear him speak.

"Some days I wonder. The director has walked us through the warehouse three times and never let us get closer to the tablets than three feet. I did bend over the one in question and show the erasure marks to him with a hand-held magnifying glass—I felt like Sherlock Holmes speaking to Detective Lestrade." His sigh came across the digital lines loud and clear. His disappointment stabbed me in the heart.

He'd been gone five days. *Five days!* And he was no closer to coming home than he had the day he left.

In the meantime, I'd learned the new routine for the Easter Parade and a simpler opening number that didn't stress or strain me too much. Dancing was coming easier. But I'd also had to learn a solo dance just in case I landed in jeopardy again. No back up, no props, just me and the music showing the judges how much I'd improved on my weaker talent.

Singing opera was easier.

Even so, Paul had choreographed ninety seconds of a waltz from Margot Tremayne's soon-to-open-on-Broadway musical. It was called the ghost waltz for a reason and perfect for me to dance solo with a pretend partner.

"I used to like Turkish coffee," Dylan sighed. "But I'm sick of it now. If we don't get in to examine that tablet today, I'm going to pull a Topkapi."

"A what?" I'd reached the door to the rehearsal halls and paused outside to finish the conversation.

"Old movie reference, it's about a break-in of a famous museum to steal a priceless artifact. Quite exciting."

"Well I hope it's not too exciting. I want you to come home in one piece with the precious information on that tablet."

"Will do. Ooops, gotta go. The director is returning, and he's got a wad of keys in his hand. Let's hope he has good news."

"Goodbye," I said and we thumbed off at the same time.

Feeling a bit less lonely for Dylan I made my way to the little rehearsal hall in the back. The room was deserted. Paul had left a note on the music system saying he had an emergency dentist appointment. I should work on the ghost waltz by myself.

I chose to do this one barefoot. Shoes just got in the way.

The blue tooth player connected to my phone. As soon as I heard the first note of the opening measure, I made my way to the center of the room, facing the mirror and counted the notes.

"Four, five, six, and one." I rose onto tiptoe and stepped forward with my left foot.

Color and light wavered in the mirror.

The music flowed around the gentle phrases.

Blue and red sparkles drifted with the music.

My breath caught in my throat.

Grief and survivors guilt stabbed me in the gut like a long, serrated carving knife.

"Brit? Jocie?" my two dead sisters and back-up singers performed my dance better than I could. They still wore the glittery gowns from our last gig in Las Vegas over nine months ago.

I looked behind me to make sure no one was there.

The apparitions danced only in the mirror.

CHAPTER 23

"Who are you, Mr. McQuilleran?" Museum Director Sahin asked between sips of yet another cup of coffee—sitting beneath an awning at an outdoor café this time.

Dylan halted the process of taking a drink. If he had to finish this cup the acid in his stomach would come back up and melt the metal table between them. Slowly he replaced the tiny cup in its saucer and placed the chinaware on the table. The bitterness of the brew overshadowed the enticing aromas of roasting meat kabobs over an open fire, the exotic spices coating fried eggplant, and the inevitable goat's milk yogurt.

"Excuse?" he asked. He did his best to present a bland face to the man he'd courted for days.

"Late last night I received a telephone call from my prime minister who had just had a call from your prime minister in London. It seems I am ordered to allow you full access to the cuneiform clay tablets. Not only may you touch the artifacts with bare hands,"—he shuddered in near horror at the desecration—"but I am to make available an array of electron microscopes and other equipment to you."

Thank you, Abby! Dylan nearly crowed with delight.

"So, the question remains: Who are you?"

Sahin's mouth turned down and his chin jutted forward in determination. Dylan knew he wasn't going to gain that precious, unfettered access without a plausible explanation.

There wasn't one.

"When in doubt, go with the truth," Ignacio said, replacing his own coffee cup on the table. He'd barely drunk any of it.

"The truth," Dylan said flatly. As improbable as most people would regard the Guild, and as much as the members guarded their privacy, sometimes he had to dribble out a little information.

"Have you ever encountered a demon, Director Sahin?"

The man's pudgy face paled and took on a doughy texture.

"Ah, I see you have. Signore Bocella and I represent the International Guild of Demon and Vampire Hunters. The tablet we need to examine is the key to calming the devastating storms that have lashed your coastlines for the past month. There is a demon at work." If he gave Tiamat her proper title of Goddess, Director Sahin would probably soil his trousers. "This one is stronger and more primal than any that might have been trapped in your museum's artifacts."

Three fat raindrops hit the awning above them. Sahin cringed away from the sound as another dozen drops pelted them, then more and more until the shower headed toward deluge. In less than a minute, a river ran down the middle of the cobbled lane.

"The tablets are more than six thousand years old!" Sahin protested. His heart wasn't really in his words.

"They come from a time when people respected magic and sought ways to use it for the good of humankind. What kind of demon did you encounter, and what kind of damage did it do?" He needed to know if and how it was subdued before working with the precious clay tablets. If it still haunted the museum, it could interfere with their work. "The StormMother has a long reach," he muttered.

"An oil lamp, pottery with copper inlay," Sahin replied. "A Djinn that smashed many fine amphorae from a much later period. The local mullah came and banished it. I did not watch to know what he did. I was too busy trying to keep treasures from our past from toppling to the ground under the force of the tornado and the earthquake spawned by the Djinn. It did not succumb easily." He visibly shuddered. When he shook his head free of the memory a tear shone in his eye.

"When did this happen?" Dylan's insides began to shimmy. He didn't know if it was excitement or dread.

"Twenty, or maybe twenty-two years ago at the summer solstice. I try not to remember too many details though I can still feel the weight of one of those amphorae as it tilted and tried to smash into the floor. I caught it..." Sahin held up his hands in the posture of catching something above his head and bracing himself.

Dylan gulped, recalling Mike Fisher's explanation to Celia about why she was the target of the Storm Mother's current agenda. An intense storm. A mating frenzy. Celia had turned twenty-one last March, near the vernal equinox.

"Was there a storm at the time the demon... went berserk?"

"Yes. Wind and rain fiercer than seen in generations."

"Sir, I will need to see the oil lamp. The mullah did put the Djinn back in the original container?"

"I knew you would need to examine the lamp the moment you told me who you are. And no, it is not the original container. That one was lost in the localized flooding from the storm. Is that demon the author of what you hope to find in the tablets?"

That shook Dylan to his core. Could it all be that simple? Did the original mages use the magic of a Djinn to contain the StormMother?

Dylan shook the serviette free of his lap and tossed it onto the table. "Let's find out. Shall we retire to your museum, it will offer us much better shelter than this delightful café."

The three men hastened across the cobbled street to the employee entrance of the museum. Still, Dylan's hair, shoulders, and shoes were soaked by the time Sahin juggled the door open. It felt like Ireland in spring.

With one foot inside the door, his head exploded. *Ghosts, Dylan. My sisters are haunting me!*

He had to fight to stay upright and not double over in sympathetic pain. *Call Abby, beloved. Or your dad. I can't come to you right now though my heart feels like it has ripped out of my chest. I won't be whole until I can hold you again. I'm too close to answers that will end this once and for all. I have to stay!*

He heard only sobs from her.

~

"Mei Mei!" Paul called as he dashed into the rehearsal hall and knelt beside me. "Mei Mei!" He touched my shoulder tentatively.

Somehow, I clawed my way out of the knot of grief and guilt Brittney and Joycelyn left behind. It took more energy than I thought I had left to roll over and stretch my back out of the fetal ball I'd crawled into.

The ghostly music stopped. Paul must have canceled the endless loop of repeats. My girls faded leaving me clutching a handful of blue and red sequins.

"Ghosts," I whispered.

"There are no ghosts here, Mei Mei. Just me." Paul's grip on my shoulder grew stronger.

I drew strength from him, even as I noted his slight lisp from a numbness left over from his dental appointment. He was still vulnerable. But not as much as me. I kept my hand clenched tight against my chest. Red and blue sequins. I'd worn white that fateful night, Joycelyn wore red, and Brittney wore blue. They'd died in those sparkling gowns, but they hadn't been buried in them.

Red and blue sequins, all that was left of my girls, of our trio, of... Mummy's wrath.

She wasn't my Mummy anymore. She was Tiamat the StormMother who cared nothing for me or my family. She cared nothing about anything except her personal agenda.

We had to stop her. For Joycelyn and Brittney.

Anger began to churn in my gut, replacing the paralyzing grief.

"I know the death of your back-up singers must have hit you hard,

Celia. Grief is natural. The music brought it all back to you. It happens sometimes."

For some perhaps. I didn't think most people endured the gut-ripping stabs that affected me. Most people didn't see ghosts ten months after the fact.

I didn't think ghosts left behind physical remnants of their presence. One of the sequins cut into my fingers. They were real. Very real indeed.

Something strange was going on. I thought I knew who was behind it all.

"Take me home, Paul. I can't work today."

"Celia, you are a professional. You have to pull yourself together. When the going gets tough, the tough keep dancing."

"I... Not here. Any other room, but not this one, and not that dance." He was right of course. And that was his job, to partner me through the competition and keep me going when I had nothing left to give to the dance.

"This is our last number together, Celia. Next week you'll have to work with another contestant."

"If I survive." That was always a very real possibility. My dancing was weaker than anyone left in the competition. But my voice was stronger.

"That is why you must pull yourself together and practice. You can't win unless you master this dance and every new dance to come. You have to practice, Celia."

"You're right." He offered me a hand up.

I took it and dragged myself to my knees, then to my feet. My balance failed and I fell against his chest. His arms went around me, and he kissed my temple.

He offered comfort.

I needed comfort. Dylan was half a world away.

I'm here, Celia.

Can you come home soon?

Tomorrow. The next day at the latest. We have access to the tablets, but more questions than we started with. He closed the link between us as his enthusiasm for the project overrode his concern for me.

I hope you know how to banish ghosts as well as demons and vampires. Big Pink and shape changers pale in comparison to what Mummy has conjured this time.

What I really wanted was to bring my girls back to life.

Even Mummy couldn't do that.

But I had real sequins clutched in my hand.

Dylan watched Sahin transfer the fragile clay tablet from its glass case to the workbench. He wore cotton gloves and a surgical mask so he would not breathe directly onto the artifact. Ignacio took a deep breath behind his own mask, closed his eyes, and touched the edge of the tablet with one bare finger.

Dylan held his breath behind his own mask and waited. And waited. And waited.

Eventually Ignacio withdrew his tentative touch and shook his head. "I sense nothing. The piece is too old."

"You've worked with pieces almost as old," Dylan snarled. He marched over to stand beside his colleague. Keeping his gloves on he transferred the piece to the huge microscope at the workstation with the computer and the electron microscope behind them. "How do I turn this thing on?" he asked Sahin. *I don't have time for this. I have to get back to Celia!*

The museum director hastened to his side. With a few clicks of keys, the computer screen flashed to life showing a blurred red-brown surface. "What do you wish to focus on?"

Dylan brushed a finger over the center of the script where the clay surface beneath the slashes and dots was too smooth except for a few tiny waves that indicated something had been erased before the clay dried and the text became permanent. For two heartbeats he was grateful the original scribe had not fired the tablet as he would a pot or a lamp. The heat of the kiln would have destroyed all traces of the man's presence.

The screen focused and the lines of text jumped to life. Dylan had memorized it before he'd left Los Angeles. He knew the accounting of fifteen coins for the work of twelve Magi.

"There, Ignacio. I need you to touch this line. See how the text is deeper than the rest of the account. This is where the scribe obliterated something and made certain it took six thousand years to discover what he hid."

Ignacio shrugged and peered at the screen, then at the ancient markings. "I have the oddest feeling that I'm going to need the demon infested oil lamp in order to discover something."

"It's right here," Sahin said. He unlocked another glass case, right next to the tablet's home and brought the triple-fist-sized lamp to rest within easy reach.

Dylan felt the psychic shudder coursing through the Italian.

There was one thing he could do to help. Dylan's Hunter training came into play as he mentally grounded himself and placed a firm hand, fingers splayed, on the Ignacio's left temple. The creators of the Vulcan mind meld from *Star Trek* had gotten something right. Instinctively he set his phone to record and placed it beside the tablet. "Read the man behind the script," he whispered. "His mind is a part of what he wrote."

"I'm afraid. I have never been afraid of reading an artifact. I've handled thousands of them for the Guild."

"Have you ever dealt with anything this old?" Sahin asked. "You have to be careful not to lose yourself in time as you delve deeply into another realm." He sounded as if he knew what it was like to be psychometric. Maybe he had to be one in order to truly succeed in the field of archeology.

Ignacio shook his head, then stopped the gesture abruptly. Resolutely he placed his left, ungloved hand around the lamp and gritted his teeth. "No, I cannot let you out of your prison just yet. I need your help. When we are finished, you and Sahin will discuss the terms of your freedom."

Through his physical link with Ignacio, Dylan's gut boiled with impatience. The lamp rocked back and forth as the spirit trapped within banged on the interior. Mentally he sent soothing waves to the being, as he would send them to Celia. This time he crossed realms and dimensions rather than mere miles.

When all is said and done, you will not have to face the StormMother. We will find a way to send you home, free of your confinement and safe from her.

The Djinn loosed something akin to a belly laugh.

I will face the StormMother with you. She will answer to me when she listens to no one else.

"How'd you know…" Ignacio asked.

"I've dealt with more than one demon in my life. This one is older and more powerful, but he has the same need to go home… to go to his beloved. Just like I do."

Ignacio pressed one finger on the tablet, right where Dylan had indicated.

Waves of fear and gibbering panic set his teeth to chattering and chilling his blood and bones.

And then words and phrases spilled forth from Ignacio. Dylan only understood bits and pieces: two for this, two of that. All in twos. Symmetrical even numbers to counteract the chaos generated by a single being. *Twelve.*

Then the need to hide it all so that no one, ever again, would have to face down the terrible rage of Tiamat. But the Djinn who had orchestrated the spell also had to forget, and so the twelve Magi confined him to the lamp. Or so they thought.

The story of Aladdin had to come from somewhere.

CHAPTER 24

Two more days I endured without Dylan. Aunt Abby (the hated nickname was addictive) dismissed my experience with ghosts. Ghouls she understood. They were vicious and harmful and had to be banished. Ghosts were too often a trick of lighting and imagination, usually combined with a mental disorder. They were also insubstantial and couldn't hurt humans.

Obviously, she'd never experienced a ghost. I expected more from her. My survivor's guilt, loneliness, and grief hurt a lot more than she imagined. I think her augmentations must have destroyed anything within her resembling empathy.

Dad, on the other hand, became instantly wary when I shared my news with him. "I don't like it. Not one bit. I raised those girls as my own daughters. I knew them as well as you did, Celia. They went to their graves without guilt or remorse. They lived quiet, honest lives. They loved life, but not so much they'd linger beyond death. The timing is too coincidental. There is something more at work here than our grief over the loss of two innocents."

Then, my father, the practical, logical, computer expert began hanging medicine bundles of garlic and sage around my hotel room and trailer. No rosemary or rue, lest those two herbs invite spirits into my life.

Mom turned over the management of the flower shop to my sisters and came to stay with me. My one remaining roommate moved in with me (drat I had to pick up after myself again) and my parents took over the second bedroom. Double drat, with Mom in the house I had to keep the living room picked up as well. But swimming laps with Mom every morning while Dad cooked breakfast made up for the inconvenience.

Sunday night came around again, my last competition with Paul. In the green room, I leaned against him while I searched the camera feeds before the show. Mom and Dad sat in their usual places. Dylan was not behind them, or beside them, or anywhere the camera panned the audience seats.

You said you were coming home today! I sounded petulant and childish to my own ears. Thank all the gods and goddess throughout history that neither Paul nor the judges heard me. They'd know how nervous I was.

They'd know that I dreaded having to dance solo and possibly conjure the ghosts of Brittney and Joycelyn. My knees grew watery just thinking about it.

Turbulence over Rome, London, New York, and Chicago. You'd think Mummy doesn't want me to come home with the little surprise I have for her.

He was on the way! And he had something with him that might put an end to the Tiamat-induced-nightmare we lived with.

He went dark then, there in the back of my mind and my heart, but no thoughts leaked through. Maybe he didn't want Tiamat eavesdropping. He'd learned as much about shutting me out as I had him. But he left that gossamer thread between us whole, strained but whole.

The audience lights blinked a warning. Time to sit down and stop talking.

All of us in the green room took a joint deep breath. We were down by more than half our original numbers. Reaching out and holding hands in a loose circle came too easily.

"Places," the stage manager whispered from the doorway.

Silently, we made our way to the darkened stage. We all wore black and black veils over our faces. A sheer black curtain separated us from the main portion of the theater.

Then a single, low cello note vibrated, growing louder and building musical tension through the vast space.

I loved it. Margot Tremayne really knew how to manipulate music to draw out the most emotion. I could learn a thing or two from her.

That one stray idea broke my nervous, looping thoughts.

Paul and I struck our pose for the opening of an abbreviated group number to *Danse Macabre*. Halloween loomed this week.

Spotlights flashed, lingering only a second on each couple before moving on. We twisted our bodies in unnatural ways that flowed into a smooth and coherent dance.

Ninety seconds can be an eternity. Or last only a heartbeat.

The audience was on their feet with resounding applause.

For the first time in the competition, I completed a dance number without having to think about every step and nuance of movement. I just did it.

I barely had time to enjoy the response when I spotted Mummy. (She might be Tiamat, Goddess of chaos and creation, but she'd been Mummy to the family for so long, I couldn't forget the relationship.) She didn't hide in the second balcony. No. She sat in the fourth row at the end of the long apron. She might as well have stood center stage.

I will not let you intimidate me!

Paul clapped me on the back directed me to the platforms at the top of the grand staircase for the show opening. I turned my back on Mummy, not even thinking about her. Paul and I barely had enough time to catch our breath and remove our veils before our names echoed around the audience and we stepped lightly down the steps to take predetermined places on stage.

Introductions, blah, blah, blah. Nothing new. We all plastered smiles for the camera, all the while thinking more about costume changes and our first number.

"We have a slight change of rules," Little Miss Bouncy said on a breathy whisper followed by the squeal of feedback from her handheld microphone. She *still* hadn't gotten the hang of using the thing properly.

I held my breath. Rule changes upset me more than seeing Mummy in the audience.

"Next week the remaining contestants will be performing two numbers each," the host said with appropriate dignity and a proper distance between his mouth and the mic.

That was not exactly new. We expected to double up when the number of contestants was reduced enough to fill the time of the two-hour broadcast.

"The first number will be performed with a pro—just not the one they have partnered from the beginning. The second number will be with another contestant." Miss Bouncy made that sound ominous.

But it wasn't. Dancing one number with a seasoned pro was a good thing, even if I couldn't have Paul as a partner. I trusted Paul to keep me grounded, on count, and to not drop me on a lift. Having to get used to two new partners was a little tricky with only one week to prepare.

"You can do it," Paul whispered. He clutched my hand and squeezed gently. "I'll be around to help you rehearse if you need me."

I smiled my thanks.

Then we had to hasten back to our trailers to change while the show ran a commercial and presented the pre-recorded package of the highlights of our week of rehearsals. In my opinion the snippets of arguments and flubs lacked the usual flare from when Dylan supervised how they were put together. "Who's going to notice?" I kept asking myself.

Where are you?

Coming in for a landing at LAX. Probably won't make the show, but soon after. Blankness. He'd closed me off. Again.

Have fun with your number! He came back online for just a moment then turned his attention elsewhere.

But not totally. I touched my mouth with tentative fingertips. Dylan was with me, just silent.

"I can do this."

And I did. Paul and I sailed through the jazzed-up version of *Easter Parade*. We had fun with it, exchanging hats, tossing hats, mixing ballroom with side by side jazz. We pranced and glided and sang.

In the end, I avoided jeopardy, nearly collapsing with relief. I didn't have to do the ghost waltz. I didn't have to take the chance of conjuring up Brittney and Joycelyn. Their discarded sequins resided in a little box in the back of my underwear drawer to remind me of the danger awaiting me.

I really, really wanted Dylan at my side when I confronted my ghosts again.

Snarled traffic around the airport. My taxi is at a standstill.

Dylan cursed in Irish Gaelic, his mother's language, the first one he'd learned and the one that came most readily to his tongue.

"Sorry, can't do nothing," the taxi driver shrugged, taking his hands off the wheel to gesture expansively at the lines and lines of stalled cars ahead and behind them. "Dispatcher says a sink hole swallowed a dozen cars and runs the full width of the freeway."

Eight to ten lanes with a median of another ten feet or more.

Mummy at work again.

Dylan swallowed the next round of vulgarity that he wanted to spit. Hands shaking he threw two twenties on the front seat of the cab, grabbed his backpack and the waterproof tote bag containing the Djinn in a specially padded wooden box—and hadn't that been fun getting it out of Turkey and through U.S. Customs even with reams of paperwork provided by Sahin—and jumped free of the taxi. Thankfully they were in the middle lanes and he didn't land in the mud of the verge.

Rain and an icy wind lashed him with particular ferocity. "This isn't Ireland!" he yelled and shook his fist at the sky.

"I grew up walking in this kind of weather," he told himself and set off at an easy lope to the closest exit behind the taxi.

I'm coming, Celia.

Silence.

Celia!

Only me, Hunter. You'll have to deal with me before I let you taint my little girl, Mummy cackled in the back of his head.

~

I endured Dylan's squelching through a mud puddle on the verge, and his slide down the embankment beside the freeway exit.

I winced as cold seeped through his loafers and socks to chill his feet all the way to his nose.

"It's not like Dylan to not check in," Abby grumbled, flicking her index finger against the side of her phone, as if she could jostle loose a lost communication.

"He just lost a shoe and his phone," I replied on a sigh. "He's making his way toward a streetlight on the corner of... Damn it's raining so hard we can't see the street signs!"

My feet shuffled restlessly with my need to go to him, dry him off, keep him warm.

"How many lives has this temper tantrum cost?" I snarled at everyone in the room.

Just then Lynette, my last remaining roommate emerged from our bedroom, tugging two wheeled suitcases behind her.

"Let me help you with those," Dad rushed to her assistance.

"I've got it, Mr. Fisher. The studio limo is waiting for those of us eliminated tonight. We're booked on the red eye to New York." She kept her eyes on the floor and her shoulders limp with disappointment.

"Don't bank on that, dear," Aunt Abigail said. She hastened to Lynette's side and draped an arm around the girl's shoulders. "The weather is frightful, and a lot of flights are being canceled. I'm not sure if the limo can even get to the airport." This was the gentle, caring godmother I'd grown up loving, not at all the steely, cold, and efficient Director of a guild of paranormal Hunters.

"The TV report said the back edge of the storm is passing over us now. I had a text from the driver, he knows some back streets that will get around that horrible traffic jam, the sink hole, and the landslide." Lynette shrugged. "We'd better make it. I'm looking forward to being interviewed on live TV. That's one of the benefits to lasting as long as I did on the show."

"Good luck," I called to her from my station by the glass doors facing the pool. I couldn't see the blue-green water from here other than a pale smudge from the underwater lights.

"Think you'll last three more shows?" She looked up from the floor to engage my gaze. We both knew how much we'd struggled with this competition. She was a dancer but only an okay singer. We hadn't been able to help each other, or bond with our differences.

"I don't know," I replied softly. "I expected to go home tonight."

"But you didn't. Good luck. Maybe I'll see you around New York. I intend to stay on a couple of weeks and audition for everything and anything that comes up." She slapped on a broad-brimmed hat that might shield her from some lashing rain but would probably blow off between the lobby and the limo.

"I'll try to call and meet up with you next week."

And then she was gone. Aunt Abigail went with her, solicitous and nurturing. But my godmother kept her phone in one hand and checked it constantly.

"You know that I'm still listed with the union as your agent and business manager," Dad said once the room was clear of outsiders.

Mom didn't look happy as he fetched his tablet and flipped through to a new screen.

"Yes. Up until now I haven't needed anyone else." A nervous flutter started in my tummy. I wasn't sure if I wanted to know what he had to say.

"I waited until Abby wasn't here, because she does still officially work for Bryant Thomas."

I nodded for him to proceed.

"We just got a couple of interesting emails." A grin tugged at his mouth. "Are you interested in recording an album of mixed classical and popular music? Similar to Sarah Brightman and Catherine Jenkins, but with your own unique style?" The grin became a full-blown smile that stretched to his ears and his eyes.

I flicked Mom a glance. She still looked hesitant.

"Is it dependent upon me winning the competition?" The nervous fluttering in my tummy became an entire flock of seagulls trying to take off.

"No, it is not," Dad said. "It's a classical label noted for their high-quality recordings and production. In fact, they want to wait until the end of the show to begin rehearsals to make certain your entire focus is on the album, not on the competition. But they'd like to sign you now and announce it the day after the finale."

"Yes. Negotiate a decent advance, but don't be greedy." I found myself rising to my tip toes and dropping back again, over and over. I'd bounce higher when Dylan was beside me, safe and warm.

Soon my love. Just a few more blocks.

Blocks in L.A. could be half a mile long.

"There's another email." Dad fiddled with the tablet some more. "Do you want to star in a touring production of *The Merry Widow*?"

Mom still didn't look happy.

"What if I win? Aren't I obligated to Margot Tremayne's production?"

"Yes, you are. So, you have to decide on taking a chance on losing so you can do a touring production that may never make Broadway, or take a chance you'll win and go right to Broadway." Dad lost a little of his smile.

"The touring company won't wait?"

Mom moved to my side and pulled me in for a one-armed hug. "Think about how hard you've worked for this competition," she said, facing Dad and speaking more to him than to me.

"The touring company is set to open in Miami in three weeks. Their lead developed a fungal inner ear infection. She can't hear herself sing and her balance is screwed. You'd have to fly out tomorrow and jump right into rehearsals the next morning."

"Leaving her with only thirty-six hours to learn the script and the score," Mom reminded us both.

"The score is no problem. I only have to hear it once while looking at the music. It's the script, staging, and choreography I'll have problems with. Can I take Paul with me as a personal coach and find him a role?"

"Not likely." Dad shook his head and stared at his tablet.

"If we don't stop Mummy before then, Miami will be under water in three weeks," Mom said. Usually she was the dreamer and Dad the practical one. Not tonight. She really didn't want me to go to Miami.

A sound outside the glass doors made my heart leap to my throat. Dylan!

Those few blocks must have been short ones.

I hastened to open the sliders. He nearly fell against me, his hair and clothing a sodden mess. Dark circles bruised the skin around his eyes and his teeth chattered. His hair dripped thick streams of water.

I wrapped my arms around him, as I relieved him of his backpack. He clung to the tote bag in his left hand as if his life depended upon keeping his grip on the cloth handles.

"Where's Abby?" he asked.

"I'll get her," Dad said and turned toward the door.

"Take this. Don't let it out of your hand until you pass it to her." Dylan held out the tote.

Dad pried it loose from Dylan's cold fingers and opened it enough to peer inside.

"What is it?"

"A genie in a bottle that will save us all."

That decided me. I couldn't fly to Miami tomorrow. I had to stay in Los Angeles with Dylan and Aunt Abigail. We still had a fight with Mummy to save the world whether I won the competition or not.

"If Lynette is still in the lobby, Dad, ask if she's interested in *The Merry Widow*."

Just as I was turning away from the glass sliders the murky light from the pool shifted to sparkling red and blue. The ghosts of Brittney and Joycelyn rose up from the depths and drifted toward me, mouths open as if singing. But I could no longer hear their voices

CHAPTER 25

Celia screamed. Mike and Jeannie clung to each other in paralyzed, mute horror.

Dylan whirled around to face the pool. His medallion heated up and throbbed. In his peripheral vision it burned white hot against his skin. He fished it free of his shirt. Would it repel ghosts, or was it only a warning?

The sparkling blue and red forms didn't need lights to make them glow around the edges and from within.

His link to Celia told him more than he wanted to know.

"They're real," he said, holding her close. In his own ears he heard the lilt of Ireland and relived the fear and pain of dealing with the ghoul just before his nanos went berserk.

"I... I wasn't sure anyone else could see them. Or that anyone would believe me," she whispered.

"They are real, or as real as a ghost can be. Insubstantial," Mike added. He still held the tote bag with the Djinn and the clay oil lamp.

The blasted genie remained inert. No help there.

Not worth my time. I'm destined for bigger things. The Djinn yawned.

Dylan wasn't certain he actually heard the genie or if he imagined it. either way, he'd have to figure something out. Fast.

"Why is my medallion glowing?" Abby asked from the doorway. "Oh!" Following our gazes she stared at the apparitions rising out of the pool in horror.

"By Bridget and St. Patrick and all the saints in heaven, preserve us," Dylan prayed.

The ghosts paused and exchanged a look.

Not much taller than Celia, they somehow looked bigger.

Celia ducked from beneath his shoulder and ran into her bedroom.

"CeeCee!" her father called. "You can't run away from them. They'll follow you through walls!"

"S'okay," she replied breathlessly, returning with a small white jewelry box. Dylan caught a glimpse of red and blue shiny things, like the sequins on the ghostly gowns.

Deep chills ran up and down his spine. Goose flesh raised on his arms. His already cold feet became like ice blocks sealing him in place, unable to move, even if he dared.

Celia opened the sliders an inch, maybe two.

Dylan reached to stop her, but the ghosts had stopped moving forward. Their mouths still worked as if singing. Celia crooned a soft note, like the opening of a lullaby. Brahms had nothing on her.

She took a deep breath, preparing to loose another note. At the same moment as the song burst forth, she flung the contents of the little box at the ghosts.

Tiny bits reflected the little bit of light around them, twisting and scattering and somehow...

Somehow the sequins stuck on those once gorgeous performance gowns, filling in spots he hadn't been certain were unadorned.

Except the new bits of red attached to the blue gown and the blue sequins filled in a spot on the red gown.

The ghosts drifted backward and sank into the pool.

The lights inside and outside the room flickered and died, along with the rain.

Dylan caught Celia as she collapsed.

The still open sliders allowed a breath of fresh air to penetrate and clear the suddenly overly warm suite.

～

"They aren't gone, just temporarily mollified," I told my gathered family: Mom and Dad, of course, Aunt Abby, and Dylan.

Dylan. Yes, he was family now, as much a part of me as my parents and Aunt Abigail.

"Can we continue this discussion after I clean up a bit?" Dylan asked around chattering teeth. He still dripped, all over the floor and me. But I couldn't separate myself from him yet.

"Upstairs and into the shower, boyo," Dad said.

I glanced toward my bedroom with its own shower. Much closer than two flights up. Dad shook his head. "Not yet Celia. He needs dry clothes and you two aren't married." He sounded stern and over-protective.

I'd give him that. For now.

Aunt Abby sat in the comfy armchair, feet tucked under her and the sodden tote bag in her lap. Mom walked warily around her, circle after circle. Her mouth worked as if she sang, but I heard no words. An ancient containment spell?

If I could work magic with song to heal, why couldn't she, also a siren, work magic to keep whatever was in that bag within the bag?

With Dad and Dylan upstairs, I was the only one in position to answer the door when Bryant Thomas arrived. Sleeping toddler on one shoulder, bulging diaper bag dangling from the other. He touched my shoulder in greeting, then nodded to Mom and Aunt Abby. Tense silence pervaded the atmosphere of the room.

I returned my attention toward the pool. The rain and murk had slacked off a bit, along with the wind. Did my ghostly nieces require a storm to reveal themselves? I couldn't remember the weather on the day I first saw them.

I considered turning on the music for the ghost waltz to see if they'd return to me, but I wasn't sure I wanted them to haunt me.

They'd been gone ten months and the hole in my soul had just begun to heal.

"What is so important, Abby, that I needed to leave my snug home? Do you know how impossible it is to find a sitter after Nanny has gone home for the night at the beginning of her vacation?" His eighteen-month old daughter still slept with her fist in her mouth on his shoulder. "If I have to be here, so does my daughter."

Mom rushed to take the child and gently removed her hat and coat. Then she set her down on one end of the sofa, covered in her own blankie. The little girl barely stirred at the disturbance.

Mom looked as if she wanted to stay beside the child but gave up that place to Mr. Thomas.

The producer looked beyond annoyed, but his deep sigh at the end of his question told me he was resigned to the inevitable. Once a Hunter always a Hunter. Just like Dad. The Guild never truly released its own.

"Dylan has brought us a genie in a bottle and an ancient spell to contain the StormMother. Again," Aunt Abby replied. She still did not disturb the tote bag.

"Oh? How much did that cost you?" Mr. Thomas perched on the end of the sofa. He placed one hand on his daughter's back, reassuring himself that she was safe and still sleeping.

Aunt Abby glared at him. "It cost more than you want to know to pry this out of the hands of the Turkish government."

He swallowed a grin. "By the way, Celia, as happy as I am that you will return next week, I would have enjoyed watching your interpretation of the Ghost Waltz. You know I've performed it?"

"Yes, I was aware of that. Paul and I watched the tapes of you and Janet Dryer before we choreographed it." That dance had been the start of the rumors about him and the talk show host. He'd still been with the mother of his daughter then. But his wife was gone now. Taken by the plague weeks before the vaccine became available.

My gaze returned to the pool and I lifted my heels, prepared to run and hide. Or maybe welcome Brittney and Joycelyn. I couldn't tell at that moment. My insides felt exposed, raw, burning as if ripped by a ritual blade.

At that moment, Dad used his key to return with Dylan in his wake. In clean clothes and freshly shaved, he looked a lot better than he had half an hour ago. He still hunched in on himself as if guarding against a chill that began in his belly.

I put the kettle on for hot cocoa—I always kept a box of instant packets with me.

"Are we all here?" Dad asked.

"Not *all*," Dylan said. He came to the kitchenette and gave me a hug and a kiss on the cheek. "We'll need twelve people, in precise pairs to pull this off. But for now, we have enough to draw up plans."

Since I had caught glimmers of his plot while he flew halfway around the world, I knew what was missing. "Six thousand years ago, Mummy was alone. Now she has two backup singers to strengthen her resistance. Before we confront the StormMother we have to put Brittney and Joycelyn to rest, in peace."

"That will take more magic than I can tap into," Aunt Abby said flatly.

"Ghosts," Dylan said, air and strength leeching out of him. He draped an arm around Celia's shoulders and nearly stumbled to an armchair. He'd make room for her beside him even though the chair was designed for one person. Good thing Celia was carrying his hot chocolate along with hers or he'd have spilled it and required another clean up. "I really don't like dealing with ghosts." He sat and buried his head in his hands, elbows braced on his knees.

"These are ghosts, not ghouls," Abby admonished him.

"Are you certain, Abigail?" Mike asked. He had taken up a position beside his wife.

She reared her head up at that. "No. No. My girls would never…"

"They aren't our girls anymore," Mike soothed her, stroking her hair, so like Celia's soft waves in a no-nonsense pixie cut, but darker and sprinkled with gray.

Dylan had a glimpse of what Celia would look like as she aged. He wanted to be beside her as that happened.

With a steady hand and a clearer mind, he took the cup from her and sipped the restorative beverage. "Don't suppose you've got a wee bit of somethin' stronger to add to this?" He grinned at her.

Bryant Thomas groaned. "Is there anything that a wee bit of Irish whisky won't cure?"

"Not much, boyo," Mike replied.

When no one moved, Celia shifted beside him.

He placed a hand on her thigh to keep her close.

"Dad, there's a bottle of Irish in the cupboard above the fridge," she said, winking at Dylan.

"Celia!" Mike roared.

"I'm over twenty-one, Dad. And I like Irish coffee. Accept it, I'm not fifteen anymore."

Growling and grumbling, Mike fetched the bottle and added a dollop of the water of life to each mug around the room.

"So, why am I here, Abby? I'm too busy to go chasing ghosts and I'm certainly not up to facing the StormMother without a lot of back up," Bryant Thomas said.

"You won't be alone," Dylan said. He finished his cocoa and set the cup on the floor by his feet. "The original spell included twelve Magi."

"Where in the hell are you going to find twelve sorcerers?" Bryant exploded.

"We won't be needing twelve *Magi*," Dylan said. He clutched Celia's hand tighter. "They contained Tiamat for a while only because she was willing to cooperate. I'm guessing that she burst free of her restrictions a long time ago but didn't bother meddling with humans other than to conjure storms and let them work their damage naturally. Now she's directing the storms and conjuring more and more of them. There's anger in her patterns of destruction. A lot of anger."

"Climate change," Jeannie whispered.

"Mummy told me that she considers humans an infestation that is destroying her earth. She's been trying to convince me to join her so that she... we... can wipe out humanity and let Earth recover."

Everyone in the room shivered. Celia's magnificent voice could counter anything Tiamat could throw at her. But would her mind hold up under the onslaught?

"I think the spell was weakened by the lack of diversity in the original contingent of Magi. They all had the same talent and they worked for money, not for love of humanity."

"Who do you suggest?" Abby asked sharply.

Dylan pulled his phone out and taped into the notes he'd compiled on the long flight home.

"First, there is a Djinn in the clay oil lamp in the bag." He nodded toward his carry-all. "He was present at the first spell and has indicated an interest in helping again."

"In return for what?" Bryant Thomas was on his feet, fists clenched. "I've dealt with those tricksters before. We can't trust it."

"I trust *him*. All he asks is our assistance in sending him home. Just like E.T. and the majority of the demons I've dealt with."

A chuckle rippled around the room.

"What will be different? The Djinn was there the first time." Abby speared him with her gaze.

He could almost see the wheels turning inside her mind. Abby was back. Madame Director would find a solution, like she always did. She might be an annoying dictator with only the welfare of the Guild in mind, but at heart she was an efficient CEO looking out for the best interests of all her employees as well as the organization. She'd find a way to do this.

"The originals were all Magi, with only the interests of Magi at heart. I propose a variety of people involved," Dylan explained. "We need balance and diversity and each of our participants will have a greater purpose than their own survival and bank account."

Jeannie gasped. "I don't know if I can sing with magic anymore. I've barely sung at all since Celia and the girls were born."

"You'll have me beside you, Mom," Celia said. "And Dad and Mr. Thomas."

"That's four," Abby said. "We'll need eight more. Who?"

"Two Sirens. Two retired Hunters. Two active Hunters if you can find one who can sing," Dylan said.

"Archie," Abby and Bryant said at the same time.

"Who's Archie?" Celia asked.

"My former accountant who turned out to be quite a musician. Anyone who can place second in the St. George competition must know music well enough to sing adequately." Abby grabbed Dylan's phone and scrolled down the screen.

"The St. George!" Mom and I gasped at the same moment. "That's the most prestigious keyboard competition in the world! Where'd you find so fine a musician?"

"Like she said, he started as her forensic accountant, there's more money in manipulating numbers than directing church choirs and playing jazz in clubs on weekends," Bryant said. "He told me that his Hunter augmentation improved his talent; that he couldn't have passed the audition let alone competed without it."

Abby took back control of the conversation, consulting the list. "Bryant, you'll need to contact Janet, your pet psychic vampire. I will join her on each end of the semi-circle as representatives of paranormal. I presume we can count my surviving a third augmentation a paranormal talent."

"No," Bryant said quietly.

"Yes."

"Janet hasn't returned my calls in over a year."

"Then I'll call her," Abby said succinctly. "We'll need two mundanes. I suggest Margot Tremayne for one."

Bryant nodded at that. "After her adventures with with Archie and a demon anchored to an antique piano, I think my music director will be willing to help. Who else is knowledgeable of the Guild and our missions?"

"My administrative assistant, Marci, will be happy to help us I'm sure."

"That's ten," Mike said.

"The ghosts of Brittney and Joycelyn," Celia said flatly.

"That makes a nice balance of mundane and paranormal," Dylan said. He held Celia's hand firmly, making sure she knew she wouldn't have to face her ghosts alone. "First we have to find them and bring them over to our side of this fight." New fears fluttered in his gut. Why did they have to be ghosts?

"How do you propose to drag them out of purgatory and back to the corporeal realm?" Mike asked.

"They're ghosts, not ghouls," Celia whispered to him. She had picked up his inner fears through their link. "My ghosts, not yours. It was a ghoul who bit you and sent your nanobots into a squiggling mess back in Northern Ireland. Ghosts are insubstantial and mostly benign." She said this like she had intimate knowledge of ghosties and ghoulies and things that go bump in the night.

Maybe she did.

Jeannie dabbed a tear from her eye with a fingertip. "If only I could hold them one more time and properly say good-bye..."

"Sounds like a spirit journey is called for," Abby said. "Choose your transportation, datura or argot."

CHAPTER 26

Dylan stepped out of the shower the next morning muttering and mumbling about hallucinogenic drugs inducing a spirit journey trance. He really did not like Abby's plans for him.

He reached for fresh underwear in the top drawer of the dresser and froze in place. "Do I know you?" he asked the shadow in the corner chair by the sliders.

Hastily he donned his undergarments to fortify himself. No man wanted to confront an enemy naked.

"You will know me better in the coming days," said a deep-voiced man in English with only a trace of a middle eastern accent that he couldn't place.

The unknown quality of the accent intrigued and frightened Dylan.

He turned slowly, mind working overtime trying to place the inflections geographically and failed. He felt as lost as his first day deciphering Greek without a tutor to guide him. He'd been eight at the time.

"Don't you recognize me yet?" the shadow asked. He turned so that Dylan could see his profile, long straight nose, lowering brow, thick dark hair pulled back into a ponytail.

"I saw you outside the studio gate the day I evicted Stevie."

The shadow touched two fingers to his brow in a casual salute. "And since then?"

"I overheard the people in the press room welcome someone named Anshar. That's not a name in common usage. I had to research it."

"Never was a *common* name. You'll find it on a few scraps of writing from old Babylon." Anshar stood and moved closer to the sliders letting dawn light illuminate more of him.

"Anshar, ancestor of the gods. I've seen your face on a dozen ancient coins that were too worn to give a date or a kingdom."

"You *have* done your research." The man smiled.

"It's part of my job."

"Agreed. My granddaughter's safety is another part of your job. Where is she by the way?"

Dylan checked his link. She juggled bundles and bags of stuff and a full cup of coffee as she headed toward the rehearsal halls.

I could use an extra hand here, she told him, sounding grumpy.

Sorry, you'll have to manage on your own. Stop and take a few gulps of coffee.

It's too hot to drink. She sounded downright surly.

I love you anyway. Ooops, was he supposed to say that yet? Oh well, it needed saying.

He flashed her an image of his visitor.

Fred?

Um...

He was our invisible playmate until we were about seven. Maybe nine. Saved me from bullies a couple of times.

Why Fred?

Joycelyn said the name fit him. Brittney and I accepted it.

Try Anshar.

The link went blank. Still there but devoid of thoughts.

You still there?

Of course. That might be his real name, but he never spoke it. He was just Fred.

Have a good rehearsal. I've got to go.

What about tonight? A bit of panic edged into her voice.

Leave the logistics to Abby and your father, and maybe Fred. Pick you up at your trailer about five.

"So, Fred, why are you here?"

Anshar raised one eyebrow. "I should have guessed that you and Celia have a telepathic bond. Good. You're going to need it to protect her." He sat down again. "Got any coffee?"

"Only a generic American blend. Not Turkish."

"That will do. I can't handle the acid of Turkish coffee in my gut anymore." He stretched out his average length legs and placed his linked hands behind his head. "It's good to sprawl a bit. I could use some breakfast too."

"I usually eat in the canteen at the studio. You are on your own for food." Dylan finished getting dressed and set the coffee maker to dripping, enough for two BIG travel mugs full. "So, if Celia is your granddaughter, that makes you Poseidon as well as Anshar."

"Different name. Same man. The Greeks think they own my myth because they were the first to write it down, but I'm a lot older. They got some of it right." He got up and paced restlessly, checking on the progress of the coffee as well as the lack of activity around the pool.

Dylan had slept through Celia's morning laps with her mother.

"Am I correct in guessing that your normal abode is that little clay lamp?" Dylan rummaged through the collection of stuff in the dish drainer until he found his favorite travel mug, and the spare he used only when he left the good one in the car.

But he had to wonder about sizes and dimensions, material and physical. Anshar looked to be on the small side of average height and build for a modern man. In ancient times he'd have been quite tall and imposing. But what he saw before him, in his hotel room, had to be just a manifestation of spiritual being.

"Yes, and I thank you for bringing me here. I only get a day, maybe a day and a half, out of the pot at any one time, and I have to allow for astral travel time. I have a number of homes around the world, but I had to be in that Turkish museum for you to find me. By bringing me to Celia and Jeannie, I have more hours each transition to do what needs doing."

Dylan's mind jumped around some more seeking connections among multiple myths. The nanobots in his brain behaved themselves and made leaps of faith seem logical.

He sat down in the chair that Anshar had vacated.

"You've got the rest of today to teach me to speak Sumerian and how best to accomplish... whatever it is we need to do to tame Tiamat."

Anshar leaned back his head and loosed a belly laugh. "My dear boy, you cannot tame Tiamat. You can only persuade her to try a different approach. That's my job in this adventure. Then I'll go back to my pot and my big screen TV that is my window on the world. I'm basically lazy and coming out to deal with my beloved mate once every few decades is about all I can manage. We usually get a new siren or merman out of the encounter though."

"Logistics he says," I muttered as I juggled my dance bag, shoes, purse, and coffee in order to get the door to the rehearsal hall open. "Leave the logistics to the pros. They'll get it all laid out and call me when they're ready." My inner voice as well as the words I spoke out loud took on a snarling quality.

I didn't really enjoy talking to myself. Today I needed to hear my thoughts because Dylan wasn't listening.

I could eavesdrop on Dylan's strategy meetings, but I had no input unless he voiced my concerns. And something about the outline of the spell bothered me, I just couldn't pinpoint it.

But no, I had to continue with rehearsals and performances, interviews, and promotional ads, as if the next thunderstorm wouldn't flood all of Los Angeles and set fire to any building above four stories.

"It's my voice that's supposed to anchor this mess, I need to be part of the planning process." The sticky door gave with a jerk and I nearly fell into the big hall where this week's guest choreographer stood at a whiteboard, marking it up with exotic symbols.

My mind flipped as quickly back to cuneiform dots and slashes and then to hieroglyphs to Mayan story in icon markings.

Dance steps, Dylan informed me.

I know that. What do they mean?

I need more than a cursory glance.

Pffft. I blew him a raspberry.

The link between us collapsed.

Fine. I needed to rehearse.

The immensity of our plot to overthrow the StormMother punched me in the gut. I had no time to rehearse. I needed to save the world.

That's my job. Now you do yours. Remember to smile and point your toes.

Pfffft

"Ah, Celia, there you are. I wanted to work with you a bit before the group descends upon us," Mavis Davis (I assumed that was a stage name) the choreographer said, barely looking away from her arcane markings on the whiteboard.

"What kind of demon are you conjuring?" I blurted, staring at her black, red, yellow, and blue scribblings.

She laughed loud and long, throwing her head back in glorious abandon even as she reached for a green marker. A purple one rested on the lip of the board. Six colors. Six remaining dancers and singers.

A few more minutes and I might gain a sense of the movement she diagramed.

My gloomy mood lifted. The sun peeked out from the thick cloud cover and brightened everything.

"You could call dance a demon. It gets under your skin and clings tenaciously even after the old body gives up." Mavis rubbed her knee, then shifted her self-massage to her lower back.

She flicked her hands at me, and I set down my burdens, but not before I drank long and deep of the blessed coffee. I burned my tongue but it gave me life-saving energy. Then she positioned me in the center of the room facing the mirror. I didn't even get a chance to change my shoes.

"Right arm up, rounded in a classic ballet pose." Mavis shaped my position with gentle hands like molding a sculpture. "Right leg anchoring you, turned out and stretched from toe to hip, one long flowing line that obscures the differences of muscle and bone and skin."

I had to smile at the grace she imbued in my body. I don't think I could do it on my own, or even with Paul coaching me.

"Now the left side will be just the opposite." She jerked my left arm out and down, wrist flexed, fingers splayed.

"That's ugly. In comparison," I remarked.

"Exactly. Now extend the left leg, let your muscles go slack and the knee bent about half, toes on the ground, slightly turned in and heel thrust out." Again, she shaped me the way she wanted.

"That is opposite to everything about dance I've learned in the past two months."

"Good that you've learned something. You've struggled so much with the dance portion of this competition I want to showcase how you've grown. I'll do the same with Gaylord on the vocals. He's learned to add a lot of dynamics to his singing and expanded his range."

"He's one hell of a dancer," I agreed. "Classically trained in ballet, he makes even our pros look... unfinished." Not to mention the way his dark skin glistened under the lights and his tight butt and long legs made every costume a second skin.

"I think I'm dancing with him this week." Oh boy that would be a challenge, but I loved the dramatic contrast of my fairness to his dusky masculinity.

"Does that mean we are contenders?" I asked, suddenly suspicious of the extra attention. Bryant Thomas hadn't intimated anything about pushing me to the forefront last night. He'd only repeated that anything crazy had to wait until the show concluded and I was free of contractual obligations. Three more shows. Even if I was voted off this coming Sunday, I'd have to return for the grand finale, along with all of the original contestants.

"All of you are contenders at this point. From ten dancers and ten singers we are down to four and four. The chaff has been winnowed out. Just don't fall flat on your face and you could end up in the final two."

"I never imagined I'd get this far."

"Then start imagining and follow me." Mavis stood in front of me and paced out a routine of six measures. Not hard, but awkward with the twisting between grace and clumsy.

I'd just managed to get my feet to go where they should all the way through when the rest of the cast stumbled in, boisterous and eager to get started.

"Hey, we made it this far. The only way is up!" someone shouted, and we all echoed the sentiment.

This morning I felt I'd made the right choice to refuse the *Merry Widow* role. I had better things in front of me, once I mastered the balance of the bizarre poses in this dance.

Balance. That's what was wrong with the spell. The balance was off.

Dylan, you didn't count the Djinn. He makes thirteen. A chaos number.

I heard his mental groan. *The original Magi didn't count him. That's why the spell broke down.*

He's a paranormal. You have to remove either Aunt Abby or this Janet person. I don't know her.

Neither do I, but Abby and Bryant do, and so do Archie and Margot. We have to trust her paranormal talent. Abby isn't truly paranormal. She will throw off the balance. We can't have her opposite the Djinn. She'll be better placed as a normal opposite Margot Tremayne.

You want to foil her plans, or shall I?

She loves you. You'd better tell her. Maybe she won't wring your neck and toss you in the midden.

I groaned inwardly as I made my way to the next rehearsal.

After rehearsal I met Dylan by Elevator B. He didn't bother hiding the eleven-digit security code on the box. He knew that I could pull it from his mind any time I wanted it.

Then the pattern caught my attention. Aunt Abigail's mobile phone number matched the lock box. Interesting.

I wondered how many people—or how few—could reach her by that number, and therefore access her private office.

Then I realized how many times I had passed this corner of the admin building, usually on the run, and never noticed the shadowed elevator. The deep overhang on the north side of the building almost guaranteed it was always in shadow. The one time I'd been in her office, after banishing Big Pink, I'd been gagging and stumbling, my dad half carrying me.

My godmother hid in plain sight. Typical of her and of my parents.

Once the elevator door had slid silently closed, Dylan pulled me into his arms and kissed me long and hard. The pressure of his mouth, the mobility of his tongue, and my own longing robbed me of breath and will.

"It's been too long since we've been alone," he whispered as he pulled me fiercely against his chest, his hands kneading my back.

His fingers found the tight knot below my left shoulder blade and I nearly collapsed. The muscles released under the pressure of his grasp.

"I thought you were holding that side a little high," he said on a chuckle, just as the doors opened again on floor five.

How had we traveled so far, so quickly? Most elevators in L.A. seemed especially slow. I guessed leisurely rides up or down provided opportunities for deal making discussions in relative privacy.

We stepped directly into the reception area of Aunt Abby's lair. Marci, her administrative assistant worked her keyboard with due diligence. She pressed Enter before turning her attention to us.

She blinked at Dylan once, then raked me with her gaze from toes to crown. Her upper lip didn't quite lift in a sneer. "You don't have an appointment," she said to me.

"I have an open appointment with Mrs. FitzWarren," Dylan replied.

"And your purpose?"

I couldn't tell if she disapproved of me or of us for interrupting her meticulous schedule.

"Important," Dylan said and led me to the wide double doors that might have graced an Irish castle as some point; stout enough to withstand a battering ram. He kept one arm around my waist as he knocked once, then twisted the knob.

It opened to his touch.

"Ah, Celia." Aunt Abby rose from her huge chair behind her desk. The monstrous furniture set up a formidable barrier between her and intruders, almost as intimidating as that door. "And Dylan. What brings you here during your lunch hour?"

She must know my schedule as well as I did.

"We've discovered something wrong with the choreography for the spell," I blurted.

She raised her eyebrows in question. Bryant Thomas could do the one eyebrow thing that had been known to make people babble explanations without hesitancy. Aunt Abby's expression was almost as good.

Knowing someone was better at intimidation helped me straighten my spine and stand taller.

Dylan's arm stayed in place, thankfully, giving me courage I didn't know I could muster.

"The Djinn makes thirteen. That's a chaos number. We need to eliminate one of the people chanting the spell to make room for him."

"Of course. We'll remove Marci and I'll take her place. My augmentation doesn't really make me a true paranormal." She sat back down and pulled up a new screen on her computer.

"You're really okay with this?" Dylan asked, as amazed as I was.

"Naturally. We need this to work the first time. We don't get second chances with the StormMother." She began typing, ignoring us. Clearly, we'd been dismissed.

"We'll need to promise Tiamat something to get her to listen to the spell and absorb it," I said. My voice rose in volume and pitch, meant to break through her mental barriers.

"What?" Aunt Abby jerked her head back to me, startled to find me still standing before her, Dylan glued to my side.

"Magic isn't enough. We have to promise her something to get her attention."

"Where did that come from?" Dylan asked, surprised he hadn't discovered this from my mind.

"The idea came to me when we entered the elevator, but then you… um… demanded all of my attention."

He nodded, grinning.

"Offer her something like…?" Aunt Abby interrupted us.

"I'm not certain. She's not going to settle for playing with Poseidon/Anshar and begetting water nymphs and sirens and mermen," Dylan said, running with my ideas.

"She considers humans an infestation now. Six thousand years ago we were just an annoyance."

"Climate change?" Aunt Abby asked, raising her eyebrows again.

"Probably."

"Let me think about this. Go eat something before your next rehearsal." With that, we were clearly dismissed.

"Oh, and you two are going ghost hunting Wednesday night, not tonight. That will be the waxing first quarter of the moon." Her words followed us as we exited.

CHAPTER 27

Dylan prowled the underground chamber of the largest crypt in an old cemetery. Spanish, he thought. The red-tiled roof and adobe walls of the church above this burial place looked old enough to be early eighteenth century and the inscriptions on the burial niches were engraved in a script from that era. His augmented vision allowed him to read with only the light from three fat candles left burning in appropriate wall niches; probably left by Abby or one of her minions when she set up this meeting.

If a ghost wanted to feel welcome, this place would do it.

The hairs on his arms stood up as a chill crawled along his spine.

"You know, Abby, I really don't like dealing with ghosts," he said to the empty and stale air of the crypt. Ghosts reminded him that he was not with his mother when she died. If she remembered to haunt him, would she be her old self from before the dementia claimed her mind? He wasn't convinced Ma had left her cottage, even when they took her to a home for memory-care patients. He'd sold the place as soon as he could. The new owners had complained about strange noises emanating from the kitchen, as if Ma still tried to bake soda bread every morning before dawn.

There were other people he'd lost too, ones he didn't want to confront in the after-life. Joycelyn and Brittney were gentle and forgiving in comparison.

"You don't like this any more than I want to deal with *these* ghosts," Celia said descending the wrought iron spiral staircase. She hugged herself, stuffing her hands in the front pocket of a heavy, hooded sweatshirt.

He changed his trajectory abruptly to meet her as she stepped off the last stair. She pressed herself against him, keeping her arms close, warding off her inner chills. He wrapped his arms around her, easing his own dread by holding her close.

Celia was real. And she was here. Not some half-seen wraith.

She kept her mind closed to him. Not a severing of their link, just putting up a barrier.

He leaned back enough to scrutinize her expression. She turned her face to the side, pressing her ear against his chest.

"What?" he whispered, taking care to keep his voice from echoing in the closed chamber.

"Brittney and Joycelyn and I were raised as sisters, triplets. We have the same birthday. We had no secrets. We shared everything from our first crib to the same hairbrush minutes before the StormMother struck and killed them."

"I know this must be hard for you, but surely they should hold no menace toward you."

"I survived. They did not."

Dylan pulled her closer.

"Could the StormMother have corrupted their love for you after their death?"

"She is Tiamat, goddess of chaos, StormMother, and their multi-great-grandmother. I never could keep the generations straight, so we settled on grandmother long ago. Who knows what powers she wields?"

"Who knows the depth of her hatred of humankind?" He had to know more about the actual entity known as the StormMother before the final confrontation, three weeks and two days from tonight on the full moon with a high tide at midnight and a storm brewing offshore.

Abby and Bryant had chosen the mouth of the Columbia River where a massive amount of fresh water flowing west met the rising waves of saltwater pushing east.

A chaotic place at the best of times.

"That is why I am more afraid of this ritual than even you are, Dylan. But I recognize the need to have my girls as allies when we confront Tiamat."

"Why tonight? Why won't Abby let us wait until just before the confrontation?"

"Time runs differently in the beyond. Or there is no time. I don't know. Mom says it won't happen right away."

"How much experience does your mom have with ghosts?"

"I don't know. Her life before she married Dad is a mystery to me. They never talk about it. I only know that at the end of their adventures, Mummy came to their aid. Then she made them promise she would be a part of their lives and the raising of their children. We didn't hide from her, we just made it terribly inconvenient for her to visit."

He sensed her smile at that. Her memory of Mummy jumping into the swimming pool that had just been chlorinated and ejecting herself upward in a wall of angry mist flashed through his mind. It became his memory, as if he'd lived through it standing beside (or inside) Celia at the time.

And Anshar had stood in the shadow of the slatted eight-foot fence at the edge of the yard, laughing his socks off.

"I'm surprised Mummy doesn't have burn scars from the chlorine when she manifests as human," he said.

As much as he wanted to continue holding Celia he knew they needed to proceed with tonight's ritual.

"Let's get started. Where are the others? Do we need more candles?" he asked, checking the three already burning. They each were nearly a foot tall with sturdy wicks and showed no signs of guttering.

"A trio of lights for a trio of singers." Celia's voice sounded flat. She'd never sing with her sister/nieces as a trio again.

The ache in her heart became his.

"Mom and Dad and Aunt Abigail are parking the car. Margot Tremayne and this Archie person, whom I have not met yet, are in transit."

"That's seven. Is it the right number for this séance? It's not even." Dylan's gut fluttered at the prospect of blowing the ritual and conjuring the wrong ghosts, and then having to do it all over again.

"I think Aunt Abigail has asked Margot to sit this one out. But she and Archie are sort of attached at the hip, so she'll be here and monitor our vital signs from outside the circle."

Dylan nodded, his mouth suddenly too dry to speak.

You can bring me in, Anshar reminded him.

I want you kept a secret from Tiamat until the final moments.

Dylan felt a grunt of agreement from the ancestor of the gods.

Then his fears took a backseat as footsteps clanged on the metal stairs.

"The cavalry has arrived." Celia pulled away from him.

He grabbed her hand and pulled her close again, claiming a sweet and lingering kiss to fortify himself against the coming ordeal.

"I'm not going anywhere," she said when they finally separated.

"Remember that when you meet your girls and they beg you to join them."

The cloying odor of burning frankincense rose from compressed cones that Aunt Abby lit while she chanted in some ancient language I did not understand. I didn't even want to turn the ceremony into song.

Mom's mouth worked as if she too was trying to make sense of it all.

My entire body itched with the need to move, but not with the need to sing.

"This is wrong," I said too loudly.

Mom's body sagged in relief. I knew she agreed with me.

Not willing to put up with this nonsense any longer, I stood from my cross-legged seat on the floor, thus breaking the circle. Dylan leaned back, bracing himself with his arms. He breathed easier than he had a moment ago.

"Do you realize what you've done?" Aunt Abby snarled.

"Yes, I do. This is all wrong. Neither Brittney nor Joycelyn will respond to... to..." I waved around the entire crypt. "To this."

"I agree," Mom said. She rolled to her feet awkwardly, using Dad's shoulder to brace her balance. She hadn't had weeks of intense dance training like I had to ease the process. "My girls spoke American English, not this ancient mumbo jumbo. And they were both allergic to incense." She coughed and sneezed to emphasize the choking mist that filled the underground chamber.

"And they were both claustrophobic," Dad added, climbing to his feet stiffly. I knew he had arthritis developing in his knees. Now we all knew it.

"Stop and think a moment before we start again," Aunt Abigail protested. "Tiamat has control over the girls. She originated in ancient Sumer. She spoke a nearly forgotten language that Dylan has partially resurrected. She had frankincense and other trance inducing..."

"We want to entice the spirits of my sisters to join me. All you are doing is reinforcing Mummy's hold over them. We need to take this outside, around a pool, with the scent of barbequed hot dogs and potato salad and beer. That was their favorite thing to do. Come on, Dylan. I think I need to do this alone, with just you as my guide. The rest of you can go back to bed."

I pulled Dylan to his feet and led him up the iron staircase that creaked and clanked with every step. Hadn't I read somewhere, somewhen, that paranormals were repelled by iron? I certainly didn't like the feel of it against my hand. Maybe that was just the cold and rusty dampness that lingered on the railing. Maybe it was poisoning my siren blood.

I didn't care. All I needed at that moment was cold night air freshened by an offshore breeze to clear my lungs of that nasty crypt.

Mom and Dad followed close on our heels. Archie and Margot came upstairs more slowly. Aunt Abby stayed behind long enough to extinguish the candles and incense.

"I have a pool at my house," Margot said simply. "You two are welcome to use it, but I don't know that I'm up for a barbeque party this late." She yawned and leaned her head on Archie's shoulder. He looked sixteen, fresh-faced and immature. But I guess that was just his augmentation and inside he was mature enough to attract a sophisticated conductor and composer. Somehow, I'd never thought the musical director for Bryant Thomas Productions was into boy toys.

"Tomorrow night, I'll host the pool party at your house, if you don't mind, Margot," Dad said "Somehow I don't think the phase of the moon has anything to do with how the girls will respond."

"But... but..." Aunt Abby protested. The streetlights from the church's parking lot cast odd shadows against her thin face, making her appear almost skeletal.

I shuddered and strained to banish that image.

"We'll invite Bryant too," Mom said. "He'll have to bring his daughter and I can play with her. Too bad Janet Dryer won't be here. She's scheduled to fly in to Portland just before we travel to the mouth of the Columbia River in three weeks. We'll make do. Brittney and Joycelyn didn't know her so she isn't necessary to entice them out of the netherworld."

"And bring the genie," Archie said.

"Fine with me. I'll make the potato salad and light the grill if you all bring the rest." Margot yawned again. "See you at seven." She tugged on Archie's hand and they disappeared into the shadows. I thought I caught a glimpse of them necking in the parking lot beside her car. They obviously had more important things to do tonight than participate in this half-assed séance.

I wondered if I could sneak up to Dylan's room tonight after Mom and Dad fell asleep.

When this is all over, he whispered to me. *When we can take our time and not have other peoples' schedules ruling us.*

~

Thursday was a bitch of a day concentrating on dance and staging in the theater, quite a different situation from endless repeats of the same steps in the rehearsal halls. The floor was different, the perspective was different. I had to concentrate on where the cameras stood. They were inert today, without even operators to swivel them, just there, silent sentinels to remind us of the wider audience of television viewers.

Wednesday would have been better for a séance if Aunt Abby had staged it right. I'd spent most of that day with Gaylord and a vocal coach. Piece of cake for me, a grueling grind for him.

Now we reversed strengths. I tried to capture some of his mood, reveling in the open freedom of the stage. Instead, all I could think about was how much Brittney and Joycelyn would have loved this competition, even from the sidelines, and how they would never get to enjoy it.

By the time I returned to the hotel, all I wanted was a shower and a nap. Mom was in the pool, Dad in the hot tub. The smell of saltwater, even though it was just an addition to the chlorine, pulled at me, begging me to join them. So I cleaned up, put on a swim suit and dove into the deep end where Mom frolicked. She played a game familiar to all of us: drop a penny then try to retrieve it with toes or mouth, never the easy way with fingers.

Ten minutes of stretching my body properly in water, and I switched to soaking with Dad. He had never been as strong a swimmer as the rest of us.

Then Dylan joined us. His long, lean body looked marvelous in swim trunks. I took a moment to appreciate his musculature. But he looked as beat as I felt.

"What's wrong?" I asked, as much to inform Dad of the problem as to ask the question out loud.

"Trolls on social media." He ducked his face in the water and scrubbed away his fatigue lines with his hands. "Remind me never to use publicist as my cover story ever again."

"Almost as bad as computer malware?" Dad asked.

"Worse. Malware just corrupts a computer. Trolls infect entire societies. One malicious adolescent becomes all wise and powerful because he decides contemporary dance needs ballet slippers rather than bare feet and therefore the entire show is bogus and inept. One hundred thousand viewers agreed with him just because he tweeted his mindless thoughts." This time he closed his eyes and rested the back of his head on the lip of the tub.

You aren't meeting my gaze. What's wrong?

You have to ask? In a couple of hours you and I will be marching into Never Neverland and trying to retrieve two ghosts who are tight in Mummy's grasp.

Yeah. That.

"Cut it out you two," Dad snarled. He didn't put a lot of menace into his words, just enough to hint that we were excluding him. "Not polite."

"You and Mom do it all the time," I returned.

"We are not as obvious about our private conversations." He huffed.

"Oh, yeah! Then how come every time you look at each other with that quiet intensity you excuse yourselves and retreat to your bedroom with the door locked?"

I shoved a splash at him.

He shoved the water back, but his aim was off—or maybe it wasn't —and a wave of water covered Dylan's reclining head.

He sat up startled and spluttering, He assessed the situation and used both hands to send water in two directions, drenching both of us.

Mom joined us and giggles ensued until the remaining contestants erupted from the hotel and joined us in our childish game.

Much too soon, the alarm on Dylan's phone waiting on one of the tables reminded us that we had an appointment.

CHAPTER 28

Dylan hummed the baritone line of the sheet music Celia plunked onto the picnic table on Margot Tremayne's flagstone patio. Old, sad memories flooded through him. A melancholy tune from World War I, sung on both sides of the trenches and barbed wire. A sentiment shared in multiple languages, each claiming it as their own. Timeless...

The aroma of hot dogs on the charcoal grill, burning tiki torches, and yeasty beer faded, to be replaced by fragrant pine, chestnuts, and Ma's alcoholic eggnog. His last Christmas at the cottage in Ireland before he had to send Ma to a home when it became too dangerous for her to live alone with her addled and mostly absent mind. This song, sung by a Welsh mine choir with a strong tenor soloist had played on the wobbly tape player in the background on that sadly memorable holiday and on the day six months later when Ma went away.

The same song had played on the same music device in hospital while he recovered from being nearly crushed in a car accident. Dylan's best friend, Jamie, had died instantly when he'd flipped his father's convertible into a ditch. Dylan had been twelve and Jamie fourteen. He could barely reach the pedals let alone drive the car safely.

The angels had sung that peaceful song while they tried to coax Dylan out of his body and into heaven to join Jamie. But they'd sung it in Enochian, a language he had to learn before he could speak it to gain entrance to the pearly gates.

He had awakened from his coma convinced he had to learn more languages in search of the elusive tongue of the angels.

"What's this?" he asked, not daring to read more than the opening lines of music. His blood ran cold, and his face flushed with conflicting memories.

"A favorite closing number we sang at almost every concert," Celia gulped and blinked away tears. "Mom sang it to us as a lullaby when we were growing up. She said it was the only thing that would soothe us when we were teething."

Jeannie cuddled Bryant Thomas sleepy baby against her shoulder. She'd grown fussy as the evening came to an end and she needed her blankie and her crib.

"Guardian angels God will lend thee, All through the night," Jeannie and Margot crooned the lullaby in perfect soprano/alto harmony. The baby settled, sticking her thumb in her mouth.

"Do I need to hire you as a full-time nanny?" Bryant asked as he took his daughter to a lounge chair at the end of the picnic table.

The women's voices soothed a baby and cut through the friendly chatter around the lovely pool—painted a deep blue rather than the ubiquitous turquoise.

The deep blue of the horizon beyond the Pearly Gates.

"I... I don't think I can do this," Dylan choked out. Then he remembered to close his mind to Celia's probing curiosity. But not before she sat down at the table directly across from him, forcing herself between her mother and Margot.

"'Twasn't yer fault, Dylan." Celia sounded as Irish as his Ma.

Everyone else stilled. The thrumming in Dylan's ears continued with the background of that pervasive song.

Darkness crowded his peripheral vision until all he could see was Celia, a pale spot of lightness in his darkened life.

"'Twas always my fault. Jamie said so." He let the soft lilt of his mother's native land ride heavily on his words.

"Jamie stole his father's car. Jamie was driving too fast and out of control. You were just along for the ride," she told him what she'd gleaned from his mind; what he knew but could never quite believe.

The nanos in his brain started to panic.

The angels had said he needed to join Jamie. Angels never lied.

Or did they?

His head and thoughts calmed down.

He grabbed Celia's hand and held on for dear life as he fought to remember every detail of that coma, all those years ago. He needed the true memory, not the nightmares born of survivor's guilt.

"Jamie was the son of a lord—who was the younger son of a more important lord and he was paid to stay in Ireland, away from polite English society. Therefore, Jamie was always right and no one, NO ONE was allowed to deny him what he wanted. And he wanted to drive the snazzy sports car his da could barely afford," Dylan said in a rush so he could get through it all before choking.

"Jamie's idea. Jamie's actions. He died, drowning in dirty ditch water because of his arrogance. You survived. The angels weren't ready to take you." Celia clutched his hands tighter.

"But the angels..."

"They spoke a language that some ancient astrologer made up in a drug induced vision," she finished the thought for him.

"John Dee left extensive writings on the nature of the language and the phonetic pronunciation. I learned it, though he never did. I deciphered it. I..."

"You can forget it."

"But how did I know what it was when I was twelve and in a coma?"

"Because you just remembered and shared with me that you learned about Queen Elizabeth's sixteenth century astrologer in school the week before the accident," Celia said. "Now you have to confront and banish Jamie's ghost just as I have to confront Brittney and Joycelyn and get them out of the StormMother's clutches."

Celia continued to hold his hand as her mother began singing that damned song, soft and lulling, a soothing counterpoint to the agony of his thoughts.

The others joined her, keeping their tones low, a gentle backdrop. Somehow more candles and torches sprang to life. Even the bloody genie in his clay lamp joined the song.

The world closed around him, them. Just he and Celia, their thoughts mingling, their blood flowing back and forth between them at the junction of their hands. All he could see was Celia, her pale face and hair a bright beacon leading him through the tangle of his memories and their purpose in summoning ghosts tonight.

She became a sparkling tower of strength, a defense against the darkness.

The surrounding blackness grew lighter, became a swirling mist that swallowed them.

~

Celia, where are you?

Hold my hand, love. Hold tight.

I'll never let you go!

I know.

With that thought I knew that Dylan and I walked, side by side, linked in mind and body. Together we could face anything. Even Mummy.

But first we had to dismiss a small dark blob oozing toward us from the side, slightly behind us; the place of a stalker seeking our visual blind spot.

Dylan noticed it first.

He's not worth the trouble of acknowledging, I whispered into his mind. *He's not happy unless he's making people miserable. Don't be his victim any longer.*

Victim?

Victim, Anshar, lounging in his clay lamp, echoed.

Dylan stiffened and turned slightly to face the vicious blob. *Begone, James! You were a parasite when alive. I'll not let you suck me dry again.*

The darkness shrank and faded, then oozed back to wherever it had come from.

I closed my mental eyes, seeking the direction we needed to go. This place of eternal mists had no up or down or front or back.

"Where are you?" I called with both my mind and voice, pushing magic into the words, going against everything Mom had taught me about control and remaining human.

And there stood the StormMother, tall and commanding, looming over us like a titan generated by roiling clouds. The mists became cresting waves, a strange and bizarre light turning their foamy crests into sharply defined prisms, as if every color ever conceived concentrated in those strips of light.

Mummy's vaguely ancient Greek draperies took on the same colors, mixing and separating at random. She held a trident, stolen from her lover Poseidon/Anshar/Fred. Her long, dark hair fanned out around her head in writhing tendrils, sometimes seaweed, sometimes eels, sometimes jets of curling water currents.

Wind and rain lashed us.

This was not the society matron who graced our family with her presence when she wanted something.

This was Tiamat, goddess of chaos, mother and center of all storms.

"You may not pass into my realm!" Her voice rebounded through my head and the thick air. "Your sisters are *mine!*"

Dylan took one step ahead of me, still tethered by the link in our minds and our hands. He'd banished his ghost along with his survivor's guilt. Here was the Hunter I knew hid beneath his frailties. This was the Hunter who wrestled werecrocs, and drowned werewolves to save me. Together we had banished a bubble gum monster. This was the man I'd fallen in love with.

"This is not your watery realm, Tiamat," he shouted defiantly into the wind.

Guardian angels stand beside thee, all through the night.

"We seek those who drift aimlessly in the afterlife. You have no power over us, or of them. Begone!" He held his free hand up, fingers making an arcane symbol I didn't recognize. But Tiamat did.

She screeched and waved her trident as a giant wave engulfed her. Outlined in the foaming water was a snarling, bearded, male face, Poseidon, or Anshar, or whatever name he chose at the beginning of time. Master of the waves, lover of storms, and in need of *his* trident.

All through the night.

The air stilled and dried.

My throat itched to lift my voice in a strong descant to the murmuring tune behind us. Anshar held the strong bass line, anchoring us all in the music. Up I soared, finding the third and fifth notes that harmonized and highlighted the melody. I picked out Mom's voice as she rose to match mine. Dad led the others along the melody, keeping them together and synchronized.

Sparkling light ahead of me caught my attention.

Two more voices joined the song, weak and wavering, unsure of the high notes and reluctant to drop into a low chord for emphasis.

My girls.

I matched them, bringing our trio back into tune.

The sparkles took form; red and blue rounding out my own pristine white. My casual capris and camp shirt had transformed into a pale performance gown of sequins and silk that molded and flowed elegantly around my body.

Still clinging to Dylan as a lifeline, I beckoned my girls to stand with me. They started forward, looked backward and then to each side, pausing in uncertainty.

"Come!" I begged them.

"Join us," Dylan pleaded.

"We need your help," I added.

Still they hesitated.

I sang to them again, and again, begging them to complete our trio. Joycelyn's voice cracked, straining to find the right note.

Brittney, always the follower, lost my guiding voice and took refuge in Joycelyn's jarring disharmony.

I clamped my hands over my ears. The notes were all wrong. This journey was all wrong. I lost touch with Dylan.

I was alone in the silent mist. I had no music left inside me to find my way home again.

CHAPTER 29

"Celia! Wake up Celia."

In the distance, Mike Fisher's commanding voice pulled Dylan out of his music-induced trance. Music: more powerful and illuminating than any drug John Dee drank to find the secret language of the angels.

Dylan lifted his chin from his chest and brought the real world back into focus. His Guild training took over and snapped him awake. The music no longer lingered in his head. Guilt no longer eroded his heart.

He looked around, assessing as many details as his augmentation allowed.

He no longer held Celia's hand. Her fingertips twitched and arched mere inches from his own. Desperate to reclaim her and the bond that bound them so tightly, he covered her hand with his own.

Slowly she lifted her head from the tabletop where she'd collapsed, blinking slowly, rhythmically until she grounded herself again.

Her fear that she'd lost her music, that Brittney and Joycelyn had taken it to the netherworld when they rejected her, filled him with a new and different kind of panic.

"Are you okay, Celia?" Jeannie wrapped her arms around her

daughter, pulling Celia's head to her own shoulder as she would a child.

Mike hovered nearby, rubbing Celia's arms, trying to infuse warmth into her.

"Dylan?" she finally captured his gaze, needing him as much as she needed her family.

"I'm okay. Are you?" he said, trying to penetrate any lingering fog in her mind.

"I... I think so. Where... where are they?"

He knew she meant her sisters, not the rest of the gathered band of supernatural adventurers.

"They went back," he answered. He had to put an immediate wall up against her gut-wrenching sadness.

"Not completely," Archie added. He stood behind Margot, one hand on her shoulder. "I seem to have developed an affinity for ghosts after my adventures at the Vienna Opera House. I sensed their presence when you confronted them. They are still around, just trying to avoid attention."

"Then let's leave them to stew in their own conflicting emotions for a while," Abby said. She blew out a fat candle on the end of the table that had lost its brilliance and smelled of fresh sea mist.

The others extinguished the rest of the fragrant wax columns, turned on the patio lights and started gathering the detritus of the barbeque. Bryant juggled his sleeping baby and a diaper bag. Clearly the evening's activities were over.

"What day is it?" Celia asked. She clutched Dylan's hand more tightly.

"Thursday," her mother replied.

"You still have two full days of rehearsals to get your bearings before Sunday's show," her father added.

Celia groaned. "Mr. Thomas, is there any way you can ensure that I get sent home Sunday night? I don't think I have the strength to continue with the competition."

"No." The group gasped.

Dylan smiled to himself. He understood why she'd asked. But he also knew that the group outrage meant Celia was closer to winning than she thought.

"I will not rig the outcome of any of my shows," Bryant Thomas insisted. "If you choose to fall flat on your face and sing off key, I will mark you down on points far enough to make sure you can't recover enough to continue."

"Celia would never do that," Jeannie insisted.

"Dad, have we signed the contract for the recording offer?" Celia shifted in her place on the uncomfortable bench.

Dylan wanted to move to her side, but her parents occupied those places.

"The contract came through my email this morning. I haven't had time to read it yet."

"Forward it to my legal department," Bryant said. He took out his phone, one handed, and made a note. "I can't have one of my contestants signing a phony offer or a badly one-sided deal. It's in her contract that any offers that come in during the competition have to be cleared by my office."

"And I recommend that you don't sign anything until after the final show to see if anything better shows up," Margot added. "Or you can negotiate a bigger advance."

"That's good advice, Celia. Please don't throw the show, and don't sign, even if it is a good and honest deal," Dylan said, tugging on her hand a bit to make sure she listened.

"I guess." She looked at each of the attendees, including the genie in his lamp. "If I'm going to dance and sing and be bright and cheerful tomorrow morning, I need to sleep now."

I'll sleep better if you lie beside me and hold me tightly.

One look at protective Mike and Jeannie told Dylan he'd get to do no more than sit in a chair beside the bed and hold her hand until she drifted off.

As she had held his hand when she healed him with her song.

～

Two more days of intense rehearsals. I danced with Gaylord, I sang, I ate what was put in front of me, I slept upon command (alone) then did it all over again.

As was his habit, Bryant Thomas made his rounds from rehearsal to rehearsal, taking a note here, a correction there. Bucking us up with encouragement when we flagged and laughing at our practical jokes—especially those where he was the victim. Halloween had passed, but leftover ghoulish props sprang about on bungee cords, startling the unwary.

I found myself laughing in near hysteria.

"Exhaustion is part of the process. There will be times when you have to put on your smiles, bandage your bleeding toes and blistered heels and continue on through six or eight performances a week while rehearsing the next show in between," He warned us as he picked plastic goo out of his hair. "Laugh whenever you can and carry it in your heart to share with your audience."

And then he shooed us away to our next round of interviews and costume fittings.

I got good scores Sunday night and had mixed feelings about staying or being sent home. And because I thought I no longer cared if I stayed or went home, I'd relaxed and rather enjoyed the performances, a song and dance routine with Gaylord, another with the group of all the remaining contestants and a solo song. I chose "You'll Never Walk Alone", from *Carousel* to show off my dynamic range and the emotions of grief. I blasted the audience with anger, sank into despair, and settled on quiet fortitude. Perfect tens for the number. A full performance, but not as grueling as singing for an entire evening in a nightclub.

The judges commented that because I was more comfortable with the routines, I'd performed better than ever. I was amazed anyone had noticed.

Just before the results, Bryant Thomas announced another change in our routine.

"Next week the remaining three in each category will each perform their audition piece, but with added choreography or song."

I almost gagged. *Old Devil Moon*, when sung properly was as demanding as any aria. Adding dance to it could break me.

"You'll have your original partners to lean on," Mr. Thomas added. "But this will have to be a chance to show off what you have learned during the weeks of the competition." He sat down again, waving to the host to continue with the elimination.

Paul grinned at me from the sidelines. He'd ensure that the choreography was as memorable, and as challenging as the song.

The remaining competitors in each category lined up, holding hands in a chain, bound together by two months of working closely together. I didn't want anyone to go home. After tonight we had only two more shows to survive before the final determination; one dancer and one singer would go to New York and take up roles in Margot Tremayne's musical.

On Broadway.

With the reminder of what was at stake, I wanted to win. I wanted to win so badly I could taste the glory and the triumph. And I wanted Gaylord to win the dancer competition because he and I danced very well together, and I wanted that partnership on Broadway. And I wanted to win so that I could give Dylan a home base in the linguistic melting pot of New York for his work as a Hunter with the Guild.

Then the spotlight began to rove among us as Little Miss Bouncy read through her dramatic lines recapping tonight's performances and the judges' comments.

My tummy clenched with nerves.

The spotlight paused on Gaylord and me.

"You are safe!" the host proclaimed.

I nearly fainted in relief.

At that point I didn't care who stayed and who would join us next week in the semi-finals. I was in the top three.

Something sparkly in the upper balcony caught my attention. Red and blue sequins. Did my sisters truly applaud me from the audience?

I hoped so.

But then I spotted Mummy, aisle seat, first row, second balcony. If my girls were really here tonight, they were still firmly in her grip. They'd sing with her on the night of the full moon, not with me.

~

"Damnit! I can't play when it's this cold," Margot Tremayne wailed as Dylan entered the big rehearsal hall, ten minutes before the contestants were due to arrive.

"Let me play the music. You direct. It's what you do best," Archie Driscoll said in a voice designed to soothe. The Hunter newly arrived from quelling ghosts and ghouls and things that go bump in the night in Vienna, massaged Margot's gloved hands.

Dylan noted the thin, white, supple leather that covered her hands well past the wrist. His augmented eyes realized that those gloves compressed as well as warmed, like a person with arthritis would wear.

"Excuse me, Dr. Tremayne, I need you to sign off on this week's ad campaign," Dylan interrupted the strangely intimate moment.

Archie gave him a one-fingered salute. One Hunter acknowledging another; equals on this paranormal playing field.

"It's not supposed to be this cold in L.A. Even in November," Margot continued her litany of grief. "I made my home here so I wouldn't have to put up with the cold."

"It's only in the mid-fifties," Dylan protested. His Irish blood found the day quite balmy. Why, the breeze of ten miles per hour with gusts to twenty, hardly qualified as a wind let alone a cold one.

Margot speared him with a fearsome gaze.

He made a point of not cringing. Instead he held forth his tablet with a stylus for her signature.

She cringed as her fingers wrapped around the digital pen. "I can't do this today. I trust you, Dylan. Just go ahead and put out whatever ads you need to in order to satisfy Bryant." She withdrew her hand and placed it back where Archie could continue his deft massage.

"Sorry, Margot. This week's show is all about your ghostly

musical. You have to approve every word of media release ahead of time."

She exchanged a pitiful look with Archie. "Okay, love. Dylan, you aren't seeing this." He grabbed the stylus and scribbled a good approximation of her signature on the bottom of the documents, then he initialed in three places.

"If I didn't just witness this, I'd say that our resident musical genius just signed these," Dylan sighed, amazed at the brilliance of the forgery.

"You didn't just witness anything," Archie reminded him.

"I got what I came for. Now, go back to work so we can get on with staging the opening group number to the now infamous ghost waltz." He left humming the haunting lilt of the finale of the musical that had run for two years off Broadway and was now being revived on Broadway.

As he walked down the hall toward the exit, Celia and the other contestants and their professional partners wandered toward him in a giggling group. She smiled at him then turned her attention back to her companions. *Love you!* she sent to him.

He smiled and nodded to the group, working colleagues as far as they were concerned. Seeing Celia preparing for rehearsal sent his imagination to visualizing her in the lead of the musical. Not a hard image to hold at all.

And he wanted it for her. Badly. She belonged on Broadway. Her vivacity would light up any stage, even without magic.

The image of Margot's pain remained with him. A gifted musician, she'd nearly lost everything to a demon attack years ago. Only recently had she come back from the brink with Archie's loving care and her own fortitude breaking through mental, and physical barriers. Banishing the piano demon once and for all didn't hurt either.

Now the unnaturally cold weather played havoc with her pain and therefore her mind.

All over the world freak storms claimed the lives of the homeless, of fishermen and sailors, of timber workers, anyone exposed to the elements. Floods, fires, and power outages claimed more lives.

The StormMother's work.

If she viewed humanity as an infestation destroying her world, then she was making a good start on clearing out some of the excess population. The plague had taken a good many more. He shivered in memory at the ever-mounting statistics until a vaccine had become viable and available.

But at what cost to the survivors?

He began working through the ancient spell he'd found in the cuneiform texts. Neither the original language nor his translation flowed in the correct meter. He was missing something.

Forward on the left, touch, step side right, three counts. Backward on the left, together, side on the left, another three counts. A waltz box. I knew that step.

My partner released his grip on my left hand and swung me under his arm until I could reach for the hand of the next man in line. Repeat with the new partner.

We did this four times until we were back to our original partners. All the while, the professional dancers and singers wove through us in their own routine. I couldn't watch them for clues as their steps didn't match ours. And neither could any of the other contestants.

The choreographer, Bryant Thomas, drilled us in this simple pattern until even the clumsiest of the non-dancers got it right twice in a row. For once that was not me receiving the brunt of the dance master's stern criticism.

"You've been here nine weeks, surely some of these steps must have sunk into your tired brains. Now repeat that chain again!" Mr. Thomas shouted.

Margot grinned from behind the upright piano. She held the music in her gloved hands while Archie played the *Ghost Waltz*. He hadn't been introduced and so remained anonymous to all but me. He really was a good pianist, drawing nuances of the waltz out of the rudimentary instrument.

"Next step," Bryant called. "Please play it, Mr. Driscoll. The rest of you listen closely."

Archie rattled some jazzy chords and upped the tempo. Interesting. The recording I'd practiced with hadn't included this variation.

I liked it. From the grins on the faces of the other contestants and the pros who filled in the numbers to the group routine, I guessed they liked it too.

"Singers, follow my steps. Dancers, consult with Dr. Tremayne on how she wants the phrasing of the lyrics," Mr. Thomas directed.

And so we continued, swapping singing and dancing roles, pushing our muscles and pulling notes out of the depths of our souls.

This opening number for the semi-final performance would be a showstopper. And if we didn't get it right, the head judge would note it and consider it in our final scores.

By the end of the three-hour rehearsal I felt like I'd learned the three minute twenty-five second number. Despite the dropping temperatures outside, we were all drenched in sweat.

Only a three-minute routine you say? A lifetime on stage. And then I had two hours with Paul working on choreography for *Old Devil Moon*, and tonight two more hours with Mitch, a tap dancer contestant. We'd drawn a menacing jazz number from the middle of the ghostly musical, a lot of rapid steps and jarring notes to demonstrate the fear generated by the haunted mansion setting of the play.

This was not going to be an easy week of rehearsals. Good thing I had plenty to distract me from the upcoming confrontation with Mummy.

I just wished I'd been able to pry my sisters out of her clutches. I didn't even have the sequins the girls had dripped like breadcrumbs to hang on to.

Breadcrumbs!

Damn, I'd thrown them back at my sisters so they couldn't find their way back, or I couldn't follow them to be with my girls.

Double damn. I should have seen the breadcrumbs for what they were.

Instead of joining the crew for lunch in the canteen, I dashed over to costuming. "Millie, is there any way you can add red and blue sequins to my "Devil Moon" costume? And sew them loosely so some of them come off?"

The venerable costume designer gave me the stink-eye that would rival Mummy any day for intimidation.

"I know Bryant Thomas of old. And I know his weird taste for things that go bump in the night, so I'll do something. But from what little I've heard, and more I've guessed, you'll need to drop more than a few white sequins from your ghostly waltz number. Why don't I just secrete a handful in a pocket and you can blow them toward the audience as you exit, like blowing someone a kiss." Millie was much more amenable than I thought.

So I hastened back to the canteen to grab a yogurt and a ham sandwich and a cola and some extra bottles of water to take to the afternoon session.

CHAPTER 30

"I need someone to go to the craft store and buy me a whole big bunch of sequins," Celia announced as she burst into Abby's office without invitation or warning from Marci out front.

Dylan sensed her bewilderment at the wild array of maps, whiteboards, and flip charts strewn around the big room. Even Abby's beloved, pristine desktop was littered with weather reports and tide charts.

Celia stopped and stared at the disarray. Dylan didn't think she spared an eyeblink for the presence of her parents, Archie and Margot, and Bryant Thomas. The portable keyboard in the corner where Margot played a dozen variations of a simple, rhythmic piece she interpreted from his translation of the cuneiform text seemed normal and organized compared to the rest of the chaos.

"You realize this is just a mnemonic teaching song, don't you? John has ten bushels of barley and Mary has three bushels of wheat. How much can they sell the grain for?" Margot chanted then added a series of complex chords to the choppy tune.

Dylan was the only one who laughed.

Then, since he was closest, he took a moment to uncover the genie in his clay pot on the credenza under the window. "Do you have anything interesting to say about that, Anshar?"

All he heard in response was a snore. The fluttering bustle around them seemed to bore the supernatural creature.

"Sequins?" Jeannie asked, moving from a flip chart filled with arcane symbols that might be ancient music notation, to stand in front of her daughter. "Whatever for? There's going to be so much wind on the promontory I don't think sequins will stay anchored to anything." She tilted her reading glasses up to rest on top of her head like a hairband while she scrutinized Celia.

"That's just the point, Mom. Brittney and Joycelyn have been leaving behind a trail of sequins, like breadcrumbs. And I threw them back at the girls, I rejected their offering of a trail to find them, or for them to find me. We need them on our side of the ritual to make it work. I need to entice them back with my own breadcrumbs."

"On it," Bryant said, pulling out his phone and texting someone. Then he cocked his head and looked puzzled. "Millie says you've already requested sequins on this week's costumes."

"That's only a start. I need a lot more. I think we should all carry them to the ritual while I just blow them around a bit at the performances."

"Okay. I'll have Millie order a case of each color and put it on Abby's bill." He grinned as he texted some more. Fortunately, his back was to Abby.

"Now just a minute, Bryant…"

"Millie will get them wholesale. Better than emptying out the local craft store.

"Well, I'm glad you all are enjoying this. Frankly, I'm scared spitless!" Celia stamped her foot and turned to leave.

Dylan caught her arm before her mother could stop her.

"We're all scared, Celia," Mike called from his post beside Bryant at a blow up of channel charts tacked to the wall.

"If this doesn't work, the world is going to drown in sea water or dust or fire and ash. I've already got a full dozen agents in Australia countering fire imps where they can. Usually we need only two to cover the entire continent," Abby said in a voice as close to soothing as Dylan had ever heard.

"I'm... I'm sorry. I have to get back to rehearsals." A tear glistened in Celia's eyes. "I don't feel like I'm doing anything important."

"The contest is important, dear." Jeannie took Celia's arm and shook her head in a warning to Dylan not to interfere. "While you are competing, you are keeping Mummy distracted. She needs you to win. Therefore, she is keeping L.A. safe for you."

"Can't prove it by me," Margot grumbled, putting her hands into heated gloves, the kind used by football fans in Wisconsin.

Celia paused and slipped away from her mother. With two flicks of the electronic piano buttons, she added a primitive drum to Margot's teaching song. It echoed a heartbeat.

"Oh!" Margot's eyes brightened. "That's what it needed."

Celia returned to her mother's side, a satisfied twinkle in her eyes.

"We are relatively safe, anyway. We're in a temporary sanctuary while we plot and plan." Jeannie concluded her reassurance. She closed the door behind her as she led Celia away for some private mom/daughter time.

"L.A. might be safe, but Fisherman's Wharf in San Francisco just broke away and is floating down the bay," Archie grumbled, looking up from his phone.

"What will the StormMother do if Celia loses the competition?" Dylan asked. "Will she gather Celia to her bosom in commiseration and try to turn her disappointment to rage? Or will she give up on her as a failed siren who won't even use her magic to win?"

He hated to think about how Tiamat might react to reversal.

"There is no predicting how Mummy will react. Logic is not part of her makeup," Mike said, hand paused above his chart, pen ready to strike but not quite close enough.

Use her lack of logic against her. She is chaos. Give her only order, Anshar said from deep within his pot. So he had been listening after all.

~

I had a plan. Well, more like a few guidelines rather than a real plan. And I had a goal. I wanted... no, *needed* to win this competition no matter what Mummy and my sisters had planned.

"You know, Dylan, I *like* people. I have no reason to join Mummy's crusade to eliminate them all."

"Good. I'd like to be around for a while." He smiled and bent to kiss my cheek. Then he slapped my bottom playfully to urge me out the door of my trailer and toward the stage door.

I could get used to him being around all of the time. Even our emotional and mental link didn't make up for having him close enough to touch and hold and kiss and... Well, we'd get to the more part later.

Bryant Thomas had changed the choreography of the opening number enough to ensure that I was the last one to exit. On the last lingering note from the cello I turned and blew a handful of fairy dust —white sequins—to the audience. In my mind I sent a plea to my sisters for them to return to me, apologizing for my earlier failure to understand their offerings.

Of course, between numbers, the stagehands swept up the sparkling offerings. The bits of decoration could send a misplaced step out from under a performer and wreak havoc with their ankles. But they left them in a tiny pile against the wall behind the proscenium arch, as instructed.

As I ran off stage from the *Devil Moon* number, I trickled blue and red sequins behind me as I fled the stage for my trailer and the final costume change of the night.

Dylan was there to help with zippers and hooks and eyes. "Is it working?" he asked as he gave me the once over and nodded approval of my slinky emerald green skirt and bias draped sleeveless top.

"I can't tell. I haven't seen Mummy or the girls in the audience." I braced a hand on his arm while I bent to adjust the elastic of my green character shoes. They had more pointed toes than I liked but gave a decent illusion of classy heels that I could actually dance in.

"I'll be in the audience, probably beneath the overhang of the first balcony, wherever they can fit me in. Either your dad or I will escort you back here at the end. We don't want you alone right now, only ten days from the ritual." He gave my tiny, veiled hat, not much more than a cap, a tweak to make sure it sat correctly and wouldn't come off during a set of rapid chaîné turns.

No sequins to worry about for this number. I needed to concentrate hard on nailing the steps with the tricky syncopation. In the haunted mansion musical this piece of fear and anxiety closed the second act and was crucial to the plot. I needed Margot to notice me as a contender for the lead role on Broadway—presuming we all survived the ritual.

Dark stage, my mark, a tiny X in glowing green tape showed me where and how to stand at stage right, and the music began and the lights came on, dim and vague. Mist from a fog machine swirled about my ankles and rose to my knees in a creepy illusion of the mysterious moors surrounding the haunted house. I almost wished I hadn't read *Wuthering Heights* last summer.

And then I took my first hesitant step forward, drifted in a wary circle and moved toward center stage, searching my surroundings for danger. I sang the choppy lyrics reciting the reasons for my fear. My partner mimicked me from stage left. We bumped into each other and both screamed. The music took over and we jazzed our way through the unsettling number.

I focused on my feet, my voice, and my partner, blending us all into performance.

Only when the music stopped abruptly, and we took our bows to a standing ovation did I have time to look up. My eyes sought and found Dylan right away. He stood in the shadows beneath the first balcony overhang just as he'd said he would. He raised his eyes. I followed his direction with my gaze and froze.

There, first row center stood Mummy wearing my white, sequined performance gown, (or a damned good replica) flanked by my sisters in their red and blue dresses. None of them looked happy. None of them applauded.

And then they turned their backs on me.

Rainwater dripped from the catwalk onto my face but nowhere else.

CHAPTER 31

After the announcement that I had top scores for the evening and would compete in the final the next week, I felt like I needed to run. Run away from the bright lights and cacophony of noise I couldn't control; run away from people clawing at me, needing to touch me; run away from Mummy and the chaos that followed her.

But I couldn't. I had to stay and smile for the cameras and the media people thrusting microphones in my face. I had to stand still when Bryant Thomas put his arm around my shoulders while cameras churned pixels into images. Then I had to accept Mom and Dad kissing my cheek and holding me tight.

"Mummy was here," I whispered into Dad's ear while he clutched me too tightly. Dylan, of course, already knew. He knew everything about me. I was okay with that. But right at that moment I needed, desperately, some alone time.

And there he was in his professional head of publicity role, clearing out the dozens of extra people in the Green Room, punching the send button on his ever-present tablet so that each person with a press pass received a package of statements and canned interview clips.

Within a moment or two the room emptied, leaving only Dylan and me.

"Let's get you out of that costume and into something comfortable. Then I'm taking you out to eat and not telling anyone where we are going. When was the last time you ate, anyway?" With one hand on my back he ushered me back to my trailer.

"I think I had a yogurt between dress rehearsal and the show."

"You think?"

"That might have been yesterday."

"My point exactly. You need fuel and then early to bed. Tomorrow you start work on the finale."

"What about...?"

"Hush." He kissed me to silence my thoughts.

"We'll worry about the ritual later. Plenty of time. Friday of next week."

"Black Friday. The day after Thanksgiving I'm going to be standing on a frigid jetty in an Arctic wind with ten-foot waves crashing around me instead of shopping. I'd rather be shopping."

My shiver of revulsion had to telegraph as well as our link how much I hated the crowds in a mall. Give me a nice little boutique in old town wherever or the internet any day rather than the mall.

"We'll worry about that next week. Which do you prefer, steak or spaghetti?"

My stomach growled telling me he was right. But at that moment the thought of food churned in my gut.

"Shrimp scampi and pasta primavera it is, unless a veggie omelet wins out before we get to the restaurant," he replied as he shoved me into my trailer and closed the door behind me. "You have ten minutes before I come in and get you."

Dinner was fun. Dylan and I talked about his years of growing up on the fringes of Northern Ireland, trapped between Catholics and Protestants. "Mom was Anglican, a Prot, and got me into a good Cathedral school and choir. We sang in Latin as well as Old English with a smattering of the Gaelic. I guess that's part of what got me started in my field."

"I don't think growing up in Cleveland trapped between normal and paranormal felt much different. I did all the usual things, sang in the choir, cheered the football team, starred in the school musicals, but we didn't go to church as a family—though I think Dad went on his own to a mid-week service and men's Bible study sometimes."

Dylan looked at his plate and the remnants of his own veal parmesan.

"You never talk about your father," I murmured, twirling my fork idly around a chunk of broccoli.

"He died in a mining accident in Wales when I was four. Mom fled back to her parents' cottage with me. A car accident took both my grandparents when I was fifteen." A solid stone wall went up around his mind. I couldn't penetrate memories that had to be painful.

There were other ways to pry information out of him, through backdoors and side issues.

"Is that why your name is the Welsh spelling rather than the Irish?" Curiosity burned in the back of my throat like a note that needed to be sung but hadn't found its mates in the chord yet.

He nodded, his eyes looking more than a bit moist.

"And the McQuilleran name? That's Irish."

"Hunters change their identity every ten years or so, certainly after an augmentation. I couldn't quite let go of 'Dylan' though. It's only one of two things I have left of me da." He fell into the lilting accent of his youth.

"And the other thing you have of your father?" I already knew that Dylan had a rich baritone voice, maybe he'd inherited that from his Welsh connections. Every collier in Wales seemed to sponsor its own choir. Music was so deeply embedded in their culture it oozed out of the pores of every one of them I'd met.

Before he could answer or I could voice my next dozen questions, a gaggle of middle-aged ladies approached our booth with shy caution. I raised a genuine smile at them. I'd learned that posture from other fans over the weeks.

"Excuse me," a tall brunette of ample proportions said as she clutched her shoulder purse tightly to her abdomen like a talisman, or armor. "Are you Celia Fisher from the *Here I Come, World* show?"

"Yes I am, and no I cannot reveal the results of tonight's show." We recorded from five to seven for live broadcast on the east coast. These ladies were about five minutes away from the opening number on the local channel.

"You're our favorite," another lady said. She thrust a clean restaurant napkin at me. "Can I get your autograph?"

"Of course." I found a pen in my clutch and signed five napkins with appropriate flourishes.

"Good luck tonight!" They called as they dashed into the bar section. Three big screen TVs were all tuned to the opening music and flashing clips from previous shows. My fans joined a crowd, all eager to watch. They announced my presence in excited voices with fluttery hands.

That seemed to trigger a flurry of open staring and furtive whispers from the other patrons.

"I knew this place was too public." Dylan signaled our waitress for the check—she hovered near the bar glancing back and forth between the TV and me for confirmation of my identity.

"Am I going to have to get used to this?" I asked, placing my knife and fork onto my plate in precise alignment—my uncharacteristic neatness felt like a new defense against Mummy. I stared longingly at the last piece of shrimp in a nest of pasta and gooey sauce. Then I defied Dylan's urging to leave and stabbed the shrimp, swirled it in the sauce and popped it into my mouth. I chewed it lovingly on the way back to the car.

"Yeah, I think you will have to get used to being noticed in the future, especially if you do more TV. Broadway will kind of hide you from mainstream America, but after next week you'll be hopping from network interview to variety shows to commercials."

"You sound like you know I'm going to win." I stopped in the middle of the parking lot, suddenly aware of how much backstage manipulation actually went on.

"I don't have insider information. I just have observations and sensitive hearing to nuances in discussions. Margot is rewriting the starring role in the musical to fit your voice. And Archie is arguing with her that she has to leave the vocal range where it is so someone less talented can sing it on the road show or when your contract runs out and you move on to other roles."

"Oh."

Fireworks went off in my brain as my tummy bounced with joy.

Then it all fell flat as a new spate of rain dumped on my head. "How will Mummy react?"

"Don't know and don't care. I'm only planning on making an airtight ritual that will control her."

Then I realized that the scintillating spots strewn across the parking lot were not raindrops refracting in the streetlights. They were sequins. Hundreds and hundreds of sequins scattered in every direction.

I bent to inspect them closer. These were no ordinary costume decorations, crenelated plastic discs with a metallic sheen. They were tiny bits of sea glass in a rare shade of green akin to the color of my eyes. I couldn't walk into a craft store to find these gems.

They had come from Mummy in pure defiance of the breadcrumbs my sisters had left me.

Dylan walked into his office cubicle Monday morning, ready to begin work on the last round of press releases before the end of the competition. He had three dancers and three singers in contention for starring roles in Margot Tremayne's musical. She'd retitled the work *Manor Hauntings*, reset it on the Yorkshire moors, and moved it back in time from contemporary and horrific to early Victorian—beastly costumes to dance in but at least the ladies didn't have hoop skirts—and she'd given the entire piece a feeling of Bronte gloom lightened by a great love story with a sort of happy ending. If you could call the grief-stricken groom committing suicide to join his bride in the afterlife a happy ending.

But then the secondary leads, best friends of the primaries, stepped forward with their own love story and danced and sang in the moonlight.

Only the *Ghost Waltz* remained untouched and the new ending had him near tears when he watched a recording of an early rehearsal.

Celia in either female role would leave the audience breathless.

Only he and Bryant knew that the grand prize of the competition had been expanded as Margot got to know all the contestants and appreciate their talents.

Whistling a jaunty jig, he set his laptop down and turned to fetch a cup of coffee. The rising sun crept through the open blinds on the windows and set his cubicle ablaze in green light. Like the parking lot last night, Mummy had gifted him with a taunt that he would fail at the ritual. Sequins littered the blinds, the floor, his desktop and his chair. Everywhere he looked he saw sea green, like he was underwater.

Except that today's offering were ordinary sequins, not precious sea glass. Only the strange color was odd. He'd never seen this shade of green sequins except by custom order designed to match a special, and expensive costume.

He found a large zip lock bag in the kitchenette with the coffee maker. Carefully and meticulously he collected every single one of the sequins, making sure he neither bent, nor broke any one of them.

Sequins everywhere. In my shoes. In my coffee cup. In my bed! All week long I found sea green sequins littering my life.

This time I saved every damn one of them, even crawling around under my bed in the middle of the night, which didn't please Lisa much after she moved back in while prepping for the final show which would feature all of the contestants eliminated over the course of the show.

Mummy never did anything for fun. She always had an agenda, I just had to figure it out.

Then on Thursday morning when I sat on the floor of the rehearsal hall to change shoes, I found a single red and a single blue sequin in the mix.

The world stilled around me. A week ago, I had summoned my sisters' ghosts and pleaded with them to support me.

A week is a long time in the real world. Who knew how long it felt like in the other world?

I checked the clock on the wall above the music station. Paul would arrive in ten minutes to go over my "free style" number, a solo piece involving both song and dance meant to dazzle the audience and the judges. Later we'd work on a revamping of our "worst" performance during the course of the show to demonstrate how much I'd improved. The opening group number was a piece of cake meant to give every single contestant in the original line-up fifteen seconds under the spotlight. Remembering when to stand still so the others could shine was the hardest part.

Ten minutes to convince Bryant Thomas I needed to rearrange the entire show.

I burst into his office unannounced and breathless from my run across the studio lot.

Fortunately, he was alone with his nose buried in a pile of papers that looked like resumes with head shot photos. Maybe applicants for his next show.

"I need ninety seconds of solo time!"

"Explain." He scooped the papers into a neat stack, tapped them against the desk to even them out and then placed them face down to his left.

I dumped the shoe full of sequins in the middle of the desk.

He raised an eyebrow in question. "I see I'm not the only one receiving Mummy's attention."

"Look at them closely." I held my breath. I didn't have a lot of time but in this case showing him was easier than explaining.

He fanned the one hundred plus bits of sparkle into a single layer.

"One red and one blue."

"After a week of nothing but sea green. Joycelyn and Brittney are trying to communicate without Mummy realizing it. I need to let them know I understand the meaning."

"I don't have ninety additional seconds to give you."

"But... but..."

"But you can change your free-style. Clear it with Paul and get the music to Margot."

"All I need is Archie playing solo piano, muted and in the distance."

"Have the experts handle it. I have other things to do."

"May I make changes with my costume?"

"Clear it with Millie. I will not risk my life approaching her with last minute changes. If she quits on me, I lose the opportunity of an Emmy nomination. And she will draw blood from the most unpleasant of places." He hunched over protecting his abdomen from a metaphorical attack.

I could live with that.

"I'll sew a thousand green sequins in place by myself if I have to."

"You may have to."

CHAPTER 32

Dylan watched Celia from the pool deck as she used a hot glue gun to affix sequins to a piece of fabric with a peel off paper backing. He guessed there was a design drawn on the paper that showed through the fabric. In his milling around the studio, including the costume department, he'd learned a few things about decorating ball gowns, like prefabricated glittering, fragile, designs that could be assembled separately, then sewn onto the gown at the last minute. Later the sequins could be removed intact and the gown and the trim repurposed.

The lights were out in the other rooms of the residence hotel. Celia's parents had moved to another room for the week now that the other contestants had returned for the finale. Celia had roommates again rather than hovering chaperones.

Dylan tapped on the glass sliders.

Celia startled and looked around, eyes wide and wary.

Then their link took hold and she smiled before her gaze focused on him.

Warmth filled him with a quiet joy.

He pointed upward toward his own private room.

Carefully she set down her project and unplugged the glue gun.

Then she slipped out the sliders without bothering with shoes or a sweater.

L.A. had returned to more normal weather these last two days. Mummy was probably consolidating her energy and gathering resources to counter the coming ritual. She had to know something was coming.

Taking Celia's hand, Dylan led her up the outside staircase and along the hall to his room. It opened with a touch and they scooted in before some late-night wanderer could spot them.

He wasn't exactly certain how they managed it, but their growing relationship had not yet hit the rumor mill which ran Hollywood. He was in a position to discover such rumors even when people didn't want him to overhear gossip.

"What?" she asked quietly, still holding his hand and gazing up at him with those crystal green eyes that melted his soul.

He bent his head and kissed her, long and slow, and lovingly. Gentle. Affirming his emotions rather than aggressively passionate, though passion for her gripped him harder than any other woman ever had before.

"There's something you should know before the performance tomorrow night," he said softly.

She cocked her head in a listening posture rather than question him.

He led her to his worktable by the window. In the middle sat an old-fashioned cassette player he'd found in a thrift store solely for his purpose tonight.

Anshar's lamp sat beside it, a silent observer.

"Sit, please."

Celia lowered herself into the armchair and leaned back, eyes still tracking his every move.

"This is the second thing I have left from me da." His accent was back in place, full and unchecked by decades of work to mitigate it. He sounded like he'd just flown in from Belfast.

Biting his lip, he pushed the play button, then dropped onto the edge of the bed, the only other place in the cramped room where he could sit.

A single piano note gave the pitch. Then a solo tenor voice crooned the soft lullaby that had lasted through the ages.

Sleep my child and I will tend thee
 All through the night.
 Guardian angels God will lend thee
 All through the night.

A ghostly voice out of his past wrapped them in the solace of music and the love of a man for his child.

"That's the only recording of my father singing. There may be others when he was just part of the choir, but that's the only solo I know he sang. They performed at the Eisteddfod in Cardiff the year I was born, and they won their division." A recitation of facts.

Celia's chin quivered and a tear trickled down her cheek.

"You have a third thing of your father's."

He raised his eyebrows in question.

"You inherited his voice."

"No. He sang tenor. I'm a baritone."

"You could sing tenor with training and practice. But you gave it up when your voice changed, and you became more interested in languages than the music. I've heard you sing. You have the same quality of tone and perfect pitch. Cherish it. Use it to honor him. And digitize that recording so that it will last."

Then she left him alone with a few vague memories and a lot to think about.

∽

I approached my mark beside a cradle at center stage fully intending to push magic through my song. Catching the ghostly attention of my sisters seemed to require it.

But the wobbly recording of Dylan's da singing the time-honored folk tune at the most prestigious of choir competitions in Wales, and winning, haunted me, as he haunted Dylan.

There was magic in the music, in all music. Being a siren wasn't necessary; only the love of the music inherent in the singer, the pianist, the conductor, all those involved in producing a pure sound that touched the heart mattered.

And so, I spread the chiffon batwings of my sleeves, a knot work of sequins outlining my angelic silhouette, with a single red and blue sequin beneath the swirling design over my heart, and I floated through the simple ballet Paul had choreographed for me, a solo piano guiding me through the melody. And then I sang from my heart, with only the magic of love and grief guiding me.

I became the guardian angel of the music my sisters and I cherished. Dylan's da had been his guardian angel over the years manifested in that cassette tape.

If Joycelyn and Brittney were going to come back to my side for one night of the most important magic ritual of our lives, then they had to come on their own terms, for love of me. My magic might call sailors to wreck their ships, but I would not use it to call my sisters back from the grave.

Dylan waited for Celia in her trailer. She had another costume change before the results of the competition. After that heart-rending free style piece he had no doubts that she'd win.

After what seemed an eternity, but in reality was less than five minutes, he heard her fumbling with the door latch. He opened it for her and drew her up the two steps to the main floor. Before she could say anything, he cupped her face lovingly and kissed her. Tingles worked their way up from his gut to his hands, to his heart. "Thank you for giving me back my father," he whispered, then held her close, engulfing her in his arms.

"You are very welcome, my dear. But I have less than ten minutes to change." She wiggled out of his grasp and slipped into the bedroom. "Can you get my zipper?" She presented her back to him while she fussed with the majorette costume from the first episode, the one that needed the most improvement.

"How are you feeling about the performance so far?" he asked, admiring the way her muscles stretched out from her spine, strong muscles honed by swimming and more clearly defined from the stretches required of dancing. He couldn't help himself running the back of one finger the length of her back.

She shimmied beneath his touch then leaned into him. "I wish I had time to indulge," she sighed. Then she straightened and slipped out of the angelic white froth of a gown, completely oblivious to her nudity. "And I feel like I... reached my target audience."

He had to hold his breath. Of course their link meant they shared a lot and she might not even be aware of how enticing she was.

By the time he'd gained control of his lust, she'd pulled on the majorette costume and reached for the pink overalls that covered it all for the first few measures of the dance.

"Shoes." She pointed to the floor of the minuscule closet.

"Pink tap shoes?" he asked even as he reached for them. He'd memorized everything she wore from repeated reviews of the show recordings.

"What else. Sandals first, I'll put on the taps once inside the studio. Can't scuff them by running across the blacktop."

"I've been thinking a lot about the coming ritual. A big part of banishing demons is knowing why. What is their motivation? So I have to ask myself 'why is Mummy angry with life'? Her reactions are more than distaste of humanity from pollution and climate change. She's angry at life."

"Probably because she was born of chaos. Chaos is who she is. Humans and nature in general seek order and routine. The swallows returning to Capistrano on the same day every year drives her crazy.

But for the birds, safety and comfort are born out of routine and homing instinct. Gotta go." She stood on tiptoe to kiss his cheek.

And then she was gone, leaving the trailer empty and lifeless.

Tomorrow a cleaning crew would come through and scrub the place with bleach to remove all traces of her residence. By the day after, someone else would occupy this trailer as a dressing room for a different show.

In an hour they'd know which singer and which dancer would perform the lead in Margot Tremayne's musical.

Dylan couldn't suppress his smile. After that free style performance, he had no doubt who would win the singing category. Celia Fisher had embodied music and given new meaning to its purpose. Music was as essential to life as breathing.

Mummy had to learn that and not reserve music for causing death and chaos on rocky shores.

"Of course, you won, Celia," Bryant Thomas said. He took his place behind his desk in his office directly after the show. All of the finalists and our families had gathered for a glass of champagne and a myriad of papers to sign before we caught the red eye for New York. The next morning we would all appear on the network morning show.

I was tired just thinking about it. But I was excited and exhilarated too.

I won!

"The moment I heard your first note six months ago at the auditions I knew you were a contender. The growth you showed from your dancing in week one to week two told me you were more than a contender. Congratulations to you. And to you, Gaylord. Your dancing is exquisite and the way you paired with Celia pretty much cinched both of you as winners."

Gaylord reached over and engulfed me in a hug.

Behind me, Dylan bristled. I sent him reassurance. Gaylord was a beautiful dancer, a handsome man, and not at all interesting to me.

Dylan was the only man I wanted, the only man who had interested me since my first crush in high school, and in retrospect that boy had to work to keep my interest beyond the first sloppy and clumsy kiss.

I had to work to keep my hands off of Dylan since I healed him and we formed our telepathic link. But I'd been aware of him, intrigued by him almost from the first moment I'd met him, way back in the first week of competition while he directed media interviews. Now I waited breathlessly for the day after the big ritual when I could claim him as my own. Forever.

We drank our champagne, signed contracts and releases, received our bonus checks and returned to the hotel to grab our bags and head for the airport.

Look out, Mummy. Here we come.

CHAPTER 33

We enjoyed a lovely Thanksgiving dinner at the house in Cleveland with my much older sisters, Anemone and Zinnia, and their families. Teenage nieces and nephews bickering over video games, the guys arguing over football, (that felt like a rite of passage for Dylan entering the family, because he was constantly checking his phone to watch a soccer game between Florence, Italy and Baden Baden) and the women elbowing each other for space in the kitchen while we chopped and stirred and measured and mixed the various dishes required for the big gorge-out.

I felt like I'd earned the right to eat as much as I could, but part of me was longing to keep my current weight for Broadway.

After the ritual.

My part in the day's festivities? I don't cook. I can, but I don't, unless compelled. There were already too many cooks in the kitchen. So, I communed with the Djinn in my father's quiet study. The Djinn. Who knew that my childhood invisible friend Fred was actually the ancient Babylonian god Anshar, aka Poseidon, aka Mummy's mate?

By communing, I mean I leaned back in Dad's oversized office chair and stared at the plain, lidded clay lamp. Oh, and I hummed the simple melody of the ancient chant Dylan—with Margot's help—had deciphered from the scrap of cuneiform text.

What is that ugly sound? Came the voice from the lamp.

"Margot called it a teaching song, a rhythmic chant that probably followed a mnemonic: A is for apple kind of thing." I replied.

Boring.

"Wait, is that you, Anshar?"

Well, duh.

The voice sounded achingly familiar. I knew this... being.

"When did you learn slang?"

I keep up.

"You know that Josie and Brit and I made you up."

A stream of gray mist tinged with sea green flowed from the spout of the clay lamp. Quickly it coalesced into the short man of Mediterranean coloring and a beak-like blade of a nose. He wore an outlandishly colored tropical shirt with khakis and leather sandals. As I watched the transformation, he pulled his long hair into a ponytail that hung half-way down his back. *Fred.*

"No, my sweet. You did not make me up. I just played the elusive shadow to stay a secret from Tiamat." He looked around for a chair and settled for one hip on the desk corner.

As much as I wanted to hug him and bring him back into my life, I knew our time was short—I'd heard Zinnia fire up the portable mixer to whip the mashed potatoes—and I had to get answers. "What can you tell me about Tiamat?" I asked. Now that he was talking, I might as well milk the conversation for all he was worth.

"First off, my real name is Anshar. In ancient Babylonian it means 'ancestor of the gods.' That's as good an explanation as any, but I think Dylan already told you that. From the time before time, your grandmother and I have been in love and lovers. We just can't stand to live together."

I giggled at the thought of Mummy living in the suburbs baking cookies for her paranormal children. I'd met couples who loved each other dearly and lived separately, some of them the pros on the show.

Alpha personalities both, neither willing to make the day-to-day compromises of sharing space.

"And?" I pushed him.

"And, when humanity began to gather into city states, ethnicities, and co-operative trading partners, Tiamat nearly went insane at the thought of such organization. Even I became disgusted with her temper tantrums. She never did learn to compromise. The closest she came was allowing your mother to marry a Hunter. Still she demanded to be part of the family with a voice in the raising of your sisters, and you and your nieces."

"So that's why she kept dropping in unannounced, at random intervals."

"But she never stayed long because your parents made their home terribly inconvenient for her."

We both laughed at that.

"You helped with the original spell to contain Tiamat," I finally said, slowly, carefully, doing my best not to offend him.

"Yes."

"But she broke loose."

"Yes."

"It has taken six thousand years for her to build up enough momentum to become globally destructive."

"Oh, she could have done that long, long ago. She's just been waiting for the right descendant to come along and join her."

"Me."

"Yes."

The doorknob rattled. "Celia, your dad is ready to carve the turkey," Dylan called. He sounded desperate.

Fred dissipated into a cool mist again and streamed back into his pot. I felt his sigh of relief as he eased into a comfortable position and turned on his big screen TV.

I can tell you a lot more. When the time is right. He yawned. *Make certain you take control of the ritual. Do what feels right, not what the ancients decreed. A counting mnemonic indeed.*

After that I was the one to carry his lamp in a box inside a backpack all the way to Portland.

Ten people came from across the spectrum of mundane and paranormal, Hunters and sirens, a Djinn and a psychic vampire...

Oh yes, the psychic vampire, otherwise known as Janet Dryer. She landed at the Portland, Oregon airport less than an hour before we did on Friday morning. We, meaning me, my parents, Dylan, and Aunt Abigail—with the family I had to drop the disrespectful but fun 'Abby' moniker.

When we arrived, I noticed a forty-something woman with a baby and a car carrier sitting in the waiting lounge just beyond security. Handsome I'd call her rather than beautiful, still striking—no, she was arresting, turning the heads of both men and women who passed her in their hurry to move from their airplane to baggage claim.

"Janet Dryer!" Aunt Abigail exclaimed and hurried to her side for a friendly hug—baby and all.

I had to pause and stare openly. This was the same woman I'd seen pictures of from her stint on Bryant's celebrity dance show—the show where he'd stepped down from the judges' dais to dance with her when her partner fell ill.

Dylan nudged me from behind to keep me moving. "It's not polite to stare."

"But... the baby. Isn't she kind of... autumnal to have a toddler, barely a year old by my guess?"

"None of our business. She's here to round out the numbers for the ritual, nothing more."

"You know more?" I prodded his mind with my mine.

All I received in return was a chuckle.

Of course, Mom chose that moment to follow Aunt Abigail and gush over the baby. Dad heaved a deep sigh and leaned against the wall as if he knew he'd be there for a long while. Once Mom got her hands on a baby it would take an earthquake to separate her.

"Margot and Archie have taken the luggage to the hotel. Bryant is off interviewing the temporary nanny for both of us. Mine quit the first of the week. Said she hated New York and wanted to go home to

Tallahassee," Janet said. She sounded tired. "And his nanny is home with her own family for the holidays."

This exhausted, middle-aged mom had lost most of her top talk show interviewer sophistication. How was she supposed to hold up her piece of the ritual countered by my pet genie?

She'll manage, the Djinn said. *Go Bogata!* He must be watching a soccer—excuse me football—game on that magic big screen TV inside the lamp that he was so bloody proud of.

I bet that Janet Dryer wished she could rest with such enthusiasm.

Mom took the baby from her, placed the tired little guy—blue knitted cap and blankie so I guessed the child was male—against her shoulder, rubbing his back in a soothing motion. He stuffed half his fist in his mouth and quieted his fussing immediately. Sleep claimed him within seconds. Mom had the knack.

Just then, Bryant walked down the concourse with a plump middle-aged woman in tow. He pushed an umbrella stroller containing his daughter. The woman smiled a lot, watching the myriad people around her with bright-eyed interest. Short curly hair, practical shoes, and a diaper bag. The temporary nanny.

More introductions, all the while Bryant kept shifting his gaze from Janet to her baby. Was that wonder in his expression? There was a lot more to this story than we had time for right now.

"We have about one hour to check into the hotel, use the restrooms and stow our luggage," Aunt Abigail said briskly. She put aside her doting auntie role and returned to her Madame Director persona in the blink of an eye. "Then it will be time to round up the rest of the crew and head for the chopper pad. Time and tide wait for no one, even for this brigade designed to save the world from Mummy."

The wind heaving off the ocean onto a tiny promontory made landing the big helicopter a challenge. Dylan gripped his seat in white-knuckled fear. The nanobots in his brain gibbered in panic. He scrunched his eyes closed to stave off the impending migraine.

Celia seemed to gain energy with each gust. He had to remember, that for all her sensitivity and seeming fragility on land, she was born a Siren. This was her element, a storm at sea that would feed her, drawing innocent sailors onto the jagged rocks to be drowned and crushed by those towering waves.

Tonight, she had a different mission but the same sucking up of storm energy.

Across the aisle from him, Jeannie, too perked up and twitched her nose at the aroma of salt and fish and sea-wrack. Celia did the same nose wiggle.

The other passengers either gritted their teeth or dozed as long as they could.

At last, the chopper settled. The pilot slowed the rotors but didn't shut them down. He wouldn't be staying long. Lucky guy. He'd be back a little after midnight to retrieve any of them who still lived.

"May I take Anshar?" Dylan asked. Celia had stuffed her backpack beneath her seat. Maybe the Djinn could calm the rollicking robots in his mind.

"Um..."

"I need him to help me set the stage. He was there the first time and knows what went right and what went wrong."

The second sorcerer, opposite end of the semi-circle from the lead, lost his nerve and quit reciting the spell half-way through.

Dylan sensed the bored yawn from Anshar. All of his training in fighting demons and vampires told him to destroy or banish this being right now before he got loose, not enlist him as an ally. The gibbering nanobots agreed with that thought.

But Celia seemed to trust Anshar, so Dylan needed to do so too. He ran through the wording of their spell in the original Sumerian, Latin, Greek, and finally English. The 'bots shut up. For a few minutes.

Reluctantly, Celia pulled the backpack free of the protective webbing of the storage space and handed it to him. She cupped the bottom with one hand, supporting the box within. "Don't drop him."

"Believe me, I will be very, *very*, careful with him."

Her trust flowed through their link and he relaxed a bit.

"Um... you've talked to him."

"Of course. I know him of old."

He caught images of "Fred" protecting her from bullies and hovering anxiously beside the family pool when she took her first swimming lesson as an infant.

"Of course." Something tight in his gut unwound. Anshar had Celia's back, therefore, he'd also protect the rest of them.

"We need the fire right here." Abby pointed to the spot between her toes once the chopper had lifted off and she had a chance of being heard.

The storm wind still threatened to drown her out.

Lighting a fire was the job of the two active Hunters. He and Archie could not conjure fire, but they had skills that pushed into the paranormal realm to keep one going, even in this wind with wet driftwood.

One and a half meters to the right, Anshar said with determination. *We need it dead center of all the rocks, not just the top layer that's visible.*

Dylan trusted the authority of the Djinn more than he trusted Abby.

She glared at him when he started making a ring of rocks where Anshar had indicated. He ignored her and continued, with Archie's help.

"I heard the old guy even if Abby didn't," Archie said. He shrugged into his down parka. "Can we make this quick? Margot is really feeling the cold."

They all wore down coats and fur-lined caps with flaps to cover their ears. Margot wore thick gloves and tucked her hands into her pockets.

"Abby is her counterpart; she'll have to take care of her."

Archie didn't look happy at that idea. But then Janet stepped up and turned herself into a barrier between Margot and the wind. The musician hunched in on herself, conserving as much body heat as she could until they needed to separate.

With a snap of a lighter and a twist of Dylan's fingers into a ritual protection, the fire came to life and held until the dry wood they'd brought with them had heated enough to support flames without help. He'd done this many times over the years, always having a fire ready to aid his fight against rampaging vampires.

Archie built up the stone ring with two more layers of rounded rocks, fitting them together with the skill akin to a mason. "Geometrical puzzles. I was an accountant before I became a Hunter," he explained.

The full moon peeked out from behind collecting clouds as it rose above the coast range of mountains to the east. The waves calmed a bit as they neared high tide. Everyone checked their phones, or watches, at the same time.

With a nod from Abby, they took their places. Celia and her mother stood one long stride ahead of the fire on either side of the promontory. They anchored the spell at the points closest to the sea, where a siren should stand if she meant to sing a passing ship into crashing against the rocks.

Dylan and Archie took up positions behind and slightly inward from them. Janet stood behind Archie as a paranormal. That was Dylan's cue to remove the Djinn from the backpack and the box and set his lamp on a flat rock behind him. In an eyeblink he manifested into his casual beach bum persona. Somehow his long hair stayed in a tight braid down the center of his spine.

The crew stared at him in disbelief for a moment, then turned their attention back to setting the stage.

The two ghosts should come next, but Dylan had seen no sign of them. Yet.

I can entice the ghosts here, Anshar whispered into Dylan's mind.

If they don't show up on their own, Celia can ask you. It's best coming from her.

Next in line came Bryant and Mike, the two retired hunters. They stood between the paranormal and the normal worlds. Lastly, Margot and Abby stood together behind the fire, the two normals, part of the surreal world and fully anchored in the real one.

The moon rose higher.

The waves reached their peak.

And the ritual would be incomplete without Celia's ghostly sisters. "We're doomed to failure." The nanobots agreed with Dylan and sent lightning bolts of pain into his eyes, echoing the storm offshore that chose that moment to head inland.

CHAPTER 34

Dylan's migraine stabbed me in my throat, my strongest and yet most vulnerable part of my body. Without my voice I, we, could do nothing to stop Mummy.

Without knowing how I knew it, I knew in my gut and my mind that Mummy had done something to Dylan's augmentation machines. She knew he was the key component to this ritual. Without him we wouldn't have the ceremonial magic, the language to translate it, or Anshar to orchestrate it.

Stand straight and lock your knees, my love, I called to him. *Whatever happens, just keep standing and follow the ritual. We will get through this, and when it is over, it will be truly over. We'll get rid of those pesky nanobots and live normal lives, like my parents have.*

I had to leave my link to him open though it meant enduring some of his pain. I'd endured weeks and weeeks of intense song and dance competition. I'd endured losing my sisters. This was just one more *thing*.

The clouds offshore thickened and drew closer. Lightning shot through them and revealed a figure of titanic proportions. The outline of a full-figured goddess in black draperies—black, the color of death when the ancients of the Mediterranean always wore unbleached linen or wool to reflect the heat and cool the body. But Mummy had no warmth inside her; she needed to wear black to draw in the heat.

She held a writhing snake of lightning in her left hand. In her right, she held my sisters by the backs of their now tarnished sequin gowns.

"Joycelyn, Brittney, we love you!" Mom called.

I couldn't say, or sing, anything with Dylan's migraine choking me. So I did the only thing left. I yanked off my glove with my teeth, held up my hand filled with sequins, red for Joycelyn, blue for Brittney, and white for me, the Fisher triplets. I added my breath to the wind to send the little glittery circles upward and outward.

Mom followed suit with her own handful of sequins. Then each of the people behind me did the same. Dylan's puff of air was weak. Anshar made up for him with gusto and a laugh.

The frothing air sparkled, reflecting the full moon, or what little we could see of it behind gathering clouds.

Anshar became a swirling and pulsating shaft of energy and shot upward, gathering the moonlight into himself just before the clouds engulfed him.

I could not see, but I felt the shift in the wind as my sisters broke free of Mummy's grip and floated toward us. As they passed me, they brushed my throat with spectral fingers, banishing my pain. They blew kisses to Mom and Dad. Then they each brushed delicate fingers across Dylan's brow. His migraine froze in place, giving him enough relief to blow a pitch pipe.

Mom and I found the opening note.

Dylan and Archie took up the note a third lower in their own octave.

Two by two the others joined us, filling a full six note chord crossing three octaves.

Mummy snarled and belted out a screech that could not fit any human scale. It clashed with our chord. The waves picked up her tone, compounding it and making it reverberate against the rocks beneath our feet.

My teeth ached with the disharmony.

Janet, probably the weakest voice among us, wavered. Abby bolstered her with a stronger alto note. Janet found the true tone and came back into harmony.

Margot brought out a small hand drum. With a leather wrapped stick she beat the rhythm of the ancient music, mimicking a human heartbeat.

I plucked the original lyrics from Dylan's mind and began the chant. Mom echoed me in English.

Mummy threw her lightning bolt into our midst. The fire blazed high, then threatened to die.

Anshar dissolved, heading back to his lamp.

My heart sank.

A towering wave rushed toward us. I could see the foam at the top, estimating it would crest right on top of us, dragging us all out to sea as it retreated.

Not again, Tiamat. You shall not win this round! Anshar rose up again and spread out. The full spectrum of colors writhed in a column of mist.

"Begone, you evil demon!" Mummy screamed. "You have no place in this world. Return from whence you came."

Not without my mate.

I sang the spell with all my might, not caring if my voice roughened and dropped a full fifth. We needed volume and words right now.

All I could think of was the atonal teaching song.

My sisters brought forth a better song. A more important one than the chant invented by sorcerers who didn't want to share power with the goddess of chaos.

Sleep my love and I will tend thee
All through the night.
Guardian angels God will lend thee.

Mom and Dad picked up the protective lullaby.

All through the night.

Dylan and I added our own voices. We slid into harmony with the ghostly voices without even trying.

Soft the drowsy hours are creeping
Hill and vale in slumber sleeping
I my loved ones' watch am keeping
All through the night

The genie gained strength from our hymn of life. The song was important to all of us, for different reasons.

Retreat my love
To realms unknowing
Help us find a cove of sheltering
All through the night

The words came to me unbidden. Dylan grabbed my hand, linking us beyond our mental bond. My sisters knew the lyrics the moment they formed within Anshar's mind and sang along. We stood side by side, a ghost on either side of Dylan and me. Together we faced the fury of the StormMother.

The others hummed along, supporting the song that Mummy had always hated. Because Anshar could calm her with it. Because she was chaos and anger, and the song countered her with love.

An extra voice joined us, a strong tenor trained to sing from birth in the mountains and mines of Wales. A ghostly voice that blended beautifully with the rest of us.

I opened my heart to Dylan's father, his guardian angel lent to us for a time.

Margot changed the soft beating of the drum to a primitive pounding. It echoed in our blood and drew us into a tight circle around the still burning fire. We stomped our feet to the march and chanted. "Go, go, go, go."

The moon broke through the hesitating storm clouds.

Anshar gathered together his myriad colors and swooped around the storm and the StormMother in a bright rainbow of glittering sequins.

With a poof of sparkling light, a chrysanthemum of fireworks, he engulfed Mummy and they winked out.

My sisters blew us all a kiss and sought their own eternal haven.

"We love you," Mom called after them.

The natural storm, having lost the artificial push from Tiamat collapsed in on itself and withered to a few gusts of wind.

Dylan collapsed beside me, hands pressed against his temples. It felt as if we were trying to keep his brain from exploding.

DENOUEMENT

Somehow Abby organized dragging Dylan into the helicopter with me still clinging to him. I was sobbing and refusing to remove my hand from him. I wanted to throw myself on top of him, to bind us skin to skin, soul to soul. Our link had become a blank slate as he tried and tried again to retreat from the pain into a coma.

I wouldn't let him. I *couldn't* let him.

We'd promised each other a life together. Or at least a long-term love affair.

I wasn't going to let a little thing like rogue nanobots come between us.

Within minutes we flew to an ER in Portland, the closest city big enough to handle nine cases of near hypothermia and a man trying to die.

Medics rushed in with IVs and monitors and syringes for a battery of blood tests. Aunt Abigail flashed a badge and arcane ID, then directed everything. She'd anticipated this and already flown in a Guild specialist.

In retrospect I think they made a wise decision to ban me from Dylan's side while the professionals stabilized him.

Dad poured a gallon of hot tea with milk and sugar into me. I hated the taste but cherished the artificial warmth it gave me. The place in my heart where Dylan had dwelt for so many weeks remained frozen.

We retired to the cafeteria. The kitchen was closed, except for urns of coffee and hot water, but there were long tables where we could all gather.

By the sixth cup of tea and the fourth hour, I'd lost my taste for the stale brew and my tears dried. I had nothing left to give.

It was then that I finally felt the soothing presence of my sisters, brightening the room and the mood with their glittery gowns and soft smiles. They hadn't gone away when Mummy vanished with her life-mate. They'd stayed by my side all through the night. Somehow, I knew that Dylan's father kept ghostly watch over him in ICU.

Eventually Aunt Abigail's phone chirped. We all held our breath.

"He's stable and they are moving him to a room. But they are keeping him sedated. One of us may go sit with him." She started to rise.

Both Bryant and Dad held her in her chair with hands on her shoulders. Then they nodded to me.

"We all know he's done as a Hunter," Archie said quietly. "He doesn't belong to you anymore, Abby."

She bristled and began a protest. I didn't hear it. I was already at the elevator doors. In the middle of the night the lift responded to my summons immediately.

A nurse at admissions directed me to the third floor. I found his room by the brace of paramilitary men dressed in black commando uniforms standing guard at his door. Guild protection.

One guard checked his phone, also black, then nodded to me that I had permission from Abby to enter.

Dylan's face looked pale, but not bloodless. He breathed with the assistance of an oxygen cannula taped to his nose. Other than that, his body barely disturbed the drape of the sheet and light blanket covering him.

He'd been so vibrant over the last few weeks I hadn't notice that he'd lost weight, the pain behind his eyes robbing him of appetite. We'd both focused too intensely on me and the competition.

My phone pinged an incoming text. I checked it, smiled and pocketed the device.

But then his eyes fluttered and partially opened.

The full force of our bond flooded into me.

Relief robbed me of all my starch. One of the guards shoved a chair behind me so that I could collapse within touching distance of Dylan's twitching fingers. He wanted my hand in his.

"What do you think about teaching linguistics at a small private college in New York City? Abby is turning you loose, into my care."

His eyes flew open and he stared at me. I saw hope and I saw joy, and I knew we'd have a normal life together. As normal as a life in show business could offer anyway. That was all he really wanted. He'd served the Guild long enough, and well. Now he deserved retirement to the career he'd been pursuing when they recruited him.

My sisters' presence faded away. I'd found the life we'd all three sought. They could rest in peace.

Dylan's father retreated as well, content that his boy would survive and thrive, all that anyone could hope for a child.

I climbed onto the bed beside Dylan. He draped one arm around my shoulders so I could lay my head on his chest and listen to his heart beat, reassured that he still lived. We slept.

ABOUT THE AUTHOR

Irene Radford is a founding member of Book View Café. You can find a number of her books, both reprints and original titles, at the café. She has been writing stories ever since she figured out what a pencil was for. Editing, as Phyllis Irene Radford, grew out of her love of the craft of writing. History has been a part of her life from earliest childhood and led to her BA from Lewis and Clark College.

Mostly she writes fantasy and historical fantasy including the best-selling *Dragon Nimbus* Series and the masterwork *Merlin's Descendants* series. Look for her writing new historical fantasy tales as Rachel Atwood. In other lifetimes she writes urban fantasy as P.R. Frost or Phyllis Ames, and space opera as C.F. Bentley. Lately she ventured into Steampunk as Julia Verne St. John.

If you wish information on the latest releases from Ms Radford under any of her pen names, you can subscribe to her newsletter: www.ireneradford.net. Or you can follow her on Facebook and Twitter.

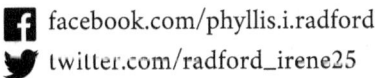

facebook.com/phyllis.i.radford
twitter.com/radford_irene25

ABOUT BOOK VIEW CAFÉ

Book View Café Publishing Cooperative (BVC) is an author-owned cooperative of about thirty professional writers, publishing in a variety of genres such as fantasy, romance, mystery, and science fiction.

BVC authors include New York Times and USA Today bestsellers. Our authors have won and been nominated for numerous awards, including: the Agatha, Campbell, Hugo, Lambda Literary, Locus, Nebula, PEN/Malamud Award, Philip K. Dick, RITA, World Fantasy, and the Writers of the Future awards.

Since its debut in 2008, BVC has gained a reputation for producing high-quality ebooks, and now brings that same quality to its print editions. Find out more and sign up for our newsletter at:

www.bookviewcafe.com